HEAD, HEART, & FAMILY

A Railers Novella Collection

RJ SCOTT

V.L. LOCEY

Love Lane Books

Head, Heart, & Family

A Railers Novella Collection

All Rights Reserved

Dedication

To my family who accepts me and all my foibles and quirks. Even the plastic banana in my holster.
VL Locey

Always for my family,
RJ Scott

Christmas

A RAILERS NOVELLA

Neutral ZONE

RJ SCOTT &
V.L. LOCEY

Ten

KARMA. IT'S A REAL BITCH. JUST ASK ANYONE.

I'd left my man and my team behind in Harrisburg and flown to—get this—fucking Tucson, Arizona, to begin treatment for my traumatic head injury.

The same city the Raptors played in.

I could open the blinds in my room here in the Draper Neurological Rehabilitation and Performance Center and see the glistening mirrored sides of the Santa Catalina Arena. Funny shit right there. Four blocks over, the Raptors were on the ice for morning skate, and I was here, trying to get my brain healed enough so I could maybe play my game again someday.

Shit, right now I'd be happy to be able to speak or read normally.

"Ho, ho, ho," I growled, closing the drapes, then pulling my sunglasses off and tossing them to the bed. Living behind sunglasses and blinds sucked. Headaches sucked. Slurred speech sucked. Seeing the pity in the eyes of my boyfriend and family and teammates sucked.

Christmas with sand and cactus sucked. I wanted to cry. I wanted to be back home with Mads, decorating our tree and shaking my presents. I wanted to be shopping for gifts for my boyfriend, my mother and father, for my brothers, and for Stan and Adler and all the Railers. I wanted things to be the way they had been before that night. Tears threatened, but I held them in. Crying only made my head hurt worse.

So, I padded out of my room and made my way to breakfast and the first of several rounds of rehab I'd be facing today. I'd been here one day and had come to realize that my brain was now as well-known with the neurologists here as my face was back in Harrisburg. This was *the* place for athletes to come when they were battling CTE-related brain issues. Most of the men here were older, retired players, lots of football players. I mean *lots* of them. I'd met three other hockey players so far, all retired, all fighting to keep a step ahead of the disease taking over their brains. Sometimes, late at night, when I was lying in bed, I'd get scared for myself and all the other guys on my team. I worried about Mads. God knows how many concussions he'd had when he was playing. Add that to his heart shit and… well, I worried about stuff now. Lots more stuff than I had before the night my head met the ice, sans helmet.

The facility held a hundred and fifty people, and not all of us were athletes. Lots of patients had come here after car accidents or other catastrophic injuries. There were head injuries and spinal cord injuries being healed. The staff seemed nice, confident in their ability to nurse me back to my old self or as close as we could get. The halls were bright and airy, the food excellent, and the medical staff top-notch. And yes, it was expensive and elite and the cream of the crop. Which was why Mads had stubbornly pushed me into coming here after my initial rehab had been completed. Two weeks at the facility, a couple of weeks back home for the holidays, then back for another four weeks. Then maybe we'd talk about hockey.

"Hey, you're Tennant Rowe, right?"

I skidded to a halt outside one of a dozen sun-rooms. As though people in Arizona didn't get enough sun just stepping outside? They needed to make rooms for sun? A tall, burly black man about my age ran at me, hand out. I smiled up at him, trying to pull some information about him from my cloudy memory banks.

"I'm Declan Fidler, cornerback for the Temple Owls."

"Ah, cool, hey man." We shook hands. God, he was cute. Short hair and a flashy smile, big wide shoulders and inkwork all over his arms. "Sorry to see you here though, dude."

"Yeah, I know that." He ran a hand over his hair. "First game of the season too."

"That sucks," I said, then released his hand. "I was on my way to the dining hall."

"I could eat if you want some company."

"Totally. Be nice to have someone to talk to who's under forty."

"I feel that."

He joined me on the walk to the dining hall, which looked nothing like the hospital cafeteria I'd been expecting when I first saw it yesterday. This place was upmarket. Round tables with cloth covers, thick royal-blue carpeting, windows that ran floor to ceiling, flowering plants in the corners, and a wait staff.

"I don't think I'll ever get used to this place," I murmured as I followed Declan to a table by the windows.

"I feel the same way," he said as we took our seats. "I mean, I grew up wealthy, my father's the chief justice of the Pennsylvania Supreme Court, and I was still blown away."

"That's impressive. Did he…?" My brain went totally blank, and I scrambled to find the proper word. "Push. Yeah, did he push to get you in here?" I winced at the slip.

Fuck this shit. Really. Push? How fucking hard it is to recall a word like push?

An older woman in a tidy uniform filled our water glasses, then asked if she could have our room numbers. All the meals here were prepared by nutritionists with an eye to the patients'—athletes in my case—unique needs.

"Big-time. He was adamant about me coming here after the initial rehab. Said that this place would do things to counter the damage that no regular rehab could do. You here for CRT?"

"I uhm…" and that skip again. Fuck. "Dude, sorry, I'm like…" I tapped my temple.

He reached over the table to take my hand. "Ten, man, do not sweat it. You should have seen me when I got here. Barely able to string four words together. Sometimes I still trip up, just like that. But it's all good. We're tough motherfuckers. We'll train our brains."

"Yeah, train the brains. Cool."

He gave my hand a squeeze and then released it. "So CRT?"

Our food was served, my platter loaded with scrambled eggs, fresh fruit, a bowl of oatmeal, and chocolate milk.

My meds also sat on my tray. Declan's food was similar, as were the meds in tiny cups lined up for him.

"Cognitive rehab therapy," he said before shaking out his napkin and laying it over his lap. I did the same and tossed down the pills. I had no idea what they were pumping into me, and I truly didn't care. As long as they got me back on the ice, they could be dumping Soylent green into my body via the milk. Man, that old movie rocked. What I wouldn't give to be curled up on the couch with Mads watching it again. "Speech, occupation, and physical therapy. You don't have any big physical issues, do you?"

"Some weakness on the left side, my arm, but it's getting better. I hardly drop anything now."

"That's good. Once the swelling goes down, things tend to get better." He took a bite from a slice of whole wheat toast. "I can't believe I'm sitting here eating with you. Cup winner, LGBT crusader. Thanks for doing that, coming out, being proud and gay. I know how hard that is. My family and team have been amazing about my being queer."

"Excellent. Glad they're… fuck, I just. Give me a sec. Yeah, uhm, glad it's good for you. I'm sorry. Sometimes I can go, like, whole days and barely fuck up, and then I'll hit this patch where my brain glitches out and… shit. Fuck. Okay, I'm going to shut up for a minute and let my neurons… fire or something."

"It's fine. I understand." And he did. I could see it in his eyes. He totally got it because he was living it too.

I wished everyone else in my life could get it as Declan did. We ate in amiable silence, not that heavy, cloaking pity blanket of quietude that my family draped over me every time I fumbled.

Therapy followed that pleasant breakfast, hours of it. Doctors and nurses, therapists, reading and tests and poking and prodding. Weights and treadmills and medicine balls. Shoving tiny pegs into tinier holes, pet therapy which was actually cool because who didn't love a dog kiss? Speech therapy was last, and I tanked at it. Totally blew it to shit with my inability to recall one simple phrase. It made me so mad I flipped the table, sending papers and pencils flying. Then, because I had no clue where that outburst had come from, I felt even shittier.

"Tennant, it's okay," the woman, who was some fancy kind of advanced speech therapist, said as we picked up the mess I'd made. "Temper flare-ups are common. It's frustrating not to be able to express yourself. We see that frequently in stroke victims."

"That was uncool. Just so uncool. I didn't... it wasn't... shit." I dropped to my ass, hands full of work sheets that looked as if a four-year-old had scribbled them down, buried my face in the papers, and wept.

Julie. Yes! That was her name. Julie sat down beside me, rubbed my back, and told me all kinds of reassuring things.

"I'm kind of done for the day," I told her, and she let me go. I walked the halls, feeling discouraged and sickened with myself. Once I got back to my room, I called home, needing to hear Jared's voice. As soon as he picked up, I kind of began babbling. A lot of it wasn't sensible, and it was garbled because I'd have to stop, think, and then restart. But through all of that, Jared listened and never interrupted. When I was done, I fell back onto the bed, exhausted, battling a headache, and sick to death of myself and my stupid brain.

"Sounds like a rough first day," Jared said. I rolled to my side, tucking my knees up, my gaze on that shiny arena where the Raptors were playing hockey right now. "Are you sure you don't want me to come out? I can get a hotel room."

"No, you need to work. The team needs you."

"You need me as well, Tennant."

"No, I got this. You can't do this for me, Mads. Neither can Ryker or Brady or Jamie or my mother. It's just…" I exhaled through pursed lips. "It's so much harder than I thought it would be. I mean, I knew it would be hard but fuck sake, I couldn't recall simple words. How will I ever be able to play if I can't…" I stopped and calmed myself down. "I hate that this happened. I hate Aarni so much for doing this to me, Jared. I never thought I could ever hate anyone."

"I know, babe. I wish you'd reconsider and let me come out there."

He sounded as sick at heart as I was. And truthfully, in that moment, I was close to telling him to fly out. I so needed his arms around me.

"Tell me you love me."

"I love you." He drew in a shaky breath. "Do you want me to come out? Just say the word."

I sat up slowly to avoid a head-rush and the pain that went along with those. "No, I'm good." I pushed to my feet and went to the window. The sun was setting now, the mirrored sides of the Santa Catalina Arena glowing scarlet and pink. "I'm a tough camper. My Mom said that to me the first time I went to hockey camp."

"Yeah? How old were you? Five months old or so?"

That made me chuckle. "Nah man, I was like six. And this camp was in Buffalo. I wanted to go so bad. I mean, I can be kind of stubborn when I want something."

"I'm well aware of that fact," he replied. Was he sitting down or pacing? Probably pacing because he was tension-riddled over me. "You were persistent about us."

"Damn right I was. I knew we'd be good." I touched the pane of glass as a smile of remembrance played on my lips. "I went to that camp, and as soon as my folks dropped me off, I wanted to come home. But Mom wouldn't let me. She said I had to be a tough camper and that once the homesickness wore off, I'd be glad I stayed."

"Were you?"

"Yeah, I loved it. Scored my first goal against Tommy Wayfarer. He got mad and cried." The lights of Tucson began to flicker to life. Someone walked by my door humming *Santa Claus is Coming to Town*. "I'll be okay. I just have to score my first goal here."

"You will."

"Yeah, I will. So, tell me about morning skate. How did the lines look?"

We talked about the Railers and about Ryker and Declan, my new therapy buddy. We talked about old movies and new songs. We talked for hours. Darkness had blanketed the city when I dozed off on him. I woke up a second later, phone still to my ear, my boyfriend chuckling.

"Wow, you snored yourself awake," Mads said, then groaned, rising to his feet I assumed.

"Shit, yeah, I fell asleep." A yawn rolled out of me. I

flopped to my side on the bed, my sight on the desert sky over Tucson.

"I need to turn in too," he said around a yawn.

"Yeah, you're a couple of hours ahead of us. I'll call you tomorrow at the same time. I love you, Mads."

"I love you too, Ten. And your mother was right; you are a tough camper. You'll begin to see improvement, I know you. You won't stop until you do."

"Thanks, Coach."

"Wiseass."

"I miss our goodnight kisses." My eyes were so heavy I could barely keep them open.

"You'll get plenty when you get home."

"Mm, loving sounds good."

"Yes, it does. Get some rest. Heal. I'll talk to you tomorrow."

"Night," I mumbled, ended the call, and then fell into an exhausted but fitful sleep. The bed was too hard, too narrow, and far too lacking in Jared Madsen's big, broad body.

Jared

WE LOST THE GAME BY A MILE. I'D FUCKED UP, LOST MY cool, and now all I could do was close the door in Stan's grief-stricken face.

The big goalie didn't force his way inside to carry on what had been a humiliating last ten minutes, and for a hopeful moment I thought he'd gone. I rested my forehead against the door, wishing I could take back everything I'd just said. Arvy and Westy didn't deserve me cornering them in the locker room and reaming them for the shitfest that was the third period. Okay, so they'd messed up, nearly taken each other out, but that was hockey, and it was my fault it had even happened. My head wasn't in the game.

I miss our goodnight kisses.

I hadn't even slept after we'd ended the call last night, not for the longest time. I missed Ten so damn bad, and I wished I was there with him right now. He would make things better, tell me that I could pull this around, and get my head out of my ass.

A thud rattled the door, but it wasn't Stan breaking his way in. Hell, he was probably just banging his head on the wood like I was.

"Sorry," he said loud enough so I could hear. "For game lost, sorry for…" His voice was low and filled with misery, but that was all he said, and I filled in the blanks. Sorry for Ten, sorry for the stress that I was piling on the team, sorry for the despair that made our starting goalie break down and start beating on a Boston D-Man. Sorry for Arvy and Westy tripping over each other to try to make things right for their coach.

Please go away.

"I'm sit right here," Stan said, and I heard the *swoosh* of his big body sliding down the door. I could imagine him, long legs spread out in front of him, the gatekeeper people would have to go through if they wanted to talk to me. People like management, the coach, the press, the team, Ten's family.

Because Stan had seen me crack tonight, had seen me lose control, and he knew, just like everyone else, that I was close to the edge.

Management had wanted to know if I was emotionally available for my work. Coach Benning had wanted to know if I wanted him to bench me until Ten came home while assuring me that this wasn't a bad thing at all. Jamie had phoned right after Ten and I had ended the call, wanting to know how his brother was, right at the moment I was at my most raw. Then Brady had cornered me before tonight's game against Boston, which we'd lost miserably, and had talked *at* me for at least thirty minutes.

You should be with him in Arizona. No. You shouldn't be with him in Arizona. Why is he in Arizona? I'm his big brother. I should be with him in Arizona. Are you sure you should still be working?

I'd managed to calm him down, convinced him yet again, that Ten was in the right place and that no, Ten didn't need his older brother there with him right now. And as for the comment about whether I should be working? I reassured him, gently and oh-so controlled, that this was my *job* and that I could do nothing for Ten if I smothered him. When I'd added that family was not allowed at the facility long term, he'd finally subsided and hugged me so hard that I swore I had bruised ribs.

When I'd checked my phone after the game and saw another missed call from Jamie and two from Ten's mom and dad, that was the straw that had broken the camel's back.

I was done with being the person everyone went to when they were worried about Ten. I couldn't be that man anymore and do my job and worry about my boyfriend all at the same time.

"We need to talk to Coach Madsen." I recognized Arvy's voice, determined and forceful. Which anyone would be when faced with an angry Russian gatekeeper. Given he used the word *we*, I assumed Westy was with him.

"Both go far away," Stan growled at them.

I could imagine the line of people waiting to talk to Jared Madsen, fucked-up defense coach and all around son of a bitch. I pictured Brady and Jamie, with their parents waiting for me to have all the answers. Right behind them would be team management not knowing what the hell to say to me. Coach Benning nodding with thin lips, and then right at the back, after all the responsibilities and people wanting a piece of me, was Ten. He'd wait patiently for me to deal with everyone, and then he'd take my hand and tell me everything was going to be okay.

But everything wasn't okay and hiding in my office wasn't going to get things done.

I flung my door open, Stan falling back in, with a round "O" of surprise. I pointed at him.

"You first," I said to Stan and motioned Arvy and Westy to stand and wait. Stan scrambled to rise, and I realized Erik was with him, appearing serious and nervous at the same time. "You as well," I said to Erik and waited until they were both in and the door was shut.

"I tried to stop him from being a gatekeeper."

"No one will move through me."

They spoke over each other. Stan only stopped when Erik took his hand and laced their fingers.

I swallowed my fears and began to deal with everything I needed to cross off the list.

"Thank you, Stan, for listening to me rant, for watching me lose my shit, and not calling me on it."

The big Russian nodded. "For Ten," he said.

That was it in a nutshell. Everyone wanted to protect me because of their love for Ten when actually maybe they should've been calling me on my lack of social skills, inability to coach effectively, and the loose hold I had on my temper. I turned to Erik.

"Erik, please take Stan home. I need to talk to Arvy and Westy, and I can handle it from here."

Stan didn't want to move, but Erik finally tugged him away, and when they'd left, I called in Arvy and Westy. They were both taller than me and wider than me, but they seemed so small standing there with sheepish expressions, and that was my fault. I'd done this to them.

"This stops now," I began, and both defenders nodded miserably. "Not you. This isn't entirely on you. I've dropped the ball, and what happened tonight shouldn't happen. Arvy, you keep your head up and stick to the plan, Westy, you stay at the net. Don't fuck with what we'd worked on before Ten got injured. You're my two best D-Men, and you were out there on the ice like two preschoolers squabbling over that puck."

"Coach—"

"I'm not backing you up like I should."

Arvy cleared his throat, but it was Westy who finally spoke for them both. "We know it's hard for you right now," was all he said. "It's okay—"

"No, it's far from okay," I interrupted. "I owe you both an apology. Now, I'll see you at practice in the morning. Get in early. We're working on speed drills, and you can stop being so damn nice to me and go back to hating me."

That was me laying it on the line. Everyone wanted to help me, to be gentle with me when actually I needed players to kick me in the ass and make me work.

Westy nodded and backed toward the door. Arvy turned and probably ran before I added more training to the schedule. I left the door open, and sure enough, Coach Benning arrived just after they'd left.

"Jared?" he asked from the door, and I faced up to him.

"Shout at me, fine me, push me to work thirty-hour days, ream me out for doing a fucking shit job. I want this back to normal before the Railers end up bottom of the fucking table, but don't take me off my team."

I sounded desperate, even to my own ears, and he

winced. He'd been just as guilty of letting things ride with me, but it reflected on him. What kind of coach was he if he couldn't corral his D-men or his defensive coach? He must've been as sick as me of hearing people excuse the Railers because of what had happened to Ten.

He pulled his shoulders back and stared at me. "Pull your head out of your fucking ass, Madsen. Get the job done."

Then he turned on his heel and left. For the first time in a long while, ever since that night Ten had fallen to the ice, I felt as though maybe I had some control. I just had one more thing to do. I closed my office door, Facetimed Ten's parents, added Brady, who was in a local hotel, and then tried to connect with Jamie as well. Only when they were all there, Jamie sweating straight from a game, did I begin.

"Guys, I have one thing to say. I can't do this anymore. I can't be the person you talk to for hours. I don't know much more than you do, and if I hear anything from Ten that I think you need to know about, I will call you or text you, but I need to concentrate on my work. I need to concentrate on Ten, and I can't do it all."

Ten's family loved me, after the initial punch-up I'd had with Brady, anyway, and all of them appeared shocked at the bluntness of my words. I almost backed down at that moment, but the exhaustion that followed me everywhere wasn't enough for me to do that. Yet.

"We're sorry," Jamie said when no one else spoke. "We're just…"

"Scared," his mom finished, and she was crying. "And we love you, and you're in so much pain, Jared."

I had to make them see what I was feeling. "I need to be strong. I have to carry on so that when Ten comes home, he just sees that we kept going for him. Am I wrong in wanting that?"

The vulnerability slipped out without me wanting it to.

I saw Brady wince. "No, bud," he said, "we all want that, and it's wrong we dump all our fears on you. We get that, and we'll fix it."

Sudden fear gripped me, I didn't want them to exclude me in their worry or treat me as if I wasn't family. I needed them as much as they needed me, only I wanted it to be more level.

"Don't leave me, though."

Jesus, I sounded so needy.

"We wouldn't," Ten's mom said.

"Never," his dad added.

Brady continued "You're family, Mads, and you're a good man. I'm glad you told us, and I'm sorry about tonight."

Jamie sighed noisily. "I might have known it was you, Brady. What did you do?"

"Fuck off, Jamie. I just talked to Mads about Ten."

"Tell me you didn't go all woe is me on Jared."

"None of your business, *little* brother," Brady snapped.

"You're an asshole," Jamie gave back as good as he got.

"For goodness' sake, boys," Ten's mom interjected. Jamie and Brady stopped. "Jared, you're right. We should all be here for each other, not just rely on dumping everything on you. Ten will come back to us at Christmas, a different man. He'll be back on his skates in the spring and fighting the playoffs in the summer. I guarantee it."

Everyone murmured their agreement, even if none of us was entirely convinced this was true. When the call ended, I felt lighter, and by the time I left the arena, I felt as if, maybe, I could be the strong one Ten needed if I didn't have to be strong for everyone else.

THE THREE DAYS between the shit game with Boston and our next game in LA were more like normal. I worked the D-Corp hard, and they gave me one hundred and ten percent. I focused on the work, tried to ignore the pit of grief that permanently resided inside me, and when our plane touched down in sunny California, I felt a win in my bones.

"Coach Madsen?"

Our GM, Dawson Brown, stopped me as I picked up the key card for my room from Layton Foxx. Layton was covering for our social director, who was currently back home with food poisoning. I was the last of the staff to get my key before he moved on to the players' allocations.

Dawson waited for me to get the card, but he didn't say anything except my name. When he moved away though he gestured for me to follow, and dread flooded me. I hoisted my bag over my shoulder and followed him down a long corridor to a small room. He shut the door behind me, and we were alone. Just me and the man who paid my salary.

"Sir?" I inquired as politely as I could despite the fact my heart was racing faster than I thought possible.

"This is an important game," he began.

No shit, it was important. Of the games since Ten's accident, we'd lost half of them. Not lost in overtime, but lost miserably. The team's cohesion was skewed, but in the last few days, the spark was back. I could see it.

"Yes, sir."

"Young James, we're negotiating three years. Thoughts?"

I had to put the name James in context. James Sato-West, Westy, pulled up from the minors to replace Max Van Hellren, a good guy, focused, fast, and not at all fucked up from me taking my eye off the ball. I'd never been asked by the GM before about contract negotiations. That wasn't my area of expertise, but I sensed there was something happening here.

"Strong, offensively as well as defensively, works hard, scrappy, focused." I gave all the words I thought he wanted to hear, but something in his expression told me that it wasn't what he needed. Westy had been the one to suffer for me fucking things up, and maybe they were hesitating because he wasn't shining as much as he could. "I fucked up with him," I admitted and winced at the cursing I used. The GM's eyes widened. "Don't lose him because of what I did or didn't do."

Dawson nodded. "Thank you, Jared."

The weird meeting was over, and he opened the door to find nearly the whole Railers team in the small corridor outside. Did they think I was being canned? They stared at me, then the GM, then back at me. The comically choreographed move made me want to laugh. I loved this team and laughter welled inside me. Not hysterical laughter, but real affection and a smile to match. I hid it well.

"You all realize you're cutting into downtime," I said instead. "This is an afternoon game. Bus to the arena is in one hour precisely. Get the hell gone."

There was a moment of silence, and then everyone

moved away, even Stan who had been glaring at the GM and still threw a warning glance over his shoulder. God save me from Russians who "know people".

"Nice to see the respect," the GM said and began to leave. Then as if he'd forgotten something, he stopped and turned to me. "The jet is fueled and waiting to fly to Arizona after the game. We need you back by tomorrow midmorning. Layton has the details."

I couldn't move, rooted to the spot. The Railers jet was going to take me to see Ten? I wanted to say thank you, but by the time I got my head around what I'd just been told, he was gone.

We won the game against LA. I wish I could say it was easy, but it wasn't. The hockey was intense, but the Railers were fierce, and we took our first road win in a long time. I barely had time to shower and dress before the car arrived to take me to the jet. Flying to Tucson Airport, I was at the Draper Center in no time. I wanted to touch Ten so badly. Needed to see him as I needed air.

Ten had texted his congratulations on the win, added a smiley face, but that had been the extent of our interaction, and he wouldn't have expected more after all the postgame shit the teams needed to wade through. He didn't know I was in Arizona. Hell, he didn't know I was outside the gate.

My cell vibrated, and I checked the screen. Ten. I answered immediately.

"Hey," he said, sounding tired. "Great uhmm..."

"Game," I finished for him, even though I knew I shouldn't. The staff here had told me I needed to let him think for himself, to grow those connections, but I was so excited to see him I couldn't help myself.

"Yeah, game." He sighed. "Are you in your hotel room now?"

"Not exactly," I said and began to walk toward reception. "What are you doing?"

"Dinner, it was… good. Talking. Tired now. Going back to the room."

I reached the door and pressed the security button. "There's something for you in reception," I told him.

"You sent me… uhm… something… a present?"

I hated the way he stumbled over the words, wanted him to be able to talk for real. *Not long. If anyone can fight this, it's my Ten.*

"Yeah, go to reception, and you'll see it."

Security let me in, and I stood by the front desk, and I waited.

Ten

I RUBBED MY EYES WITH THE TIPS OF MY FINGERS, JUST IN case this was a medication-induced mirage. Mads looked up, our eyes met, and that loving smile tugged on his lips. Hell, this was no dream.

"Tennant," he said, giving the receptionist at the desk a nod before walking to me. A chaste kiss was all I got, which was fine. The old gal behind the desk didn't need to see two people swapping spit there in the lobby.

"Fuck, you feel good," I whispered after I burrowed into his arms. "Miss you… a lot."

He pressed his lips to my hair. "I miss you too. Come on, let's find a place to talk."

Excitement coursed through me. "I know… wait, I know… there's a good place."

"Then lead the way." He released me.

I slid my hand into his. I tried to fill him in on my progress as we walked, but the words kept tangling up. Which made me frustrated, which made it harder to concentrate, which made me even madder. By the time we arrived at the solarium, I was pissed and totally tongue-tied, my thoughts ramming into each other like bumper cars. "Hey, look up here at me."

He took my chin in his hand. "We have plenty of time. There's no rush. Slow down." He put his mouth on mine, his lips soft and warm.

My eyes fluttered downward, and I let his strength and calm seep into me. I wanted the kiss to deepen but knew it couldn't. I wanted to take him to my room and have him wipe the past horrors from my mind, but that couldn't happen either.

"Okay, yeah, I'm uhm… smooth now," I whispered as I stared into his blue eyes.

He nodded, the very model of a man who had his shit totally together. If only I could have had one-tenth of his self-possession. Ever since the accident, I was borderline madman, prone to snapping at people for no good reason.

"Let's look at the city." He draped his arm around me and led me to a wall of windows. "Tell me about Tucson. Have you seen much of it yet?"

"No, not much." I let my screwy head rest on his shoulder. The smell of him and the familiar solidity of his body next to mine eased my tension. "We—me and Declan and uhm… his name is Heath something, played back when you were playing. Therapist took us to some park, walked around with us as if we were kindergarten students. Then, we came back and made macaroni art. I shit you… not. Really, arts and crafts."

I snickered, and so did he. "I love macaroni art. Ryker made me hundreds. I might still have them packed away somewhere."

"Ten grand a day and we're gluing... ziti to cardboard."

"I'm sure they're doing more than arts and crafts for you. Is that the Raptors Arena?"

I followed the direction he was pointing. "Yeah, Raptors home ice."

"You look angry."

"Well, yeah, he's there, sitting in a box watching the game. F... fucker."

"Hey, no anger. Relax," he cooed, pulling me tighter to his side.

I did a little relaxation-type breathing. Julie, my therapist, had mentioned that adrenalin and I seemed to be at odds with each other. The angrier or more excited I got, the less focus I could apply to speaking well. And I could see that now that she'd pointed it out.

"People say I should press charges. Brady, Jamie, my folks... say it. Should I?" I looked up at him. Standing there, with the overhead lights, he was super tense and tired. The fine lines around his eyes and mouth were deeper. "You okay?"

He kissed my nose. "The last thing you need to be worrying about is me. I'm fine. Some jet lag is all. As to the question of pressing charges, I can't make that decision. What I would like you to concentrate on now is getting healthy. Legal matters can wait if you decide to proceed in that manner. Focus and courage."

"Courage... an indefinable quality that makes a man put out that extra something when it seems... there is nothing else to give."

"They teaching you Herb Brooks quotes in here?" he

asked as the desert city lay sprawled out in front of us, its lights little pinpricks.

"Nah, Brady had that as a poster on his wall. You saying be courageous, that reminded me of it."

"Mm, it's a fine quote from an amazing man. Also, you're smooth now."

I took a second and thought, then nodded. "Calm helps. Nothing calms me more than being in your arms."

He inhaled and exhaled, his big chest expanding. "Same here."

I tipped my head up for a kiss, and Mads, well, he never could resist my needy smooch face. His lashes fell to his cheeks, and his lips moved over mine. Small kisses, tender things that would have led us to something smoldering if we were home. Sadly, we weren't home. We were in Arizona, at the brain place, and he would be leaving soon.

"Ten, you still up for checkers or—Oh damn! Sorry, man."

Jared and I both started. Pulling back and turning, I saw Declan in the doorway, the box of checkers under his arm.

"No, hey, it's all good." I wiggled free, smiling, and took Jared's big mitt in mine. "Mads, this is Declan Fidler, cornerback for the Temple Owls football team. Dec, this is my boyfriend, Jared Madsen."

The two big men shook hands. Jared looked a little puzzled, but I chalked that up to fucking life in general right now. I mean, I was puzzled all the damn time, too.

"Nice to meet you, Coach Madsen. I didn't know you had company, T. We've kind of been hanging out on our downtime," Declan explained, shifting the checkers box from one arm to the other. "Place is packed full of old jocks."

"Right? Like, at least I can mention... Arctic Monkeys to you and not have you think I'm talking about Mickey Dolenz in Siberia."

Declan chuckled, and we did this funky little fist rap thing that we'd come up with. "I'll leave you to have some time. Nice to meet you, Coach Madsen. T, drop by when you can, and we'll set up the board. I got some new SZA for us."

"Cool, I'm..." The wheels slipped a bit. "Down. Down with that." Another fist rap routine and Dec was off. "He's cool. Plays Pokémon Go with me. Great laugh. Totally same musical tastes. Sucks at checkers, though."

"He seems like a nice kid," Mads replied, his expression hard to read. "Let's sit. I need to plant my saggy old ass somewhere."

I patted his ass as we made our way to a taupe sofa. "Not so saggy yet."

"Feels like it's dragging on the ground behind me," he replied, then sighed deeply when he dropped to the couch.

I sat beside him. The AC was blowing down on the back of my neck. I'd have to move soon or risk a sinus headache. I was trying my best to avoid any kind of headache trigger, which meant no sun without shades, no tiny detailed reading, healthy diet, lots of water, letting my PT crew know when I felt the creeping poke of pain inside my head blossom. Things had been pretty good the past few days, and I was assured that I would, indeed, continue to improve as long as I followed the regimen.

"Did you nod off?"

I jerked back to Mads. "Oh, no, I just... drifted. I'm so

tired. Like… mentally you know, exhausted. They put me into this seat today that spins you in all different directions. Totally NASA astronaut training kind of crap, right? Then… they measured brain waves and pupil dilation, and I do not know what the hell else."

"Good, I'm glad they're doing all they can for you. It's a world-class staff." He slipped his fingers into my hair, his expression wistful. "You're the single most important thing in this world to me right after Ryker. I just… well, if you hadn't been okay, I just…" His fingers drifted down from my hair to trace the bandage on my neck.

"Hey, dude, my man, you're not being a… cheery visitor here."

"Christ, yes, I'm sorry. I'm in that mentally exhausted boat with you." He stroked my face, his gaze searching mine. "I just wanted you to know how much I love you, Tennant. You're the reason I wake up with a smile, the reason I go to bed fulfilled, the reason that I am the man I am now."

"I love you wicked mad," I whispered, putting my lips to his just one time, then nestling into him to watch the winking, blinking city be a backdrop for the winking, blinking lights on a freaking cactus in a pot the size of a dorm fridge. "Is there snow in Harrisburg?"

"A little," he replied, his words warm puffs on my scalp.

"Good." Sure, I was a Southern boy and froze all winter long, but my life was now in the North, where there were fir trees in the corner, not cacti. There was just something majorly wrong with stuffed Santas hanging off a cactus.

"I'm looking forward to you being home for the two weeks."

"Mm, yeah, me too. I don't have any presents for—"

"Stop. Focus on the happy and good and the healing. You'll be home. That's all that matters. Trust me, your family does not care if they don't get a Far Side calendar from you this year. Just having you with us will be all the gift any of us need."

He always knew just what to say to make me feel whole and loved.

TWO DAYS LATER, Dec and I were in line for the Raptors game. I had my black Jigglypuff cap pulled down low over my brow so that the folks in the Raptors jerseys didn't recognize me. I was one of the crowd, nowhere near the team, but part of me needed to see the team again, get a feel for how much pain I still had inside me. Even if Aarni was still working out his suspension.

"T, are you sure this is a good idea?" Dec asked as we shuffled in through the front doors to wait for our turn to be wanded by security. "Place is going to be loud and bright, bud."

"Yeah, it's cool. I have shades and earplugs. I just… I need to be here."

"Okay, but first sign of distress, we're leaving."

I gave him a thumbs-up, then moved along in line. We aced security and then made our way to the lower bowl. Seats here were cheap. I mean, like dirt cheap. Maybe sand cheap would have been more fitting. To say the Raptors were a team in disarray would have been putting it mildly. They were struggling to hold on to fourth place in their division. The vibe was not good in the press, lots of talk about major renovations over the summer. I prayed that the first thing that went was Aarni Lankinin. He wasn't really human enough to be considered a person, so I categorized him as a thing, an it, a nasty sludge bucket who had humiliated and hurt Bryan Delaney in ways that a bruised brain and a couple of months of rehab could never compare to.

We paused at the top of the cement steps that led down into the lower bowl. I grabbed the cold metal rail, and I drew the smell of the rink into my lungs.

"Oh, God above, do you smell that?" I asked Dec.

"Yeah, smells like dinner."

"Dude, no, not the onions and peppers, the ice. The crisp molecules of frozen water that float in the air and get drawn into your lungs. The tang of sweat and men and crowds."

"Um, you want me to leave you and hockey alone for a while?"

That made me laugh. "Nah, I'm good. Only a semi-chub."

"Ass. Hey, go find our seats. I'll get us some food."

I turned my head to look up at him. "Get something greasy. And a beer."

"Nope, no beer. Meds."

"Fuck my life," I moaned. "Fine, soda then."

We rapped knuckles, and I went down the stairs, taking it slow in case the brain checked out and I fell on my face. I'd done that the first day of CRT and wanted to die of embarrassment. My eyes had just tangled up as I was working on the stepper, and *crack!* down on my face I had gone. The docs had assured me such things were normal and would, over time, stop happening. Over time. Over time. I should maybe get that tattooed on my neck instead of the Rowe family lion.

We had choice seats, right by the glass behind the away net. The Raptors were playing Vegas tonight, and I loved the Vegas goalie. I snapped some shots of him warming up and sent them to Stan, who had a serious case of fangirl all over the team chat. Within ten minutes, everyone on the freaking team was on the chat, all talking at me at once. I promised them all that I was totally allowed to be here. I wasn't in prison. I was free to come and go as I wished. Then I snapped some pics of Declan, and Adler just about creamed his shorts when he saw the famous collegiate football player.

Dec and I stuffed ourselves on Italian subs, onion rings, and giant cups full of foamy root beer. The music and lights gave me some issues, but not enough that I wanted to leave. I slid my shades on and protected my ears with tiny pink foam earplugs, and sat back and lost myself in the game. Dec didn't know the game well, but he cheered every time Vegas scored, which was often because I'd filled him in on the Raptors and shitbag Aarni.

Ryker popped up in a separate chat, him and his new guy, Jacob, who was adorable, and then my man sent me a message. It included a photo of the Christmas tree that he'd hauled in. It was big and fat and green as shit, and according to Mads, it poked like a porcupine. Something about seeing him and that naked tree hit me in the gut. I should've been there with him, setting it up.

I'm not decorating it until you come home, Mads texted. *We'll do that together.*

I was kind of emotional, so I took a fast selfie,

personalized it with hearts and flying pink pigs and the tagline *This is my love you face* which got me a long pause before a reply came back.

Where are you?

Raptors game w D

Big, drawn-out silence between my text and the next incoming one.

Why are you there?

Hockey. Bored. Root Beer. Hockey.

Another long pause.

Don't set yourself back, Tennant.

I won't. I needed to be here, see the ice, smell the stink of it all. You know.

Yes, I do. Just… be careful.

I hit him back quickly. *See you in two days. <3 U – T*

Love you as well. I'll dig out the ornaments. – J

The Vegas goalie made this outrageous save, and the crowd went wild. I winced at the noise, even with the plugs in my ears. I turned off my phone, feeling strange and out of sorts, and let the game take me to that place it always did. Out of myself and into oneness with the ice and the puck.

Jared

I'D HAD THIS IDEA OF HOW CHRISTMAS WOULD GO SINCE Ten and I had fallen in love. The Railers were at an away game in Vancouver on the twenty-second, then nothing until the twenty-seventh, when we had Florida visiting us. Five whole days, me and Ten, obviously interspersed with family time, but mostly it was going to be about the two of us. Everything was planned.

See, there was something really important supposed to happen Christmas Day. I had this whole montage going on in my head, delicately orchestrated and timed, to the nearest second. There we would be, surrounded by gifts, with coffee and Santa cookies, Christmas music on the iPod, and I would pretend that I had forgotten a gift. Nothing big, I would tell Ten. Nothing that he'd miss if I didn't go and get it for him. He would tease me, demand his gift, and I would make him wait until kissing turned to more, and finally, I would get the gift from the drawer where it was hidden, and I would take it out and fall to one knee.

And ask Ten to marry me.

That was how it was *supposed* to go. I even had the music reaching a crescendo when he said yes.

But I didn't know if that would happen now. It wasn't because I didn't want to ask him because I did more than anything. Only, I wanted it to be special. I wanted music and lighting and mood, and most of all I wanted Ten not to be battling a headache or be spaced out or a million of the other things he was fighting at the moment. I wanted his answer to be real and right, and I wanted the moment to be something he remembered for the rest of his life.

So, yeah, the proposal might not happen that way, but unless I had the rings, it wouldn't be happening at all.

Which was why I was standing outside Rose's jewelry shop, in the sleet and snow, staring at the door as if it had poison on the handle, and touching it would kill me. I slouched into my huge puffy coat even more, yanking at my beanie, cursing at the freezing air as it bit sharply at every sliver of bare skin. I'd allowed two hours for this visit. Parking, walking through the mall, maybe getting a coffee, holding on to that delicious feeling of anticipation that I knew I would feel. But I'd used up half of that time standing at various points outside, wondering why the hell everything had gone wrong for Ten. For me. For us. I cycled from selfish feelings to having hope to experiencing despair, and as if Mother Nature knew my thoughts, she was throwing every single icy dart to get me to move inside.

Finally, when I'd moved past selfish and onto acceptance, I pushed the door open and stood inside.

And I didn't move.

The warmth burned those parts of my exposed skin that had frozen, my nose was running, my head pounding, and the garish lights on tiny trees assaulted my eyes. I nearly turned and ran.

Or at least I would have if I wasn't stuck to the floor as if there was lead in my boots.

"Can I help you?" a short woman asked me. Her badge said her name was Alyssa. Her pretty name matched her perky nose, ready smile, and long, blonde, hair that formed an angelic cloud around her shoulders. She wore the requisite holiday holly in her curls, and in each ear she had a sparkling LED Santa flashing in a discordant rhythm that made me twitch.

I wish Ten was here. Then I listened to myself. *Ten wouldn't be here anyway. I'm picking up the damn rings. I don't need Ten by my side in every difficult situation.*

"Sir?" she asked again, and there was a small frown of concern right between her perfectly shaped eyebrows. "Do you want to sit down? Shall I take your coat? It's wet through. Hang on."

She vanished then, but I still didn't move, and she was back in a flash with a mug. "Coffee, black, but we have cream. Would you like some cream? Sugar?"

All I could think at that moment was that the coffee was hot and I was way past cold.

"You should take off your coat," she said when I didn't answer and held on to the lifesaving caffeine as a hostage until I unzipped my jacket, which took forever with frozen fingers.

I'd seen Ten struggle with zips and buttons. Apparently his fine motor skills were, for want of a better word, bruised. Or at least all the nerves and synapses were bruised. I listened to the experts explain that, but I'd never understood. Not until that moment when my fingers scrambled to get the right hold.

"Cream, please," I said. Anything to get her away from me so she didn't watch me act like a freaking idiot.

She disappeared again, and by the time she was back, I was out of my coat, gloves, hat, semi-solid iced-over scarf, and stood just in my jeans and my Railers hoodie.

She handed me the coffee and second-looked the logo on the front of my hoodie and then up at my face.

"Oh my," she announced. "Coach Madsen." She held out a hand. "I am a huge Railers fan, the biggest."

I shook it as best I could, my skin prickling and numb in different places. I waited for her to make connections and for the sympathy that was being thrown at me from all sides.

God, listen to me. People just care, okay. You're a fucking idiot, Madsen.

It was just so painful to be the focus of attention when all I wanted to do was get the job done on the ice. I steeled myself for the usual, but she didn't go there at all, at least not all the way through to stammering and not knowing where to look.

"I'm so excited to see Ten back on the ice," she began, then dragged a chair out from the corner. "Have a seat. I loved the way you paired Arvy and Luka or at least, I know you don't have the final say, but we are so forwards-heavy, and sometimes it isn't all about the forwards, you know. I mean, flashy goal scoring is one thing, but when you have leaks in front of the net like the Boston game, then it doesn't matter what Stan does. He'll never be able to stop them all."

She pulled the other chair over and sat opposite me as if she had all the time in the day to talk to a half-frozen defensive coach.

"But Andrew, he's my husband, he's a Boston fan, so he loved that they shot us down so badly." She laughed then. "Of course, with all the money tied up at the front, the D is going to suffer, so I like that you're working to bring guys up from the Rush. Have you seen Taz play recently? He's on fire."

"Sorry about the Boston game," I offered because that defensive mess was on me. I know I'd taken care of it, but to hear all of this from a fan, that was pretty damn cool. The pairs had worked well, and after my admission of how I was fucking up, it seemed as if my D-Corp was going above and beyond to keep their shit together.

"It's one game, and we're still Stanley Cup champions." She held out her hand to fist pump me, and there was something about her, something infectious, friendliness, talking about the game, not about me and Ten, but about hockey. She'd grown up a Vancouver fan, having lived there as a child, but as soon as the Railers franchise happened, she was one hundred percent behind her home team. I found out she was a big Stan fan, but our goalie attracted fans wherever he went, and that she had cried buckets of tears when we'd lifted the cup in the summer.

You and me both, Alyssa.

I don't know how long we sat and talked hockey, but it was for at least two coffees, and only when I felt human did she ask me how she could help me.

"I came in to pick up rings I'd ordered online. They're under the name Jared Smith."

She grinned so wide it had to hurt. "Oh, we wondered who that would be. Never put my money on you though. Thought it might be Jared Leto, but then why would he be ordering from us in Harrisburg? Hang on a minute, and I'll go to the safe and get them. Let me take your mug."

I passed her my empty coffee cup, and she left me sitting under the blowing air. I was toasty warm, and outside the glass door, the wind howled, and the snow fell, and somewhere out there, miles away in Arizona, Ten was probably in PT or drawing pictures or practicing walking backwards.

I love him so much it hurts.

"Here you go," she said and gestured for me to join her at the counter.

I stood, and miraculously all my limbs had unfrozen, and the short walk didn't hurt one little bit. She'd unrolled a square of black velvet and carefully placed the two rings on the small piece of fabric. They were exactly as I had imagined. Custom designed with help from Gatlin Pearce, at first glance, they appeared to be simple platinum bands. Solid and secure, they would last forever. But when I tilted them to the light, the subtly engraved *J* and *T*, and the tiniest of hockey pucks, joined by miniature hearts, were easily seen. Inside was a message, exactly the same on each. *Tennant & Jared Forever.*

Tears choked my throat, and I forced them back. Tears had no place in this moment when I first saw the evidence of what I wanted to do.

"Ten will be so happy with them," she murmured, then blushed when I glanced up at her.

I'd deliberately chosen this jeweler because of how my hockey friends said it was high end and that they dealt with every purchase with discretion. But I guess she could've Tweeted this right then, and Ten would've found out, and then everything would've been ruined.

"We serve with the utmost discretion," she said and laid a hand over mine, squeezing a little. "Nothing leaves this place."

"Thank you."

I picked up Ten's. It was slightly smaller than mine. He had long, delicate hands for a hockey player, strong but slim, able to play a concerto as much as placing a wicked slapshot in the net. Still, these were men's rings, sturdy, beautiful.

"I love them," I said.

"Would you like me to put them in their box?"

I watched as she deftly gave them a once-over with a polishing cloth and placed them carefully in a single box with a double space. How stupid was it that I didn't even want the rings separated?

I paid the balance and put the rings into the zip pocket of my hoodie; my coat was still too wet. I couldn't avoid putting it back on though. Better a wet coat than nothing at all in this weather. The door opened as I left, a couple coming in, wide-eyed and full of excitement. Alyssa gave me one last smile and left me with two things.

"Make sure you take down Vancouver, right?"

"We will," I said, defiant to any person who wanted to take the win off of us.

"Have a *really* good Christmas, Mr. Smith."

The door shut behind me, thrusting me into the snow and ice, but I had this warmth inside me, a cautious flicker of happiness, and I hurried back to the car and home. Only after I buried the rings in with my socks, right at the back of the drawer, did I do what I really wanted to.

Ten answered on the first ring, as if he'd been waiting for my call.

"I love you," I said, even before the hellos.

"I love you, too," Ten said, clear as day, no stuttering, possibly one of the things he'd been practicing. "Why did you… say…?"

"I'll always love you. You remember that, right?"

The line went quiet, and I cursed to myself. Of course he remembered I love him. Why was I so fucking needy? It wasn't me in a facility getting my brain unscrambled.

"I will always love you too," he spoke deliberately, slowly, and then laughed. "Guess what I just did."

I slumped back on the sofa. "What?"

"That thing… with fingers… we had to build with plastic… bricks… the word…"

I so badly wanted to tell him that he meant dexterity, but I didn't.

"Aha! Dexterity, that's the word."

"Ryker used to love brick building," I said and chuckled. I remember huge great Death Stars and one particularly difficult castle with knights and horses. "What did you build?"

"A house," he said with no stumbling. "Only it looked… bad."

"How bad?"

"Dec said it was bad. That houses aren't… green."

It didn't even matter that Declan was part of the story. Ten sounded as if he was smiling, and really that was all I wanted; for Ten to smile.

"I've seen green houses," I pointed out. "I think Declan is talking out of his ass. I've seen pink houses, blue ones, I've even seen a few purple ones."

"Is that a... thing... in Canada?"

I had to let him have those pauses, wait for his brain to catch up with everything going on in his head.

"Ha freaking ha, Southern boy. So the house was a good one?"

"As houses go. Next I have..." He paused, and there was some talking that was muffled as if he had his hand over the phone. "Macramé," he announced with great enthusiasm. "Dec says two minutes."

That chest tightening thing happened again, and I didn't think it was jealousy of Ten talking to another man. Not quite jealousy, maybe envy that Dec could be in Ten's periphery instead, even maybe helping Ten to heal. *I'm a complicated mess of contradictions.* I changed the subject so I could cover the important things in the last few minutes before I had to wait until tonight to talk to him again.

"Are you packed yet for the day after tomorrow?"

"Uhm... packed? Why would I be packed?"

Shit. Did he not remember he was coming home for Christmas? I looked at the decorations in the boxes, and my chest tightened even more. How could he forget coming home to me?

Then the fucker laughed. "Only joking. I'm *so* packed, and I... can't wait."

"You know you're an asshole, and I really hate you," I groused.

And Ten snorted a laugh; it had been a long time since I heard that laugh. "You'll always love me."

I gripped the phone, wanting to send all my love down the line to him, imagining it winding its way down the country taking a turn in the middle and heading for Arizona.

"Yes, babe. Always."

Ten

FLYING FIRST CLASS WAS PLUSH. MY OWN SEAT BY A window, lots of leg room, a flight attendant who brought me ginger ale when my stomach got touchy after takeoff, some ibuprofen when my head started to ache from the cabin pressure, and a new sleeping mask to block out the lights when the string on the one I had came off. Her name was Melinda, and she was amazing.

"Sorry for being such a pain," I said again as she refilled my ginger ale. I knew I was being whiny. Flying with a lingering head injury was totally different from flying when a person's brain wasn't healing from a bruise. Normally I aced this jet-hopping shit.

"It's fine, Mr. Rowe. If you need anything else, please let me know." Melinda shook open the packaged blanket and laid it over my lap with a soft smile. If I'd been into women, I would've asked the tall, leggy black woman out on a date. Sure, she was older than me by about ten years, but I kind of liked a little age on my lovers.

I settled back into the well-padded seat, slid my

earbuds in, and let my tunes drown out the noise of the flight. The music was low, loud stuff made me wince, but even at low volume, Marianas Trench's fourth album *Astoria* seeped into my soul and eased it. I napped on and off for the four-hour flight, waking as we descended for the landing. My gut rolled over when we touched down, a side-effect of the TSAH, Traumatic Subarachnoid Hemorrhage, in brain doctor speak. I removed the sleep mask, eased the window blind up, and grimaced at the brilliant sun reflecting off the white snow blanketing the tarmac. *Right, shades on.*

I filed off the plane with the other first-class passengers, my Railers bag over my shoulder. I'd only brought a carry-on. Most of my clothes were still in the dresser at home. Home. The space I shared with Mads. I was so desperate to see him I had to tamp down the urge to run into the terminal. Being stuck behind an old woman with a cane as we made our way up the jet bridge kept me in check.

I stepped around the old gal once we were inside and had our bags, and amid the crush of holiday travelers, Jared Madsen stood out. He was taller than most, broader than most, and way fucking more handsome than anyone else on the planet. He raised a hand, and I raced to him, not giving two shits about the odd looks I was getting. Mads opened his arms for me. I bounced off some dude with a rolling suitcase, fumbling over my feet, recovered, apologized, and then threw myself at Mads. He lifted me a few inches, arms tight around my middle, and kissed me passionately.

"Hey," I panted in greeting when we came up for air.

"Hey." His light blue eyes glistened like tourmaline gems. "God, I've missed you."

"Same here." I ran my finger through his short, golden hair, loving the crisp feel on my fingers. "Let's go home. I want to get... all over you."

He let me down, my sneakers dropping back to the floor. "About that..."

I snuggled into his chest, burrowing my nose into the lapels of his winter coat and inhaling the erotic fragrance of his cologne mingled with his unique scent.

"Tell me the family hasn't descended," I mumbled into his coat.

"Like a flock of blackbirds on a cornfield." He nuzzled into my hair.

"Great." I sighed, hugged him tight, and then because I had to, I pulled away. "Are they all here?"

"Every single one and the dog." He lifted my bag from my shoulder, dropped it onto his shoulder, and took my hand. Some people looked at us in disgust, but a lot didn't notice at all.

"Man, our place... must be packed full."

He led me outside. The cold was so severe it made my nose hair freeze and my head ache. Mads gave me a worried frown. "Are you in pain?"

"Meh, cold headache. I'm fine."

"Let's get you into the car and warmed up."

Being fussed over was nice. The ride to our apartment was uneventful, just Mads and me talking about my therapy and the treatments they were giving me and the Railers. When we pulled up in front of our townhouse, I moaned at the rental cars in our driveway.

"Man, you weren't kidding." I sighed, wishing that my

loving, crazy family could have given Mads and me at least one hour of alone time.

"They'll all go to their respective hotels later," Mads told me, slipping his big Range Rover into park. "Well, except for your mother and father. They're in the guest room."

"Well, sure they are." I stepped out of the car to the curb because we'd been relegated to the street, glancing up at the front door with the evergreen wreath opening up. There stood my mother in the doorway, her hands clasped and resting on her chest, her smile wobbly.

I was about to call out a greeting to her when a snowball the size of a cannonball hit me in the face. I stumbled back into the fender of Mads' car, spitting and coughing as someone—it sounded a great deal like Jamie —yelled something indecipherable.

Wiping snow from behind my sunglasses with my finger, I heard my mother come completely unhinged on her middle son. The snowball hadn't hurt, but hearing my brother get chewed out was always fun.

"James Rowe! What the *hell* are you doing throwing snowballs at Tennant? What if that had a rock in it as it did that time he was seven?"

"Ten, are you okay?" Mads asked, stepping up beside me.

I chuckled, nodded, and handed him my snowy shades. "Yeah, it's all good." Jamie was in the front yard, beside Brady, both dressed for snow with coats, hats, scarves, and gloves. The sun hurt my eyes, but as they adjusted, I saw the pile of snowballs by the driveway. Typical Rowe boys' welcome home. My mother was still yelling at Jamie. "Mom, hey, it's cool! I'm fine. He totally owed me that one. I got him with a water balloon the last time we were in Florida."

"He does *not* owe you that! You're recovering from a major brain injury, and he throws a snowball at your head. You both apologize to your little brother right now." She stood in front of them, her nice warm spot inside the door left as the maternal rage had overcome her, staring up the men who had a good foot of height on her. She was so mad her hands were tightly fisted at her sides.

"Why am *I* getting yelled at?" Brady inquired. "I didn't throw it at his head."

"Because you're the eldest and should have talked him out of it." Mom pointed at him. I waited patiently, Mads at my side. "James?"

"Sorry, Ten, I wasn't aiming at your face. I was aiming at your balls."

"*James!*"

"Well, I was," he muttered.

"Christ, no wonder you can't hit the one or three hole," Brady chimed in.

The sound of kids screaming rolled out of the house. Brady's twin girls, no doubt. Jamie's daughter too, I bet.

"Oh, fuck you, Brady," Jamie fired back. "At least I can say Saturday correctly."

"Don't start with that shit. I speak just fine."

"Ah no, you don't. It's Saturday, not Saddadee."

The twins ran outside in their slippers. Their mother, Lisa #1, who was growing big and round with their second set of twins, waddled outside to yell at the girls.

Jamie's daughter started crying right after Brady's dog, Bourque, dashed outside after the children with a stuffed bear in his big jowls. Her howls bounced down the street.

I glanced at Mads. "Maybe *we* should get a hotel room and let them have the townhouse?"

"Tempting," he replied with a soft smile. "But the tree is in there waiting for us."

"Ah, well, okay, I guess we'll have to stay here then." I took my shades back from Mads and put them back on. "For the… tree."

"For the tree." He ruffled my hair gently.

WE NEVER GOT to the tree decorating. My family kind of swept us along like a storm surge. Everyone talked at me all day long, asking questions about rehab, how I felt, had I thought about checking for something closer to home for the specialty rehabilitation, had I watched that new superhero show on Netflix, and on and on and on until my sluggish brain was on the verge of shutting down.

Thankfully, the dinner bell was rung and saved me. Sitting next to Mads, I tossed back some pain pills while Brady got the girls into their seats. They were tired and cranky, miserable to be exact, which made three of us. Brady's Lisa looked to be in the same boat. If not for the fact that Mom had made one of my favorite meals—lasagna—I would have begged off and gone to lie down in our bedroom, preferably with Mads and no lights or sounds. But Mom was in full Mama Bear mode, hovering around me all day, bringing me anything I might've needed or thought I might've needed in the near future.

As always, the talk at any Rowe gathering soon turned to hockey, our teams, and how we were doing in the standings. This would, inevitably, turn into a dick-swinging contest between Brady and Jamie. I poked at the slab of saucy noodles on my plate, the thumping headache souring my appetite. Both Lisas tried to stem the hockey talk after giving me several furtive glances, but the two elder Rowes were in full cock battle mode.

"… just saying that if your attention were on the odd man skating high…"

"… difference in a one-man or two-man forecheck…"

"… left wing lock like Montreal and Detroit have used…"

"… New Jersey trapped their way to how many Cup wins and never…"

"… not every team can be a free-flowing team…"

"… get his opinion. What do you think, Ten?"

Mads tapped my knee with his. I lifted my eyes from my lasagna and was shocked to discover that Mom had cleared the table and placed a massive chocolate cake in front of me. When I glanced around, everyone at the table, down to Jamie's little girl Bethany, was staring at me. My brain slammed down as all the words spoken around me in the last half hour tried to jam themselves into my head at once.

"Uhm… I guess I'm… the forecheck is kind of, I never… the odd man… uhm, could we… I need to… fuck." I buried my face in my hands.

The deafening silence that fell over the table made my shaky breathing sound louder.

"I think it's time for Ten to relax. Too much overstimulation shorts him out a bit," Mads said, pushing to his feet and taking me by the elbow. No one, not even Bethany, who was a jabber-monkey, said a thing. "Come on, babe."

I stood, stared at the cake, which was my favorite kind

of cake, and then found my mother. Tears welled in her eyes. I turned away and leaned on Mads. He led me to our bedroom, gently closed the door, and moved around me with quiet, confident ease. I let him peel me out of my clothes. When I was down to my underwear, he got me into bed, crawled in beside me in just his briefs, turned off the light and held me close.

"Mads, I—"

"Shh." His fingers slid into my hair. He didn't rub or stroke my scalp. He just let his hand rest there.

"It's too…" I drew in a reedy breath. "Bed. Too early for… bed. I hate this, Mads. I just… want to be… me again." I wept on his chest for a few minutes, unable to string the words together to express how fucking fed up I was with the whole miserable situation.

"Everything will get better, Ten. Give it time. Your injury is fresh. Try to rest, babe. Things will look better in the morning."

I snuffled, my thoughts starting to string out and get fuzzy. The pain meds were seeping into my bruised gray matter. Sleep stole me away from Mads for several hours. When I woke at five a.m., my mouth was crusty and my throat dry. Damn pain pills gave me such cotton mouth. Mads was on his side, facing the window, deeply asleep. Not wanting to rouse him, I slipped out of bed, pawed around for some clothes in the dark, and padded downstairs in a pair of my jogging pants and one of my boyfriend's old Sabres T-shirts.

"Good morning," my mother called from the living room. She was seated on the bench in front of my old upright piano, sipping some coffee, in her pajamas and a robe, her hair brushed neatly. I made my way to her. She smiled feebly up at me. I bent down to kiss her cheek. "Are you feeling better?"

"Yeah, thanks." I lowered myself to the bench beside her. She slid around to face the piano. "My head just gets… filled up, and the injury slows… it slows me down, my responses and speech and… stuff."

"We shouldn't have all come here at once," she murmured into her mug.

"No, no, I like you here." I studied her profile. She wrinkled her nose. "I do. I could live without Jamie and Brady, but… but everyone else is cool."

That made her smile just a little. "Your brothers love you, even if they have barbaric ways of showing it at times."

"I know."

She offered me her coffee. I took it with a soft "thanks" and sipped cautiously. The warm, sweet liquid felt wonderful sliding down my throat. We sat there for a few minutes, sharing coffee in front of the ugly upright that rested by a naked fir tree.

"I've been doing lots of reading of late about how music stimulates the brain in powerful ways. Research shows that it does wonders for those who suffer from Alzheimer's or who have brain disorders."

I threw her a look. "I'm not fighting… dementia."

"No, but the therapy you're getting in Tucson is similar to that they use for stroke victims or those who are battling Alzheimer's. Would you like to try something simple?" She slowly lifted the fallboard. I stared at the black and white keys as if they were scorpions. "*Chopsticks* maybe?"

"No, I can't… even talk right. The notes will confuse me." I closed the fallboard.

"I did not raise men who were quitters." She opened the fallboard. I closed it. She opened it and laid her fingers on the keys, in position for the song I had learned when I was three or something.

"Cheater," I grumbled but took my position on the keyboard. We'd performed this duet a thousand times when I was learning to play. It was burned into my brain cells. The trick, we'd learned as I faltered along, so far behind her that the childish little song was totally out of sync, was getting my brain to feed my fingers quickly enough. She paused several times to let me catch up, but the relays from my brain to my fingers were listless. "Fuck, I just… can't. *I can't*!"

I cleared the sheet music from the music rack in raging frustration, then slammed the fallboard shut. Mom sat beside me, face drawn, as sheets filled with tiny black notes that I would probably never be able to read again, fluttered to the carpet.

"I can't… Mom, I can't do this…" I coughed, my emotions running wild, my thoughts a tangled mess.

"You will," she softly assured me, then took me into her arms. "You will, baby boy. You will. I know my son. You will."

I was glad she had so much faith in me. Someone had to believe it would all be okay in time. God knows I was having doubts.

Jared

I HOVERED OUTSIDE THE DOOR, WATCHING AS TEN CLUNG to Jean, the detritus of his breakdown scattered around them. I wanted to go in and scoop him up, tell him it was all just a matter of time, that he *would* be okay, and that he should *believe*, but he needed this time with his mom.

He'd slept like the dead, clinging to me much as he was clinging to his mom now, and when he woke, I'd heard him stumbling around the room, but he was humming. Just that soft sound of a song I couldn't even identify was normal-Ten, and I didn't want to break any tenuous connection to a time before the accident. I slipped away before either of them saw me, and got busy in the kitchen making more coffee, waiting for that moment in which either Ten or his mom might need me.

"Morning," Ten murmured, wrapping his arms around me from behind, and I tensed a little before relaxing.

Twisting to face him, I then pulled him close and held him as the coffee percolated. "What do you want for breakfast?" I asked, pressing my lips to his neck and kissing him right in that warm spot that was all mine.

"Chocolate cake," he said. His tone suggested he was waiting for me to say that he should eat oatmeal or fruit or anything that wasn't full of sugar, but the lover side of me wanted Ten to be happy, and what did one morning of acting like a kid matter?

"Me too," I lied.

I wriggled free of his grasp and cut two generous slices from what was left of the demolished cake, then placed that and coffee on our kitchen table. He took his usual chair. I took mine, at right angles to him, and we ate cake and drank coffee, all while holding hands. I couldn't help glancing at him, seeing the seriousness in his expression as he forked up the cake, and then the sheer pleasure as he sucked on the chocolate and moaned in delight. I couldn't help it; my boyfriend was struggling with a head injury, but the sounds he was making over the chocolate were pornographic, and it had been so long since we'd been together. I was lost in the sounds.

"Do you not want yours?" Ten asked.

I looked down at my plate, realized I'd hardly touched my cake.

"May I have it?" he asked and slid my plate to him, flushing scarlet, as if he could read my thoughts.

There was a stray crumb at the corner of his mouth, and I knew he'd get it, but I softly kissed it off him with a glide of my tongue over his lips, which he was happy to return. "Too long," I murmured. "I miss kissing you every day, miss touching you."

He smiled at me, and there was my Ten, his green eyes twinkling, his eyebrows raised.

"I need a shower," he murmured.

"Okay." I wasn't disappointed. He needed a shower and actually didn't need me taking liberties with him. But then he placed a hand on my thigh, squeezing it gently.

"I need help in there," he said, pushing away his plate and using the table to stand. "Can you *help* me?"

I was up and out of my chair in less than a second, guiding him out of the kitchen and to our room. We passed his mom.

"Dad and I are popping to the hotel and taking the kids out shopping. Are you okay with a day on your own?"

I read between the lines; she was giving Ten some space and peace, and that was exactly what he needed right now. She was being the responsible one, when all I was doing was expecting things from Ten when he was ill. Guilt flooded me, and it was actually Ten who answered his mother.

"Have a good time," he said, hugging his mom and his dad and waiting at the door until he saw them go. "We should move your car off the street," he said, all kinds of responsible.

I picked up the keys from the dish, but he stopped me as he closed the door.

"Shower first, okay?"

I could do this. I could be the grown-up here and help him, watch him in case he fell over or got dizzy, or needed me to pass the soap. Shoulders back, I went straight into our room and through to the shower. We'd made the new area into a wet room, with big shower heads. The whole space was built for two men, a shelf in there for his products, a small space for mine. He didn't have to know I'd been using his things while he was away, just to have the scent of him on me. Because that was sappy and stupid. Right?

"I'm taking this back with me," he announced, picking up the bottle of Dior Homme shower gel that was my only luxury. "So I can smell you on me."

My chest tightened, and I gathered him close. "I use your stuff when you're not here," I admitted.

He sniffed my neck and smiled, but then it dropped. "I hate not being together," Ten said, his sentence strong. It was as if he'd been thinking it so long in his head that it was easy to say.

"Me too." I felt I couldn't contain the emotions inside me and to say anything more would've forced me to lose control.

"Shower," he said after a while, taking off his pajamas, the ones he wore when we had company, with tiny hockey sticks in the fabric, courtesy of Jamie who never thought Ten would actually wear them. I leaned back against the sink, watching him, ready to help at a moment's notice, but he managed just fine, and I got an eyeful of a naked, sexy Ten who went into the shower and stretched tall before turning on the water. "Come on, get in," he said, his back to me. At this angle, I could see the end of the scar on his neck, which one day would be disguised with a tattoo. It was horrific to recall the blood and the deep cut, but it was a pink line now the stitches were gone, but I couldn't think about that; otherwise I would've completely lost control.

"You want me in there with you…?"

He turned to face me and smiled encouragingly. "I need your help."

I stripped in record time, flinging my clothes at the

hamper and stepping under the water. "What can I do?" Did he need me to help him balance or just support him?

"This," he said and took my hand, entwining our fingers and guiding me to his cock, which was hardening in our hold. "I need this."

Was he doing this for me? Did he see the lust in me this morning? God, was I going to hurt him? Why did he want this?

"You can't—"

"I… can. I want… this."

I watched the small frown between his eyes as he stumbled over the words. Abruptly, I knew I was right; he'd clearly practiced what he wanted to say, but now he was losing the words as we moved off-script.

"Okay," I said, "Let's just kiss, right?"

His frown grew, and then he kissed me, and I had an armful of wet and incredibly sexy Ten. I was hard in an instant, and our hands remained twined as he moved them along the length of him. I used soap to help, rested back against the wall so that I held his weight, and we kissed for so long, the rainfall of water warm on his back. He moaned into the kiss, and I gripped his butt, turning him a little so we could see our hands in unison on him.

"Jared…" he whispered, groaned, kissing me, parting to look down.

I supported him completely as he got closer and closer, his moans turning to soft whimpers and the frown disappearing from his face completely. When he came, he was quiet, and I followed not long after, just from the soft touch of his fingers. Then, showered, I wrapped him in one of our sinfully soft towels and guided him to the bed. His hair was still damp, so I rubbed off the excess water.

Normally he'd fuss in front of the mirror, but right now, he just wanted to lie down, and he pulled me with him. In towels, eyes closed, we hugged and held each other, and I could feel his smile against my skin.

"I love you," I said because I needed him to know, to be sure of me, as much as I was with of him.

"I love you more," he said back, and all was right in our world.

THE TEXT that woke me was from Ten's mom to tell us they were staying out for dinner. I sent back a kiss and a thank you.

"Who... did... was it?" Ten asked sleepily, and I rolled to face him, kissing his nose.

"Your mom says she your dad and her are staying out with the family, and we shouldn't wait to do the tree."

He smiled and yawned, stretching, and I saw the wince when he turned his neck. In this position, I could see what remained of the skate blade's cut up close. But I wasn't seeing the scar, I was thinking about the lion that Gatlin had suggested he have tattooed.

Strength. Power. That was what a lion meant to me, and that was exactly Ten.

"We can do the..." He closed his eyes. "Tree," he finished, but he didn't frown with the effort, and that was a good thing.

I rolled up and out of bed; it was two in the afternoon, and we had all of today to be together because tomorrow I was back with the Railers, thankful they'd given me the two full days to be with Ten. We might not have had a game until after Christmas, but I needed to train with my defensemen so we kept up momentum. Ten knew that; he understood.

I dressed, put coffee on, made sandwiches full of roast beef and salad, and pulled out a bag of Ten's favorite chips. We ate and smiled, and Ten was relaxed. Only when we were done did he wander into the living room while I cleared up the plates. By the time I made it in with soft drinks and popcorn, the low sounds of Christmas music filled the room, and Ten was crouched on the floor next to a box that he'd found somewhere. It was only when I got closer that I saw the logo of the facility that Ten was staying at.

Ten unclipped one side. "They make it… difficult on… purpose," he said, although the pauses between words weren't as jagged as they had been before his sleep.

I crouched next to him. "I guess that helps fine motor skills," I said, just for something to say.

He nodded and unclipped the other side, then slid off the lid and rummaged in a tangle of shredded paper, finally lifting out a brightly covered *thing*.

I wasn't sure what I was seeing and then realized it was a handmade ornament, wooden clothes pegs, bright red paint alongside brown, splashes of white, and what I was now holding was Rudolph, scarlet nose and all, made out of pegs and glue. Tears pricked the back of my eyes. This wasn't a child's work; it was neat, strong looking.

"I did that," Ten announced proudly.

Grief and pride snapped and snarled inside me, and my breath was stolen at the enormity of what I was holding. This was Ten, the most capable forward in the NHL, a star on the rise, a man who could hold a team to a high standard without skipping a beat, and he was handing me a decoration that was the pinnacle of his achievement since the accident.

It meant so much to me. It was everything.

I cried. "It's beautiful. You're beautiful. I love you." I was talking a lot, all the love that was inside spilled out in a hurried mix and mess of words. "I love you."

I hadn't broken down in front of Ten like this, not for real, not when every worry and fear pushed at me and forced the tears from my eyes.

He smiled at me. Then it became a grin, and even though there were tears in his eyes, he was okay.

He'll be okay.

I wanted to ask him to marry me right there and then, but even as I opened my mouth, something stopped me. He had to know what he was doing. He had to be able to think of the consequences of saying yes, had to know what his forever would be like before he committed.

"I love you," he said and took the ornament back, standing carefully and then approaching the tree, appraising it critically. "Here," he said and separated the ribbon so it would slip over the branch of the huge Norwegian fir.

We hugged then and faced the ornament on the empty tree.

"Perfect," I said, then picked up the larger box of lights and ornaments I'd purchased for us. Next year we could go out together and buy more, special ones, like the one we'd put up first. "When we're sixty and we put that ornament up, it will mean something," I voiced my thoughts.

Ten hooked a small gold angel to another branch as I untangled lights, which I swear hadn't been tangled when I'd first taken them off the spindle they'd come on.

He cleared his throat and looked me right in the eyes, pausing a little as he formed words, nodding. "Being with you means everything."

I was so damn proud of him I could've burst, and fuck my life if the tears weren't back.

With everything finished, we held hands, turning on the lights, which thankfully worked the first time, and I truly had never seen a more perfect tree.

Ten tugged me away and to the sofa, and we sat next to each other as Nat King Cole crooned about chestnuts roasting on an open fire.

"I want to skate," Ten said.

"You will soon." I was confident. I knew he would be back on skates one day soon. He was healing well, reports were encouraging. It wouldn't be long.

Then he broke my heart into a million pieces, turning his liquid emerald gaze to me. "Now, Jared."

"You can't, Ten—"

"I want to."

"Have they said—?"

"Please."

How could I resist?

Ten

MADS AND I SNEAKED OUT TO OUR PRACTICE FACILITY IN Rutherford. With the team on holiday leave for a few days and most of the amateur leagues on break until the new year, we figured we'd have the place to ourselves. And we did. After a quick call to the manager who was more than happy to come unlock the front door, then give Mads the key, we were in.

"Ah man," I whispered, the barn quiet as vespers in a nunnery. I closed my eyes and inhaled. Yeah, there it was. The tang of frozen water and sweat. Gross sounding, I know, but that smell was just one small component of the rush that hockey gave me. "You smell that, Mads?"

He nodded, pocketed the key, and shifted our equipment bag to his other hand. "Smells like hockey."

He got it. I caught the flare of sport lust in his blue eyes. Once an ice rat, always an ice rat.

"I'm stoked," I confessed, the ice smooth as glass, beckoning me to lace up and step out on her surface. Such a siren ice was. "Scared too… big-time scared. What if—?"

"Do you want to call it off?" Mads stepped in front of me, blocking my view of the ice. "No one would think poorly of you if you backed away, Ten."

"No. I'm not letting fear rule my life." I'd worked on that line all the way over. Every time my gut would flip at the thought of falling, I'd repeat that mantra to myself.

"Okay, then. Let's lace up and make a circle." He moved to the side to let me lead the way to the locker rooms. Once inside the home dressing area, we slid on skates, grabbed sticks and pucks, and made our way to the ice. "Here. You wear this, or we go no further than the bench."

He held out a smoky-blue helmet. "Thanks."

"Also, news of this little outing never reaches Jean's ears." He flung the gate open. "If your mother knew I gave in to your request to skate, she'd skin me alive."

"It's our secret." I stole a kiss, pulled in a deep lungful, and stepped out onto the ice.

"You okay?" Mads asked when I stood there, feeling the slide of sharp blade on ice for the first time in what seemed like years. I'd never gone this long without skating. Ever. Far back as I could remember, I'd been on the ice daily.

I glanced over my shoulder. The man wore his worry plainly. I smiled. "Nah, I'm good."

"Are you sure?" God, he was tense.

"Dude, you want me to use… a bucket like the one Stan gives Noah when they're on the ice?"

His lips flattened a bit. Then he nodded. "Right, yes, sorry. I'm being overprotective."

"It's cool. I love you. Come skate with me."

I pushed off, one foot and then the other, and there it was. The power of muscle memory, the flow of tendon and muscle, the rasp of skate on ice, and the feel of a stick in my hand. It all meshed perfectly, no gaps or stutters as my brain experienced. My body knew what to do. It had been trained for this sport since I was two.

Mads stayed beside me, peeking my way every four-point-two seconds, chiding me to keep my speed down and enjoy. So, I did, even when my body wanted to go faster. We poked around the ice, slow circles at first, then some puck-handling exercises. Nothing super fancy but enough to make the darkness that had inhabited my heart start to lift. I'd been so scared that I might not be able to do what I had done before, but I could.

"You want some cones?" Mads called after I sent the puck into the empty net for the tenth time.

"Cones?" I asked while skating to the net to fish the puck out with my stick.

"Yes, traffic cones. They're pointy orange rubber things that—"

"Okay, smartass," I called. Mads chuckled, warmly and honestly. The first sign of ease that I'd seen since I'd suggested this. "Nah, we can skip the cones." I skated to him, resting by the boards, the home bench behind him. "I think it's going to be okay," I said as I removed my skid lid. He reached over to fluff my hair. "I mean... I truly believe that, way deep down now. I've been feeling as if I was trapped... in the neutral zone since that night, you know?" He nodded. "But now... being on the ice, seeing that my reflexes are still pretty sharp, and my body remembers what to do... the future looks good again now.

Hopeful. Thank you for doing this. I know you didn't want to… I could see the fear in your eyes."

"I only want to make you happy, Ten. I'm thrilled to hear you sounding so upbeat. Your family will be too. When we tell them. In thirty years or so." He rubbed at the back of his thick neck awkwardly. He was too cute. I grabbed a kiss, or five, and then we made our way back to the dressing room to get our shoes on.

"I'm kind of hungry," I said after we locked up the rink.

"Well, I kind of made reservations for us at the pizza place you like so much." Mads slipped the key back into his pocket. "We'll head there as soon as I drop this key off at Ken's place."

"The pizza place with the stuffed crust mongo pizza?"

"That's the one."

"Okay, I love you more than like… anything."

He gave me this bizarre kind of look, as if he were on the verge of saying something prophetic like, "I am the servant of the secret fire!" or "You shall not venture further!" or any other awesome Gandalfesque epic quote.

"I love you too," he replied, took the bag from me, and walked to the Rover. After our gear was stored, I buckled up, watching Mads as he settled behind the wheel. He glanced up after snapping the seatbelt, must have felt me staring at him. "What?"

"You're acting weird."

"Don't be silly."

"You got some sort of something up your sleeve, don't you?" He gaped at me. "Did you set up something at lunch?"

"Oh. Oh, yes, I did. Damn it, you can read me too well." He grinned a little too widely.

"Yeah, I knew it. Did you get Wayne Gretzky… to come eat with us?"

"Not quite…" he answered, pulling into traffic, then purposely burying the conversation, no matter how I tried to wheedle what he was hiding out of him.

Papa Joe's Pizza Parlor sat less than a block from Ken's house. I hustled inside, the cold air and brilliant winter sun trying to give me some trouble but failing. As soon as I stepped into the packed pizzeria, I saw what the surprise was. Stan rose to his feet, shouted something in Russian that had every head in the place turning, and then rushed at me.

"My best of good friends," he gushed as he wrapped me in a bear hug that forced all the air out of my lungs. "Is big welcome back to homes." He kissed both my cheeks and then stared into my eyes. "Brain is not sloshing no more, true?"

"True, it's not sloshing, but it's kind of… dull at times."

"Pah, my goodliest friend is not dull. Maybe just stupid from big knot on brain. Come! Sit with me. We have much talks to make. Jared, you come sit too. Come! Sit! Make conversations with me."

Every patron watched us sit down. My face was hot with embarrassment.

"This is gift from Erik and Noah. They are snotty cold sick, and so I told them they could not come because you are healing your brain and would not wish a snot cold to be in your head." I took the book and smiled at my best buddy. His gray eyes sparkled.

"Go make the opening! I bet you are not sure of what it is."

"Uhm, it's a book." I patted the neatly wrapped book.

"Ah, well, good guess, but what kind of book?" He waved at the server. I opened my mouth to guess. "I tell you! Is book about otter who gets hurt playing otter games. He gets most sad and is making big mopes all over himself and Mama Otter. Then he stops being sad and with the mopes before he grows into happy face otter! The end."

"You should get a job as a book reviewer when you're done playing hockey, Stan," Mads teased. Stan glowed.

I threw Mads an amused glance. "Awesome. Thanks, bruh," I said to Stan.

"Ah, is no big thanks needed. I read to Noah many times." The server wriggled around Stan to take our orders. "They have some of pizza. Cheese crust and big meat. My friend Ten loves the big meat."

Mads choked on the sip of water he'd just taken. Oh man, the looks we got from the nearby tables. I mean, yeah, it was true I did like big meat, but for serious?

"Okay, so uhm... tell me what's up with you, bud." I steered us deftly away from big meat discussions, then ordered a large chocolate milk. Mads got a large diet cola.

"What is up is much exciting things. I am studying for to become American citizen."

"Dude, that's awesome!" I offered him my hand. He grabbed it with a mitt the size of a dinner plate and shook it up and down. "Is it like super hard?"

"Yes, many facts. But is worth hard facts to become American. There is much I wish to do as citizen that only American can do. I wish to vote so that we have good people in charge. People who do not look down on LGBT people or women or people of colors. I wish to marry my love someday and find cake for us in any bakery. This only can be done for voting, and so, I wish to vote and make my new country happy home for all peoples."

"You totally rock... you know that?"

Stan nodded. I chuckled.

"I know many things now. Like George Washington, Abraham Lincoln, and Martin Luther King Jr. make America land of free and brave. Also, I am trying to learn state capitals, but it is most hard. There are fifty!"

"Yeah, I'm aware." I sat back to make room for the pizza, which was massive and loaded with big meats. Just how I liked it. "Seriously, dude, best way to learn the state capitals is to check out Wakko's '*Fifty State Capitals* song on YouTube."

"Whacko song for capitals?" Stan threw a confused look at Mads.

"Don't look at me, must be a whippersnapper thing. Ryker would probably know," Mads said while lifting a slice of pizza to the red plastic plate in front of him.

"Ry and Jacob would totally know," I said, diving in for a slice of my own.

"Then if Ten says it is totally good, I shall find the whacko song," Stan announced with enough energy the people outside could've heard him.

It was great to be back home. I had really missed all of this. Mads, the town, my best friend, pizza, laughing, and just being able to forget the mess of the past month. If I buckled down, worked super hard when I went back to Tucson, I could be back here soon, super soon if I pushed myself. Hell, maybe I could be back on the ice in a few months...

Lunch sped past, and all too soon Stan had to go home to check on his snotty men. We hugged it out big-time, and I promised him I'd be home soon to help him study for his citizenship test.

Mads was all sprawled out in his seat, sipping coffee, looking at me over the rim of his mug. I picked up a crust that I'd left behind and took a bite out of it. I wasn't hungry, far from it, but leaving a stuffed crust behind seemed like a crime.

"Did you notice how smooth your speech has been over lunch?" he asked over his steaming coffee.

"No, guess not." Now that he'd pointed it out, I hadn't gotten too mad at myself for falling over words or the annoying logjam of ideas trying to burst free. "Being home is good for me."

"Having you home is good for me too." He put his mug down. "We have the rest of the day. Are you feeling up to some shopping?"

"Yeah, totes." I shoved the rest of the crust into my mouth and shot to my feet. Stan had taken the check over my and Mads combined protests, so I dug my wallet out and tossed a fat tip to the table.

"Whoa, slow down. Are you sure you're feeling up to it?" Mads eyed me with concern. "It's been a busy day so far. We could go home, nap, and then head back out."

"You planning on slipping your big meat to me if we go home and go to bed?" I asked, then shoved my arm into the sleeve of my winter Railers jacket.

His eyes flared. "No, of course not, you're healing. God, Tennant," he sputtered, which entertained me to no end. He could sound like such a prude at times. What a dad.

"Well then, shopping it is." I zipped up the thick woolen jacket. He sat there staring at me. "Come on, I'm fine. Better than… fine, I'm great."

"No headache or pain of any kind?"

"I'm golden." I folded my arms over my chest.

He sipped and studied me for five minutes until he had convinced himself that I was okay.

"Okay, one hour at the mall and then it's home to bed. To rest," he quickly clarified as he stood, then stretched. His sweater rucked up a bit to show me that sinful strip of toned belly. Shame he was so set on resting. I was up for more than a nap. A long, slow blow job sounded like heaven. "I mean it. No sex until you're discharged."

"Mads, that's like some indefinite time. Could be… months!"

"Yes, it could be." He gave me a knowing little smirk, patted my arm, and then headed to the door. I fell in behind him, and out into the cold we went. I squinted, then fished into my pockets for my shades. Mads waited for me to get them on.

"Which mall do you want to go to? Colonial Park or Strawberry Square?" God, he was smug all of a sudden.

"I want to talk about this… arbitrary decision you made… about no sex until I get sprung." I planted my sneakers widely on the sidewalk and made a tree. No, that was leaving. Well, I made like a tree in that I put down roots.

"Here?" He waved his gloved hands at the shoppers rushing past. "You want to discuss my decision to make sure you take care of yourself and not overdo things by rushing into penetrative sex, right here?"

"Okay, first off, I said nothing about… penetrative sex.

I was thinking about a blow job. Oh, sorry, ma'am," I mumbled when an old lady in a purple knit hat gave me a dirty look. She huffed off, and so did Mads. I pulled up roots and jogged after him.

"We are not talking about this out in the open," he told me when I caught up to him. Christmas music streamed out of a bakery door. "Actually, we're not talking about this at all." He stopped suddenly, then spun to face me. "As much as I want to, and trust me, Ten, I *really* want to, I am not going to jeopardize your recovery just to get my rocks off. You mean more to me than just something to slake my desire on. You're my whole world, and you need to take it easy. If you can't find the fortitude to curb your desires, then I'll be the bastard and do it for you because I love you and I want you healthy."

Okay. Well, wow. How did a man argue with that? "Can we maybe shower together and maybe… you know… shower together?"

His stern expression slipped just a bit. "God above, you're tenacious."

"That will serve me well… when I get back to Arizona, right?"

"Maybe a shower. *Maybe.* Right now, we're going shopping for an hour. One hour. And then its home to rest and take your meds."

"You're such a worrier." I rose to my toes to press my lips to his. The door to the bakery behind us opened, and *Santa Bring my Baby Back to Me* rolled out into the snowy street. "I love that… about you."

He wrapped me in a hug and kissed me long and hard. "You're everything to me, Tennant."

"I know."

"One hour of shopping, a nap, and then a shower."

Yeah, man, I knew he'd start to see things my way. It really was a wonderful life, even if I had a killer long road ahead of me. With my man at my side, I knew I'd make it. He did that for me. Gave me strength, a solid base, and love. So much love. Lots of fretting too, but hey, that was all part of the love package, right?

"So maybe a shower first and then… a nap?"

"*Tennant.*"

Jared

So I had a final plan of how to ask Ten to marry me. In my head, we would be by the tree, and I would smoothly go to one knee and say just the right words, and he would consider his answer carefully, and then he would say yes with no hesitation or pauses. When it came to the actual day to do it though, things weren't *right.*

First off, my knees had never really been the same since a low hit in a game against Ottawa. One torn meniscus later, and I had this fancy popping tune I could play every time I kneeled. So, gracefully to one knee was never going to happen. More like creaky old guy needing the sofa for support.

Secondly, and probably worse, was that everyone was here. Every one of Ten's family. Even though they were less in his face this time, there was no way that many people could ever be truly quiet. It didn't help that Ten had this knack for buying the perfect gifts, and the kids loved him so much they showed it by squealing. A lot. They also climbed over him, and even though we all asked them to stop, it was Ten who refused to make them get down. He held them and squeezed them like he was never going to see them again.

Thirdly, Ten still stuttered his words or at least delayed some of them. That morning, we'd been speaking politics, and he'd managed to say the word filibuster without hesitation, then stumbled over asking for butter for his toast. He couldn't form the word butter. He said his head was blank, as if there was nothing there, and that suddenly it would pop into his thoughts, and he'd feel like an idiot for not knowing such a simple thing.

And then last of all was the fact that I wanted to ask him in private. Just the two of us appeared in this perfect scenario of mine, a quiet, thoughtful proposal that meant something and wasn't swallowed up by congratulations or jokes.

So yeah, the proposal didn't happen on Christmas Day, and even though the rings were in my coat pocket and they went with me everywhere, I still hadn't found that right moment. Not only that, but with Jamie's team playing us on the twenty-seventh, he stayed over with us, and that was one more person who appeared out of their room at inopportune moments.

It did Ten good to have one-on-one time with a single brother. Jamie on his own wasn't all about teasing and sarcasm. He was caring and supportive and liked to hug. A lot. He even caught me on the way from the kitchen with a bear hug that would have been more comfortable had he not just been in a towel.

We were at the arena. This was my second visit back today. This morning had been team practice, talking strategy, working on a niggling issue I had with my third

D-pair, and I'd gone alone. Tonight, we had Florida in the barn, and Ten had said he was coming with me, saying he'd watch from the Railers hospitality box, that he would stay seated and he wouldn't overdo it. He had headphones with him and sunglasses and seemed to be taking everything very seriously, so who was I to argue? I collected him and brought him back when the team had all dispersed to their homes for naps and pregame rituals. It was just me and him in the locker room, and he'd parked himself in the cubicle on the end right next to where Stan's goalie stuff was.

"I need to talk to Coach. You okay here?"

"Go for it. I won't move."

I wanted to say that I hadn't meant he couldn't move, but I guess, in all honesty, that was what I'd meant to say. The idea of him walking around the arena and getting dizzy or lost or fuck knows what left me cold. When I had the meeting out of the way and headed back to the locker rooms, he was still there, sitting cross-legged on the floor right by the Railers logo on the carpet. He had his eyes closed, his hands resting on his knees, and I didn't want to disturb him. I knew that meditation was part of his rehab. Quiet times that gave his brain moments to heal, even as they threw him around trying to retrain his synapses. He had a hockey stick across his lap, and I recognized it as one of his, the signature part of the design on the edge. He must have left the locker room to go find it, but he was safely back, and that made me feel a little better.

I worry too much. He's a grown man.

With his eyes still closed, Ten picked up his stick and smoothly rose to his feet, his toes right at the outer circle of the logo, and then he moved, and it was poetry.

Walking backwards, he moved his stick in smooth slow circles, like a gunslinger twirled his gun, the weight of the stick evenly balanced on one hand. He went into a deep stretch, placed his stick behind his neck, and then ended up with it on the floor behind him.

Only then did he open his eyes.

"Hey," he said when he saw me watching. "How did I do?"

I wanted to tell him he was beautiful, fluid and sexy, and so damn strong, but we were at work, and people were in the corridor waiting to come in and only stopping because I had my body blocking the door. I could hear Adler grousing already, something about coaches who don't know they had a game. I punched behind me, making contact with someone who let out an *oof* and a curse. I really hoped it was Adler, the ass.

"You're doing so well," I said to Ten instead of telling him how gorgeous he was. "Your balance is there, you're moving smoothly, and you've lost nothing when it comes to handling the stick." I knew he needed to hear the technical side as well, and he smiled at me.

Then he stood up, wobbled a little, and then gave one more twirl of his stick. "I rock this rehab," he announced.

We couldn't talk anymore, because Erik and Stan had joined the waiting group.

"Ten in here?" Stan said in a very loud whisper, and someone shoved at my back. Finally, I couldn't stop the team actually getting into their own locker room and stood aside. Stan pushed past Adler, followed by Erik and Arvy, Adler grousing that he would like to get on with getting ready and would people stop shoving at him. Everyone fist bumped Ten, pulled him into a side hug, treated him as usual, and I loved all of them for that.

The only wrinkle was when Gideon "Gids" Levesque walked in, took one look at Ten, and spun to leave. I think Ten had been waiting for him, though.

"Gids, wait!" Ten called after him, and the locker room was silent. Twenty or so guys watching. Gids had nicely integrated into the team. He was no Ten, but he'd been the skater called up from the Rush to fill the bottom line as everyone else moved around to cover Ten's absence, and he'd done well. He was also probably returning to the Rush when Ten came back, but he was making the most of the opportunity, with three goals and two assists on his record at NHL level.

Gids stopped and turned warily. "I just um… need to get more clear tape," he said and had ten rolls of tape thrown at him by the watching audience. The action broke the silence, and everyone was back to talking. Except me. I watched Ten carefully.

"Your goal against Boston, the way you got around their defense, you're fast and good. Watch out for Jamie though. Idiot likes to think he's a two-way forward."

Ten held out his hand to shake, and Gids took it, a cautious smile on his face.

"Thank you. How are you feeling?" He'd blown it, asking the question that everyone else had been avoiding.

The entire room went silent again, held its collective breath, including me, which proved that we'd all actually been watching what was happening. Ten had told me enough that he didn't want to be asked how he was by everyone, and I certainly didn't focus on asking him every time I was with him.

"Better," Ten announced loudly so the whole room could hear, his not-so-subtle way of explaining to everyone at the same time. "Headaches, dizziness…. Words are something… sometimes hard. Can't wait to be back on the ice." The last part of his little speech was way more confident than the rest. Knowing Ten, it was a litany he repeated every day.

I can't wait to get back on the ice. I will *get back on the ice.*

We separated about an hour before the game, him leaving to make his way to the team box, me to do pregame preparations.

"He seems good," Erik said before he headed out to the ice for warmup. "More like Ten."

I nodded and even smiled because I'd felt a shift in Ten the last couple of days. There was a cautious confidence about him, and seeing him with a stick in his hands and the way he held it, I thought I saw a spark of the Ten who was a king on the ice.

I could imagine his eyes on me and the team from the box, worried a little about how exposed he was. Television cameras had likely caught him up there and were panning to his face as he watched the team play. It must've been so hard to be the focus of everyone's attention.

I wonder what he's thinking.

Florida sent Jamie Rowe's line out, and I gave Arvy and Westy the tap, watching as my guys managed to hold off Ten's determined brother. When they came back, they high-fived each other, and I looked over at Jamie who in turn was staring up at the box. He and Brady were idiots around their brother, but they loved Ten. Everyone loved Ten. What wasn't there to love?

We took a win from the game, a solid two points in a cramped league, and the mood in the locker room was jubilant. Ten didn't come down at that point, said he'd wait up in the box, and by the time we were done, the arena had emptied, and the cleaners were working the rows, removing the litter created by eighteen thousand fans. I received a text he'd gone down to ice side, but he didn't give an explanation, and I didn't ask. If he needed to be close to the ice and it helped his progress, then I wasn't going to argue at all. I grabbed my coat, assumed I would be meeting him and we'd be going home, but I found him sitting on the Railers bench, skates on, helmet in place, staring out at the ice.

"Just quickly," he said to me. The cleaners were finishing up in the stands, an hour or more having passed since the game. The ice was smooth and empty, but I wondered if he'd cleared it with anyone.

"Have you checked—"

"Who's going to stop me?" he asked with a wide grin. "Surely it's good for marketing to have *Tennant Rowe back* on the ice? Layton will love it. Make sure you take photos for his twitter account." He stood up, stick in hand and a determined jut to his chin. "Okay?"

I didn't have skates on, but I stepped onto the ice first and gestured for him to go past, reaching for a pile of pucks and throwing them down. He picked up a puck on his stick, made slow lazy figure eights in front of the bench, each circle taking him wider on the ice. He looked good, slower than usual, but he was skating well, natural, flowing, and his focus was perfect. He changed direction, skating backwards, pulling the puck with him, heading for the net, and I couldn't help that my chest tightened. He wasn't checking where he was going. He was heading right for the net. What if he hit it and fell to the ice? What if he hit his head? I moved toward him a few steps, even though there was no way I could reach him in time. I wanted to shout, to warn him, but I couldn't find my voice.

In a split second, with that almost otherworldly hockey awareness he had going on, he skated to the right, slid the puck forward, iced to a stop, then hooked it into the net, even throwing a mini, slightly shaky, celly as he passed around the back of the net.

"And the crowd goes wild," he announced and skated back to me to get another puck. "Number ninety-four scores!" The words were smooth, as if hockey talk was easy for him.

I checked his eyes for focus, wanted him to stop then, but Ten was determined, utterly in sync with his skating, and this time he shot from the center line, the puck sailing a little wide. He frowned, collected the puck, and shot it again and again. Seven times out of ten he managed to get the five-ounce rubber disk into the net, and then he slowly skated back, his cheeks flushed, his eyes bright with emotion. Lights dimmed in the seating. Clearly everyone had left, and it was just him and me.

I remembered the day he'd joined the Railers. That singular moment when I'd spotted him through the glass, standing there and owning the press, confident, cocky, and here he was now. He was so happy, and I knew one thing for sure. I was never letting him go. I actually fell to my knees a lot more gracefully than I had imagined I would, and he towered above me in skates, his expression worried. Probably wondering why the hell I was down on the ice.

"Jared?" He reached a hand out to help me, his smile dimming.

I rooted in my pocket, fumbling to pull out the box. There was no Christmas music, no tree, no perfectly arranged setting, but there was Tennant, me, and two platinum rings. "Marry me," I blurted. Gone was the flowery speech about forever and how he held my heart and how much I wanted him. "Ten, I love you. Marry me?"

Ten

MY BRAIN WAS SLOW. I MEAN, SURE, WE ALL KNEW THAT. A big crack to the coconut makes your head like the Hell Hole Swamp back home in South Carolina. We'd gone there once when I was a kid, maybe eight or so. Only once, because Brady had gotten it into his thick skull that he had to cross the swamp. Mom and Dad had stopped to look at some plant, and there went Brady, wading out into the muck until he was up to his armpits. Jamie and I had stood there, watching, laughing, considering wading out as well until Brady started freaking out because he was unable to slog his way through. There may have been water moccasins and alligators in that water, or so Dad had told us to keep us from going out into it. Kids really don't listen for shit most of the time.

So yep, that was my brain. Mucky as the Hell Hole Swamp. Words kind of waded out and then got stuck, like Brady. That was the case right now. Mads down on a creaky knee, his blue eyes brimming with devotion, and a box with two platinum rings in it had gummed up my reasoning.

"Are you serious?" I finally pushed out because this wasn't in the plan.

Not at all. The plan had been to live together, win the Cup, get married, travel, and grow old together. This was not the plan. The plan had been deviated from. Well, I mean the living together plan bit had been done successfully. So that kind of made the next step in the Tennant Rowe and Jared Madsen plan... fuck. Marriage. We were at the marriage stage. When had we gotten there? How? It felt as if just two days ago I'd laid eyes on Mads, on the ice, through the glass. I'd known right then that I desired him above all other men I'd ever wanted. That want grew after getting to know him again. It grew and changed, matured into affection and respect, and yes, lust. God, how we'd lusted. But amid all that wanting and growing and changing, we'd fallen in love. And now, there he was, staring at me in abject terror as I gaped down at him like a drooling fuckwit.

"Tennant? Are you having some kind of setback?" Mads asked, worry flowing off him.

I went down to one knee, mirroring him. "No, I'm good. I'm golden. I just... we did the whole thing right up to now, yeah? All of it, the good and the bad, we aced that... all that stuff, yeah?"

"Yes, we aced it all. Are you sure you're okay?"

I smiled at him, at the concern in his voice, the fine lines around his eyes, the silver that was creeping in at his temples, which made him hot as double hell. I loved all of those things and more. His laugh, his frown, the way his reading glasses sat on his nose, the width of his shoulders, the girth of his cock. I loved him so damn much more.

"I'm golden, seriously."

"Good, okay, so I hate to push you, but I have these rings, and my knee is about to seize up, and I really would like a reply."

"Yes, I'll marry you. Yes, and yes, and like a hundred thousand infinite yes to the yes times a million!" I threw myself at him, arms around his neck, and rode him backward to the ice, my mouth sealed to his. He chuckled into the kiss, a warm snuffling sound that made me wiggle closer and kiss him with even more passion.

"No one can ever say you lack enthusiasm," Mads chortled, his head resting on the ice for a moment before I slid to the side and he sat up. I brushed the sparkling bits of shaved ice from his thick gold hair. Then I pushed my fingers into the length of it and led his mouth back to mine. This kiss had heat blanketed in devotion. The sweep of his tongue over mine made me hard and breathless, as usual.

"Can I wear it?" I asked when we had to come up for air. "I'm not really up on how dudes do this. I mean… Jamie and Brady bought diamonds but…" I kissed him again because I had to.

"There are no set rules as far as I know. We can wear them as engagement rings or put them aside for the actual wedding day. What do you want to do?"

"I want the world to know you're mine… if that's cool?"

"It's incredibly cool. I like the idea of all those Tennant Rowe fangirls knowing you're officially off the market now."

I held out my left hand, eager to see him slip the band onto my ring finger. His hand shook a little, so did mine. The smooth, warm ring slid over my knuckle, the fit perfect.

I plucked the larger one out of the box, peeked at him, smiled in return, and pushed the ring down over his finger, wiggling a bit to get it over knuckles permanently scarred and lumpy from fights and slashes from opposing players.

"That's beautiful," I murmured as I admired the ring – *my ring* – on his finger. "Oh my gosh!" A thought raced through my head. I pushed to my skates and then tugged my fiancé to his feet. Wow. We were affianced. I felt so grown up and giddy. Mads stopped brushing ice from the seat of his pants to glance at me. "Do not tell Ryker yet. He and Big J are coming…" Damn it. *Take a breath. Let the excitement wane a bit.* "They're coming for New Year's and Stan's party, yeah?"

He nodded, his attention now on me fumble-bumbling around mentally.

"Cool. Don't tell him, okay? I want to lay it on him. Bust his balls a bit."

"Oh-kay, we'll sit on it until he gets home." He took my hand in his and lifted the heavy band to his lips. "But it's going to be hard not to shout about it from the rooftops."

I patted his cheek, his new whiskers rough on my palm. "Totes."

TWO DAYS later we were getting ready for the big blow-out at Stan's place. Russians love their New Year's parties, and this year was supposed to be even bigger than last year's. I wasn't sure what Stan had up his sleeve, only that it involved an orchestra and the fact that he "knew peoples" so, yeah, I didn't pry. My overactive imagination had oligarchs doing backflips across our goalie's living room. I told Mads that, and he gave me his patented "Your mind worries me" look before going back to the book about home brewing he was browsing while sipping coffee.

When the front door flew open and Ryker's shout filled the townhouse, I barreled out of the kitchen, dress shirt unbuttoned, tie in my back pocket, and gave the boys a wide grin. Man, Ry and Jacob were a gorgeous couple. They complemented each other so well, and it was obvious they loved each other.

"Dude," Ryker replied, fist-bumping it out with me. Jacob and I shook hands, the farm boy's grip strong, his fingers calloused. "You look good. How are you feeling?"

"Pretty righteous," I replied, hearing Jared step up behind me, the creaky floorboard giving him away. We stood there watching the two of them peel off their coats. Both guys had worn suits, as had been requested by Stan, and they looked fucking amazing. I had to wonder if Tan France had decked them out. Jared slid an arm around my waist. "So, um, we have something to tell you."

Ryker glanced up from something on his phone. Jacob, always the silent behemoth, gave us his undivided attention.

"What? Did Stan cancel the party? I'll be royally pissed. You have any idea what it took to get this man into a suit? Or what I had to go through to let me buy him a new suit?" Ryker's gaze flew from me to his father, then back to me.

"My old suit would have been fine," Jacob commented from behind Ryker. "Waste of money to buy a new one that I'll only ever wear once."

"Your old suit was too small and too old," Ryker tossed back, sliding his cell into the interior pocket of his gray suit jacket. "Hence the reason you needed a new one."

Jacob opened his mouth to retaliate, but I slid in, all slick and shit.

"The party is not canceled so chill with the… suit worries. Ryker." I dropped an arm around Ry's shoulders. He snickered. "We have news for you."

"Okay, so give me the news," he said, his attention flicking steadily now from Jared to me.

"From now on, you have to call me Dad." I held up my left hand to flash the band under his nose. Ryker, the poor stunned dolt, made like a goldfish for ten or so seconds and then punched me in the arm. "Dude, that's like stepdad abuse."

Ryker tried to say something, but it got all mashed up with hugs and hugs and even a few more hugs. Jacob got pulled into the embrace-a-thon. When the first round of congrats had been delivered, Jacob and I took their bags to the guest room to give Mads and Ryker some time to talk.

I finished dressing, wishing I had that new ink on my neck to cover the bright pink scar that stood out above my white dress shirt. Gatlin wanted clearance from my doctor that the wound was indeed fully healed. Maybe by Valentine's Day, he had offered to placate me. Who knew tattoo artists could be so damn strict? When we all met in the kitchen, Mads and Ryker were talking about home brewing, but both men's eyes were shiny with unshed tears.

"We good?" I asked as I fumbled with my tie.

"We're incredibly good," Mads said, gently pushing my fingers aside to neaten up the knot in my tie.

We shared a small kiss, gathered up the kids—I planned to bust Ryker's chops forever with the kid stuff—and made our way to Stan's big house. It looked as though we'd be making our big announcement to the team tonight. We'd had lots of practice. We'd told my family yesterday in a group call that went off the rails into emo-town for all involved. My mother had woken me that morning with an announcement that she'd made a Pinterest board for wedding ideas. Like, seriously? She had to ring me at five a.m. sharp to tell me about a board she was filling with wedding cake and flower arrangement ideas? I guess that was what parents did. I'd have to do that for Ryker just to see him lose his shit. I was going to rock this stepfather thing, just as I was going to rock the rehab. Right now though, we had to brace ourselves for this Russian suit-wearing party.

"Dude, if there are oligarchs there and we get jailed for collusion or some other espionage shit… and have to postpone the nuptials for twenty years, my mother is going to be pissed. Did you see how many pins she's put in that… wedding board of hers?" I whispered to Mads as we walked up the snowy walk to Stan's front door.

"Let's hope we don't end up in prison then. I'd hate to piss Jean Rowe off," Mads replied and rang the doorbell. A dude I did not know opened the door. Tall, head full of blond curls, and the same chin as Erik, he smiled at us as if he knew us, and boy, was he enthusiastic.

"Hello! I'm Bjorn Johnson." He pumped our hands

strongly. "You don't know me, but I'm Erik's cousin. I'm a big fan of the Railers."

That was a lot to process right away, but Bjorn had such a wide and welcoming smile that I immediately smiled back.

"Good to meet you," I said, and repeated his name in my head so I would remember it. Bjorn. Like the guy in ABBA.

"I'm stoked to be here. I was in America for a skiing competition in Big Mountain and stopped by on the way home to celebrate New Year's with him and Stan." He let us in.

"They made you the official doorman?" Jared asked.

"Seems that way."

Thankfully, we didn't end up in a federal pen somewhere for sharing secrets with Russians. There had been this opera singer, some friend of a friend of Stan's from the homeland, who had sung a song from *Madame Butterfly* that had left some of us hockey players slightly stunned and a little weepy. No one would admit that they'd teared up over some dumb opera song, so that went to the grave with us. They did hoot and holler and slap my back repeatedly when Mads and I made the big announcement.

It had been the best night.

Now, sitting in the desert, staring out of the window as I worked on strengthening my left side from brain to fingertips, I felt the tug of homesickness.

Midway through January and here I was still, working my ass off, alone, Declan having returned to his team two weeks ago. I missed him. He'd been someone my own age whom I could hang with, but he wanted to be back on the turf, the gridiron was in his blood like the ice was in mine. I did not fault the man. I was chomping at the bit myself.

Patience was hard to come by as my recovery sped along. Every day I'd ask the therapists and doctors when I was getting sprung. And every day they'd reply with something meant to inspire me to stick with the program. They cautioned against leaving early, which I could do at any time. This wasn't a prison. There were no locks on the doors. But—and there was that big but—if I wanted to heal those pathways the brain bleed had destroyed, I needed to stay put and put the time in here. So I did. I put the time in and then some. I missed Mads, though, and the team, but mostly Mads. I sorely missed hockey despite glutting myself on Railers games, Raptors games, hell, any NHL game I could find, and streaming all the OU hockey games. There was a massive part of Tennant Rowe that was missing.

Dedication and hard work. That was what was needed to get that chunk of me back in place. So I worked. And I dedicated myself. And I sweat and cursed and threw things and laughed and cheered myself on because...

Because I had one hell of a wonderful life ahead with my soon-to-be husband. I was damn sure going to be one hundred percent healthy for the rest of our time spent as one whole instead of two halves. Like that old 80's song that Mads liked to hum in the shower, our future was so bright we were breaking out the shades.

Epilogue

Jared

WHEN IT CAME DOWN TO IT, I HAD ABSOLUTELY NO SAY IN Ten getting back on the ice. The doctors said they were cautiously sure, which sounded like medical bullshit to me. Management had all kinds of legal documentation in place to keep him safe, but that surely was their way of covering their backs. Sponsors had major advertising in place. Even TenWatch was all in for Ten skating with the team.

I wanted him to stay at home. In bed preferably.

I may have come over a little too protective, and it came back to bite me in the ass when I found Ten rummaging in our drawer of medical things. He'd placed two bags of cotton balls on the counter, and he was still looking for whatever he needed. I immediately went to his side because he still had issues with remembering odd things, and some of the bigger words took him a while to form.

"What are you looking for?" I asked, in my best I'm-not-interfering tone.

"More cotton balls. Or bubble wrap, I don't care."

Was he hurt? Bleeding? My chest tightened, and I did a visual search of every part of him I could see. Why bubble wrap? He wasn't making sense.

"Ten, what's wrong?" I finally asked when I couldn't hold back anymore.

He very deliberately shut the drawer, turned to face me, then crossed his arms over his chest. "You keep wanting to wrap me up somewhere safe where I won't get hurt."

"Ten—"

"Let me finish. Seriously, there aren't enough cotton balls or bubble wrap to stop me getting hurt again, Mads. It's the game."

"I can't help being worried."

You can worry, yes. But ask people to watch out for me and not hurt me? That's a big fat no."

Oh shit, how did he find out?

"I don't know what you mean." I was lying. I knew exactly what he meant, but him getting hurt wasn't just all about him. There was me as well, the scared lover who wanted to protect his man.

"I know you called Coach Benton last night."

Fuck.

"I know you told him to talk about our Defensemen and ask them to protect me." He raised an eyebrow, and I stopped because there was no point in lying to Ten. He knew all my tells.

"I just wanted…"

He held his hand up to stop me.

"Also, I know you have individually asked at least seven of the team to look out for me, to which Stan immediately replied directly to me... wait, let me get my phone." He pulled out his cell and read from a text. "I'm known peoples for putting warnings on NHL website for not hurt Tennant Rowe."

I was busted.

"I'm sorry, Ten. I can't help that I'm worried."

He softened, cradling my face then. "At home we are lovers, going to get married. Here you can worry over me and love me and make me breakfast every morning. But at the rink, I need to do my job. You understand that? Right?"

His speech was so much better, no stumbling over the words. He sounded so completely determined that I had nothing to say back to him. Rationally, I knew that he needed to get back, that he was always going to be a skater. He was like a kitten desperate to get out of the house, so utterly determined and very nearly like the old Ten again.

I grasped his hand, the feel of the ring on his finger giving me a jolt of love mixed with worry. "When I sat next to that hospital bed, I thought they were going to say you were dying, Ten. I hate that I can't separate the two, but I love you, and if you let me worry just a little, then we can do this."

"But no telling people to look after me."

I sighed noisily. "Does that mean I need to cancel the bribes to the other teams?"

He laughed, then kissed me, and I wanted to stay right there in the kitchen and do this with him forever. But I couldn't, which was why I was now on the bench, watching practice and seeing my lover out on the ice in a no-contact jersey, practicing with his team for the first time since the accident. There were flashes of old Ten, a deke and spin, a poke check on Stan, laughter as he put home a goal on Stan at one end, then caught the bouncing puck as it squirted out from the net, then traveled the entire length of the rink, avoiding all of our D-men and scoring against an unsuspecting Bryan. We kept the practice light for him. He needed to work on his strength, but he had no fear.

Even after what happened, he hadn't lost his confidence.

I have to believe in him as he believes in himself.

I found him after practice, sitting next to Stan, listening intently to the big man about something that had them both smiling.

"There is news from Russia bad news mix up with good news. Many cousins over dies. Much bad news. Leaves his children with no family. So much more bad news. I go to fetch children, bring to America and makes ours to raise like American children with much clothes and phones and teenage bad angst. So big much happy news!"

"That sounds great," Ten replied and punched Stan in the arm.

"You be godfather for our new children? Spoil them, raise them if Erik and I die in tragic scuba-diving accident?"

"I'd be honored," Ten said, emotion making his voice crack.

I opened my mouth to ask if Stan and Erik had ever been scuba diving, but Ten noticed me standing there and grinned widely, high on excitement, about what I'd just heard him being asked, and probably the rush of being back on the ice.

"I'm going to be a godfather," he announced, "and you know what else? Trainers are pleased with my progress, Doc is ecstatic, I feel great, and I'll be back on the team in March, I'm sure of it."

And knowing my stubborn fiancé? He probably will be.

THE END

A RAILERS NOVELLA

Hat
TRICK

RJ SCOTT &
V.L. LOCEY

Stan

Watching snowflakes flutter by the window, I was struck by how beautiful snow was and yet how deadly it could be. Like now, it was soft and fluffy and would blow off the wings as soon as the 747 I was seated in took off. But there were snows that could cripple an airplane, sticking and freezing on the wings. Such was how many things were. Such was how my homeland could be. Russia was a beautiful country, rich with history and stunning cathedrals. The people were proud and vibrant and loving. But there was a dangerous side to Russia, one that might make my return risky. It was not a good time for gay men in Russia. The government called us terrible names, jailed us, or worse... simply for loving someone of the same gender.

I glanced at the flight attendant helping the other first-class passengers find their seats and stow their carry-on bags. He'd told me his name was Howard. He was older, distinguished, slim, with salt-and-pepper hair. His accent was British, very pretty, and he fussed over his passengers like a mother goose does her goslings. He'd assured me that, once we were in the air, he would come with the drink cart. Generally, I did not drink much. On New Year's Eve of course, but other than special occasions, athletes skipped alcohol. Erik was not much on boozing it up. We were happy homebodies.

I looked back out at the snowy airfield. Erik. I missed my beloved already, and the plane was still sitting at Harrisburg International Airport taking on passengers. I shifted in my seat, glad for the leg room that first class gave me. Also, the seat was plush, the blanket thick and warm, and the food and drinks would be above par. Sadly, I would be enjoying all of this luxury alone. Erik had to stay home with Noah. There were hockey games to play, a nanny to find, and paperwork to have in order when I returned with our new children. The team wasn't happy to lose me for the time required to make this trip, but they had given me leave to go. My stomach flipped in excitement and apprehension yet again. Ever since the call had come during the night two weeks ago, all of us had been bouncing between terror, anxiety, and joy.

Funny how a man's life can change with just one phone call.

I'd been sleeping soundly the night the news had come, Erik in my arms, our bodies tacky with sweat and semen. My eyes had felt as if they had just closed when Elvis started singing Hound Dog over and over. I had found a new ringtone app called "Elvis Ringtones" and picked a new song every week. Elvis had released many, many songs, so I could have a new ringtone whenever I wished. That night, it was Hound Dog, and it played repeatedly.

Erik had slid over me, mumbling, and grabbed my phone off my nightstand.

"It's for you. Someone saying something in Russian," he'd grumbled.

I slung an arm over his back to keep his belly pressed to mine. He let his head drop to my shoulder and his leg shimmy between my thighs. Perfection, *I remember thinking before I put the cell to my ear and everything went upside down and inside and out. Is there an "and" in that saying? I shook my head. No, I didn't think so. Inside out. Yes, inside out is right. So yes, the call had come through, the line raspy with static as the service in the small town I had grown up in wasn't good.*

It was bad news. My fourth cousin on my father's side, Anatoli, had been killed in a terrible accident involving a truck and him on a motorcycle. The two children he had looked after, children of another cousin, had been left alone upon his death, as their parents had died several years earlier. Their father from cancer and their mother from alcohol poisoning. She had been just a young woman, but her drinking was bad, as it is for many in the backwoods of Russia. When I was a child, I would look at the people of my small village and see only gray faces filled with great hardships and bleak futures. Which was why I had worked so hard to get out and make sure my sister and mother did as well. I did not want my mother to die before her time, her life dreary and sad.

The children, it seemed, had now been left to me, or maybe the better explanation was that I had been named as their next-in-line guardian. The poor children had been passed from pillar to post and had never known a stable family. The message was clear—could I come now to Leskovo and fetch them before they went into the government system. It seemed no one in the family could afford two more mouths to feed. I had sat up, stunned and shaken, unable to think of the proper words to say back to one of my uncles. I'd had no knowledge of my cousin naming me as a second guardian of his children if anything should happen to Anatoli, and I had told Erik that, after I'd blurted out some reply to Uncle Maxim about giving me time to make plans and to not allow the little ones to go to the government.

"I do not know how the government treats little ones with no parents, but if they treat them as bad as they do gay people," I mumbled as Erik hurried to dress and find me something to pull on. "I go now."

"Stan," he said a moment later as I pulled a pair of jeans over my ass, "I'm sure they'll be fine for a few days until we sort through all of this. You can't just fly to Russia and toss the kids into a plane headed for America."

"Why not? I am chosen next guardian by father. I go now. Bring home. We adopt. Make them ours. We want more children; you say so too. Now we will have three!"

I padded to the closet to find a suitcase. Erik slid between the closet door and me. "Stan, you can't go off halfcocked. This is going to be a tangled-up bureaucratic mess to wade through. We'll need a lawyer, probably an adoption representative, maybe state and federal permission. Things between the US and Russia aren't exactly stable right now. And there's the fact that the Russian government knows you're in a relationship with a man here in the States."

"Pah. I do not care. The Kremlin can suck my fat cock."

Erik rolled his pretty eyes. "Stan, the point is you can't just run over to Russia and expect to come home with two kids the next day. There's protocol that we're going to have to follow. And two kids? I mean, at once? Who don't speak a lick of English? What are their names? How old are they? What sex are they? Are they healthy? Are they immunized? I don't want any kids around Noah who haven't been immunized. What if they're mean to other kids or pets? What if you get over there and the government is waiting, and they lock you up to make a show of you, or they take you to the top of some high fucking office building in Moscow and throw you off just because you're—"

"Hush now, hush." I pulled him into my arms and held him for a long, long time. He clung to me, fingers digging into the skin on my lower back, his nose buried in my throat. I kissed his golden curls as he sucked in a long breath, then slowly let it out. "Nothing bad happens to us. We are strong family. Much love. This will be good." I ran a hand up and down his back. "We will make this good, you see. Big family means much more love and strength."

The soft rumbling of the plane rolling out to taxi jarred me from the memory. I fastened my seatbelt and turned off my phone. Howard checked on me, smiling and patting my shoulder, and then went on to make sure the others were obeying the rules. The flight was long, over eleven hours, and would afford me plenty of time to dwell upon things. Such as my mother's reaction the following day when she had learned of our fourth cousin's death. She said she'd never liked him, but she had wept softly for the children, holding Noah on her lap. Then I'd had to tell her about me being the chosen adult to take them.

It made sense to me and to Erik once we'd returned to bed the next night and talked things out as best we could. I was the most successful one in our big family. My cousins all knew I played professional hockey, and that I was now studying to be an American citizen. They had seen the images of my house, my car, my family here in Pennsylvania. I'd not pushed my wealth under their noses, but even just sharing pictures on social media, my family back in Leskovo would comment on the luxuries they saw. So, me being listed to take Anatoli's children if there was no one else made sense. Also, who didn't want to immigrate to America? This was the country of opportunity! The Statue of Liberty said so. She called to the weak and frail of other countries to come to her shores. I loved her so much, Lady Liberty. Every time we played in New York City I went to see her, and I thanked her for taking me and my family into her country.

So, me being picked seemed reasonable. I had been chosen, and I would fulfill my obligation to my family and those children. Mama had broken down when I'd told her I was returning to Russia as soon as we could arrange the legal things. Erik had been tasked with the paperwork. He was well spoken, his English smooth, and his bearing that of a prince. I was big and scary, and while my English was wonderfully better, it was still bumpy sometimes.

I'd hushed her as I had Erik the night before, assuring her that I would be welcomed back to Russia with open arms. She'd not thought so, but she had quieted when I reminded her of those two children—a girl and a boy, we had learned—who had no one to love them.

"They will need much love. They never really knew their parents, and now they have lost a guardian. They need more even than Erik and I can give them," I'd whispered to her in Russian as I'd knelt beside the rocking chair in Noah's room and held her. "They will need a sweet gam to tuck them in when their pappa's are not to home and bake *pryaniki* for them."

She'd patted my cheeks and sniffled, her chin coming up a bit. "I will do whatever they need, but you must promise to come home to me, Stanislav." She'd stared at me with eyes the same stormy color as mine. "You bring the babies home. Safe. All three of you. I will work hard with Erik to make the house ready for them."

"You are a good woman." I'd pulled her to my chest and kissed her damp cheek.

"And you, my son, are a good man."

The plane began to roll down the runway. I felt the pressure against my chest as we lifted off. Turning my head to the left, I looked out of the window and watched Harrisburg slowly get smaller and smaller.

"I will be back soon," I whispered to Erik, then pulled the shade down and patted my passport and the packet of legal papers riding in the interior pocket of my winter coat. Never had mere paper felt so heavy.

Erik
_____

"HOW HARD CAN IT BE?" I THUMBED THROUGH THE searches randomly and found an agency in London that specialized in finding the right Russian-speaking nanny. Okay, so it wasn't the US, but apparently they placed nannies in all different countries, and the US was on the list. It didn't escape me that I would be contacting an English company to talk about a Russian nanny for an American family. None of this had been easy so far. Why would finding a nanny be any different?

"We offer a full search and selection program, with all interviews, reference checks, and paperwork completed before we recommend a candidate to you," I read out loud, and waited for a comment. I had an audience. Stan's mom, Stan's sister, Galina, and Noah all sat on the sofa in a judgmental line. Stan's mom was in a major sulk because we were even contemplating bringing another Russian harlot into our house. I wasn't entirely sure she meant harlot, but it was difficult to understand her sometimes. Actually, most of the time. There was no denying that she was a doting grandma and mother, but she wasn't a young woman, and Noah was... at an interesting age is all I can say. He seemed hell-bent on pushing every limit we put in place, hence why he had a clump of hair missing from the right side of his head. How the hell had he managed to climb up to the vanity in our bathroom, I didn't know. I suspected it was a combination of using the bathtub, a box of jerseys ready to sign that he'd somehow pushed from our office, and sheer willpower.

Unfortunately, one experiment later and somehow our son had managed to shave some of his hair off. He'd been in trouble, and this was why he was part of the group all staring me down because I'd told him off. Apparently, he wanted Stan because Stan was the best dad, and I was useless. I mean, he didn't actually say that in so many words, but I could sense it from his mutinous expression and his pout.

Then there was Galina, who Arvy had dropped off at ass o'clock this morning. She'd wanted to help. Arvy had wanted to come in, but I think my glare had scared him away. He was the lucky one; there was no sense in two of us being stared at with such frustration.

I'm doing my best, okay? I didn't know Stan's cousin was going to die. I didn't know we were suddenly going to have three children in the house. A hat trick of kids that we would call our family.

"I can help," Galina said. This was the fifth or tenth or twentieth time she'd said the same thing, but she wasn't listening to me any more than Stan's mom was.

"We need someone at the house, on a semi-permanent basis, Galina. I explained that as much as we want your help, we also have to think long term."

Galina shook her head, as if she was disappointed in me for that statement. Stan's mom tutted, and as for Noah, he was still at the pouting stage. When I say thinking long term, I don't actually know what I meant by that. Weeks? Months? Years? Stan had said his cousin's children would know a little English, and that we needed a nanny who spoke Russian. Otherwise they would feel at a loss in the US. That was my job here. I wasn't the one returning to a country that judged our love as wrong, I wasn't the one who was facing red tape and danger, but he'd assured me he knew people who would help. I'd stopped asking him what he meant after I'd met the man outside Ten's room in the hospital.

Yep, clearly my lover knew people, and not outwardly friendly people but big guys with tattoos and scars and fixed expressions. Stan would be safe.

He has to be safe.

What would I do without Stan? What would my life be like without him? What would Noah do? Would Stan's mama and Galina have to go home? How would I get a nanny? Would I have to go to London? Would Stan come back to me? *What if he gets stuck there? What could I do? Would I have to—?*

"Dadda?" Noah clambered down from the sofa and held his hands up. "Carry," he demanded.

I dropped the phone and instead picked up my son. He seemed warm, but I wasn't sure if that was because of the post-haircut tantrum or that he wasn't feeling well. I wasn't sure I could handle him being ill on top of everything else. I slumped into the nearest comfy chair and inhaled the scent of Noah as he snuggled into me. He really did feel warm, but I held him close and rested my chin on his blond curls before closing my eyes briefly.

"I'm to wash," Stan's mom announced with a dramatic sigh and headed for her room, which left me with Galina.

"What will you do today?" she asked and looked pointedly at her watch. I knew she didn't mean what would I do with Noah. He had a place at the day care right next to the arena, sharing play time with Connor's children and always coming out with a grin on his face.

"Try and get hold of someone," I said and felt for my phone, which was just out of reach.

She picked it up and passed it to me.

"I didn't mean that. I meant, how will you concentrate on practice, on playing, when Stan is...?" Her eyes filled with tears, and my chest tightened. She was probably as scared as I was, and so was Stan's mama. We were all frightened that Stan wouldn't come home.

"He knows people," I said, and really that was the only thing I could cling to.

LEAVING Noah at Squirrels Nursery was hard. He didn't want to let go of me, and God help me, I didn't want to let go of him. Connor was there dropping off his children, and he must have seen the panic in my face. He managed to peel Noah off me and set him down.

"He's warm," I warned, and Connor checked his forehead, frowned, then shook his head.

"He feels okay to me." The look he gave me was one of sympathy, and I was mortified that he could see through me to the idiot dad inside, who didn't want to let go of his child.

"I don't want to…" *let him go.*

"You have to," Connor explained as if I was a child.

He was right. I had a job to do, one I got paid good money for, enough to have Noah at this private and expensive nursery and to be able to hire the best Russian nanny of all Russian nannies. Enough between us that Stan and I didn't hesitate to say we'd take the children who had been orphaned in Russia.

"I don't even know their names," I said as we walked out. I'd had an entire conversation in my head about the children and announced my findings as if Connor had been part of the head-talking. No wonder Connor was confused, but then his expression cleared.

"You mean the children from Russia, Stan's family. You don't know their names."

We reached the door— showed our passes to get in, the warmth of the practice arena in sharp contrast to the bitterness of the wind outside.

"I know Stan's cousin is Dusan, *was* Dusan, that's all. I know that Dusan and his wife died young, that the children didn't know them much, and that they were taken in by another cousin called Anatoli, who has now died." *Poor kids haven't had much of a life so far.*

We walked in silence for a short while. Then Connor stopped me with a gentle touch to my arm. "We're all here for you, Erik, you know that."

I sensed a "but" coming and waited patiently for the proviso to that sweeping statement.

He cleared his throat. "With my captain head on, you need to tell us if you're not up to playing. I don't want you out there not concentrating, not keeping your head up, getting hurt. You depend on the team, and they depend on you, and if there's anything in your head you can't shake, we can bench you for the Dallas game. I don't want you or any Railer hurt because your head isn't right. On the other hand, we're already down with Ten, and we need your style of scrappiness around the net, but if your head isn't in it…"

I wanted to be offended that Connor would even think that I wouldn't give the team one hundred percent, but even as I worked my way up to argue, my defensiveness vanished.

"I need the team; I need to play," I admitted. That wasn't exactly saying I *could* play, but it was close.

Connor studied my face for a moment and then nodded. "Okay."

That was it. He didn't ask me if I was sure. He took my response as the gospel truth, and we carried on to the locker room. Bryan, our starting goalie in Stan's absence, was already suited up, his head bent. He was staring at the floor, utterly still. There were a couple of missing faces at this practice, which was optional, but nearly everyone was there, all staring at me when I walked into the room. The questions began immediately, but I held up a hand to stop them.

"Stan is on his way. I should know more by this evening, and I'll message the group chat."

Then I turned my back on everyone, deliberately not looking at the empty space where Stan normally sat, and tried my hardest to get into the hockey zone before we went out.

Practice was odd man rushes, and for the life of me, I couldn't get the puck anywhere near the net, ringing every single one of them off the damn pipes. I could see Bryan's moves, watched him observing me with concern, and all I wanted was one freaking disc to get past him, but he didn't even have to try, I was messing up the shots myself.

Stop thinking about Stan. About Noah. About two children I don't even know and Russian nannies.

We went from shooting to corner drills, a sweaty-messy fight to get pucks out of blocks behind the net, up against Adler, who was being a fucking asshole and making my life hard. He was all over me, hazing me, pushing me into the boards, cursing at me, getting the damn puck away from me so fucking easy that I lost my shit. I cross-checked him hard, but at the last minute, he sidestepped, and I crashed into the plexi, side on. The breath left me, and I rounded on him, knowing this was him taking advantage of me not being on form.

Get your head on straight.

Adler winked at me, grinning as we went head-to-head in the corner again.

"You want some?" he kept shouting. I shook off my gloves, ready to go at him. He skated right up in my face.

"Fuck you!" I shouted at him and punched him, catching him on the chin.

"You hit like Noah!" he said and ducked as I swung at him again.

"Asshole!"

Then he danced away, still grinning, and I chased him down, both of us rolling on the ice, grabbing at jerseys and skin until he managed to pin me. "Better?" he asked, and I could see the compassion in his expression.

It was what I needed to pull me out of my funk, but I wasn't entirely over him pushing me as we switched places, and I ground shavings of ice into his face. When we both lay back, him laughing like a loon, me staring up at the rafters, he shoved my arm, hard enough that it moved me on the ice.

But at least for whole periods of time at practice, I'd forgotten about everything except hockey.

Connor cornered me after practice, and I stopped him before he could ask me. "It's all good." When he walked away, I saw him fist-bump Adler, and all I could do was shake my head.

Stan

WHEN WE LANDED AT GROZNY AIRPORT IN CHECHNYA, MY stomach flipped over on itself. Not from the descent, but from anxiety. Hand resting over the wad of official and expensive paperwork, I rose from my plush seat, thanked Howard the flight attendant, took a deep breath, and stepped off the plane onto Russian soil. Actually, I stepped off the plane into a jet chute, but it was sitting on Russian soil. Carry-on bag on my shoulder, I took maybe five steps before a man in an old suit pushed away from the wall of the sky bridge. He was stocky, bald, but with a bold gray mustache and wild eyebrows. His eyes were dark and serious. I could tell he was from the government. Government people all had an aura. I'd seen it with American government workers too, especially those dealing with immigration and Russian immigrants. I'd seen distrust in many eyes, some warranted and much not.

"Mr. Lyamin," the burly man said as he approached me. I nodded respectfully, letting others behind me hurry around us. "I am Agent Mikhailov of the Ministry of

Education for the Russian Federation. It is my honor to meet you."

"And I you, Agent Mikhailov." We shook. His hand was dry and cold, much like his gaze. "Is this normal procedure for a person coming to our country to be greeted by the government?"

"Well, you are not a normal person. Shall I speak in English, or do you still understand your native tongue?"

"No, Russian is and always will be my first language." I glanced at a couple scurrying past. They darted looks at the government man and me, then dropped their gazes quickly. "Perhaps we should go through customs and then talk?"

"Ah, you have been cleared already. But yes, come and let us go to a small office that has been set aside for us." Heart skipping wildly, I gave him a short smile and followed him. I was led to a small room with a table and two chairs, not so much an office, but rather a tiny space where suspicious people coming into the airport would be detained and questioned a bit more thoroughly. "Please, have a seat."

I sat on one side of the table, he on the other. "I am expected in Leskovo within the hour. The children await me."

"Yes, of course, the children." He sat down with a weary grunt. "Such a tragedy, orphaned and with no Russian kin willing or able to take them in. You are aware that Americans are no longer allowed to adopt Russian children?"

"I'm not an American. I'm Russian." I spoke plainly and with no anger. Our lawyers had told me that I must be respectful, and I must tell anyone who was with the government what they wished to hear, even if I had to lie. *"Embellishment is bad in hockey but good in this case,"* our attorney had told me. "I will always be a Russian." And that was true. I would also be American, and while I loved Russia, my life was now in America, where I could be me, and my children could grow up healthy and free to be what and who they wished.

"That is good to hear. Please, with your permission, may I see your passport, your visa, the adoption paperwork, and the visas for the children, Eva and Pavel?"

I passed over the neatly folded paperwork and looked at the closed door. There were no windows in this room. "You will see all is in order."

He glanced up from the papers he had placed on the steel table. "Yes, everything looks to be in order. Even the usual protocol for all orphaned children to be in the government's database for three months before they are considered eligible for international adoption has been waived."

"We have been fortunate," I replied.

He stared at me, his eyes narrowing a bit, his tongue tied because of the names listed on the paperwork before him. Important names. Friends of mine in high-ranking positions. I knew people.

"Yes, quite fortunate." He folded the papers slowly and carefully, tucking them and all the visas and my passport back into the thick legal envelope they'd ridden to Chechnya in. "Just a few more questions, and then we'll leave for Leskovo."

"'We?"

"Yes, I am to be at your side throughout. You have been granted four hours to pick up the orphans and return to America. Is there any reason why an agent of the Ministry should not be at your side?"

"None at all. Your company will be most pleasant." The lie tasted quite bad, like a bite of those tart candies that Adler passed out under the guise of sweet treats.

He smiled, but there was no warmth in the gesture. "So, you are living in America with your husband, Erik Gunnarsson."

"We are not wed, yet." There was no point in lying to the man. He had all my information in front of him, Erik's as well, and probably information on everyone in my house, my family, the Railers, and the two dogs we'd adopted.

He probably knows that we'd found BB, the brown one, behind the dumpsters at the rink, shivering in the snow. They could even have known that Mama had looked at his paws and told us he was going to be the size of a *"buryy medved"* or a brown bear.

I bet he knew that Wolfdog, or Wolfie for short, was a small Maltese mix who thought he was a big dog. He was the first one to bark at noises outside and bared his sharp teeth and growled at anyone who tried to touch our family.

I'd realized I'd lost myself in my thoughts when he pointedly coughed at me.

"Pardon me," I was polite.

"Mm, so this is a homosexual arrangement. You are aware that the presbyter of your church in Leskovo, Father Vladimir, is strongly against you taking these innocents to America and exposing them to such a reviled and repugnant way of life. He fears, as all our beloved church elders do, that if they live in America, they will not have a true Christian upbringing and will fall from the love of

God. Add in that you are exposing these children to such a disgusting lifestyle…no offense of course."

"No, of course no offense was taken," I lied again. I wanted to reach over the table, grab his head, and drive his face into my fist numerous times. But I did not. I'd been coached on this. I had known this was coming. The hatred still hurt my soul though, even if it was expected. "I can assure you and the presbyter that these children will be raised in a Christian church. I attend services every Sunday with Erik and our son, Noah."

"Yes, a Baptist church with a predominately black congregation." He sat back and assessed me closely. "That is not wholly acceptable to the Orthodox Church, but it does show us that your sinful choices may not corrupt the children we are handing over to you."

"I thank you for your gracious acceptance of our lifestyle." He smiled that dead smile, and I checked my wristwatch. "If there is nothing else, perhaps we should go fetch the children so that we do not miss our plane back to America?"

"Yes, it would be a shame for a Russian man with your skills to be stuck in his homeland. Tell me, Mr. Lyamin, who will you play for in the next Olympics?"

If the NHL let the players go unlike last Olympics, I thought.

"It would be my honor and my duty to play for Russia." I met his stare with one of my own.

"I'm sure the president will be most happy to hear that. He does so enjoy ice hockey."

With that, we rose and walked out of the airport, no baggage check—although I was sure they had gone through my one suitcase with every manner of X-ray and sniffing dogs available—no customs, and no stamp on my passport. Several men in suits hovered just a few steps away, all with that dead-eyed look, staring at me, judging me. It seemed I was to hustle in, grab the children, and then placed on a plane under the cover of darkness. That suited me fine. The sooner I had Eva and Pavel back in America, the easier we would all sleep. Sleep sounded nice. It had eluded me for over twenty-nine hours, but I was too energized to feel the jet lag yet.

The car that awaited us was a sturdy gray sedan. Nondescript in every way, and in truth, I had a moment of worry when I crawled into the backseat. If they were going to hold me, it would be now, with a long drive to a detention center that I would never be released from. Thankfully, that did not happen. Agent Mikhailov drove me to Leskovo in complete silence, but I did notice the car behind us, with the same agents I'd seen at the airport. I knew they would be armed. I was aware things could go badly, but I had to stay focused. The night hugged the countryside, and in a way, I was sad not to see the land where I had grown up.

The small village was dark when we crawled through the center of town. The roads were ugly, filled with big holes that made Agent Mikhailov curse violently. There was no PennDOT to call to report the potholes, to set out two dozen cones and for ten men to stand around and look at said holes. No one cared about this tiny village or how it was one wheezing breath away from death. We passed the small house Mama had lived in, the place where she had raised Galina and me. I stared at the little shack as we passed it, sadness filling my heart. Onward we went, to my uncle Maxim's farm. It was old and run down.

"Stanislav!" The shout rang out when I was pulled into the small two-bedroom house. Maxim hugged me and clapped my back, his mouth going steadily, explaining over again how sad he was that he couldn't take Anatoli's two, but he had six of his own and a sickly wife.

"They will be better in America," Maxim whispered, his gaze flicking from me to the imposing government official lingering by the rusty wood stove. "Mari and I tell them that at least five times a day. We've told them that they'll live in a mansion and be rich. That America is the land of dreams for immigrants."

"Yes, it is that," I concurred while Maxim steered me to the small bedroom his six children slept in. I ducked to enter, and eight terrified sets of eyes landed on me. Two children stood in the corner, ratty bags in hands, gray eyes wide with horror. Maxim's young were in beds, three to a bed, peeking at us from under the edge of their quilts.

"This is Eva and Pavel." Maxim waved a work-roughened hand at the two orphans huddled by the frosty window. "Children, this is Stan. Your new pappa."

I dropped down to one knee in front of them, knowing that my height could be imposing. The girl, Eva, was twelve, and she reminded me of Galina at that age. Long, dark brown hair and the stormy gray eyes many Lyamin have. She was lean, as was Pavel, but many poor children were thin. I smiled at the girl's defensive posture, hugging her brother to her side to protect him. Pavel was six, with short, wild dark hair and gray eyes that held a touch of mischief mixed with apprehension.

"Hello. We are most happy to be making for America," Eva said in nice English. "Pavel does not make good English. I learn from YouTube."

"You have learned much good," I told the young girl, wishing I could scoop them into my arms and hug them, but they were too wary for such displays yet. "We will all learn super good English together, even Pavel."

The boy grinned.

"It is time to go back to the airport. Your flight is leaving in under an hour," Agent Mikhailov said from the doorway. Pavel hid his face in the pleats of his sister's dress.

"Come, children, come. Get your coats on! Do not make the good man wait," Maxim said, hurrying the two children into thin coats, then pushing them, and me, out into the cold.

I turned to Maxim and handed him some money. American money, but he could exchange it. "For the food and upkeep of them until I could arrive," I said as I pushed the ten one-hundred-dollar bills into his calloused hand. "Thank you for keeping them safe."

"Give them a good life, Stanislav," Maxim said, kissed my cheeks, and then shut the door in my face. I sighed, turned, and then led the children back to the car, bypassing the men in suits who hovered even here. The children rode in the back with me, one on each side. Pavel fidgeted with the latches on his bag, an old leather thing. Eva stared into the dark, her eyes growing wide when we pulled into the airport and were escorted to our flight. For a moment I thought Agent Mikhailov would board with us, but he did not.

"Thank you for everything," I told the dour man in the old suit. I reached into my coat pocket and extracted a slim envelope that held a check for sixty-thousand dollars. The cost to adopt a Russian child had been twenty-thousand, but we had been told it would be thirty-thousand per child. He took the envelope, nodded, and then motioned for me to get on the plane. Visas and passports out, I hustled the terrified children to the boarding gate. Pavel was sniffling in fear, obviously never having flown before. Eva cooed to him in Russian, holding his hand in hers.

"Come now, little ones, time to go home," I whispered after we'd been cleared to move along by a nice lady in a blue vest. They balked a bit, both glancing over their shoulders. "No, do not look back. America is the forward looking now. You will be so much happy, you will see. Come, let me take your hands." I offered them my hands. Eva nibbled on her lower lip. Pavel hid behind his big sister.

"Will we find Big Macs on the plane?" Eva asked. That made me chuckle.

"Not on the plane, but as soon as we are in Harrisburg, Erik and I will take you for Big Macs and Happy Toy Meals."

People pushed by us. The lady at the desk was saying our flight was now boarding, and I was making deals with children.

"Good for us enough," Eva replied and slid her hand into mine. Pavel, well, he needed a full moment and a good explanation of Happy Toy Meals in Russian before he would let me take his tiny hand. Once on the plane, we were shown to first class—I supposed that big check to whoever it was in the Russian government who handled adoption fees had covered first-class seats—and settled in. Both children were seated side by side in the middle row. I had the window on the left. Eva was poking at the buttons on Pavel's small movie screen. I sat back, took a quick picture of our new family members, and sent a fast email to Erik, making sure to attach the image.

Our new son and daughter. I love them much already. Big things happen, all good but many scary minutes will tell you all. Love you so much too, and Noah. Kiss Mama. Tell her I am safe and to be brushing up on her grandma kisses. She has new cheeks to smooch. Love you soon big times – S.

Erik

I REREAD THE TEXT FOR WHAT MUST HAVE BEEN THE hundredth time. I hadn't even shared it with anyone else, selfishly wanting the moment to myself. The children in the picture didn't look how I was expecting them to. Hell, I don't know what I'd been expecting, but listening to some of Stan's stories about the poverty in his town, I guess I thought the children would be…

Disheveled? Exhausted? Belligerent?

I scrubbed at my face. I was the very worst kind of person to be judging anyone, particularly kids who had just lost their guardian and had already lost their parents before they'd even really gotten to know them. I checked the photo again, and I saw Eva and Pavel sitting next to Stan. They both had dark hair, and Eva was showing Pavel how to use the video screen in the back of the seat in front of him. They seemed small in the photo, but they *were* sitting next to Stan, and anyone next to him would appear small. I zoomed in on Eva's hand. It was so tiny, so fine-boned. Thin.

I wished I could see their eyes. Then I would know that we would be okay, that we were doing the right thing, and that they *wanted* to come here.

There was a knock on my door, "Someone here for you," Galina announced, and I opened the door to see Noah in her arms, playing with her long, dark hair. "From the Railers, I think."

I assumed it was Connor, who knew everything we were going through, and had been doing his captainly best to keep an eye on us. Or maybe it was Jared, who'd been passing messages from Ten, about how he couldn't wait to be an uncle again. I didn't think it would be Layton Foxx at my door, either. Although he'd been in the loop with all of this. We'd had a final meeting last night, steps to be taken, legal, moral, introducing the idea of us bringing two children from Russia to the US. From day one, he had told us that relations between our two countries were hard.

Layton didn't have to say a thing. I knew it was going to be rough, but Stan and I were determined. I took Noah from Galina when he asked, and he curled his little arms around my neck, smacking a sticky kiss on my cheek. I missed his curls. After the shaver incident, we had to take him on his first trip to the barbershop, to even out the mess he'd made. Bless him. He'd cried at the barber's. I'd cried when we'd gotten home.

I'm a mess right now, and I'm not embarrassed to admit it.

I went to the hall, and standing just inside, was a man I'd never met before or even seen before, certainly not anywhere at the arena. Yet Galina had let this stranger into our house?

"Erik Gunnarsson?" he said and extended his hand. I

shook it, but I didn't like the way he stared at me. It was as if he had something to say, and he looked hard and focused. He wore a suit, smart, sharp Brooks Brothers, his shoes shiny, his dark red hair cut short and tidy.

"Can I help you?"

He held up Railers' ID. "Sacha Ivanov, Layton Foxx sent me," he said. "Can we talk?"

Stan's mama chose that moment to stand next to me, her arms crossed over her chest, a mutinous expression on her face.

"Ivanov?" she began, then let out a torrent of Russian, and from the tone, it sounded threatening, although I did pick up a few American words in there that led me to believe she was merely furious with Galina at letting a stranger in the house, more than angry at this Sacha guy.

Then the man, tall, broad, and with dark eyes, launched into just as much Russian back at us, and Stan's mama lost all her bluster.

They said something else, the language too quick, the vowels too growly. I stepped back and away a little.

"The Railers organization has explained the situation to date and hired my services," Sacha began. "I know you're meeting your partner at the airport. I suggest you call and verify me with the team, and then we need to talk."

I fished my cell out of my pocket, connecting one handed to Layton Foxx who assured me that yes, Sacha was a liaison there to help us, so I ushered him in our house and shut the door.

"Noah." Galina was there, taking Noah from me, and she and Stan's mama left, and then it was just me and the tall man who could speak fluent Russian. I remembered my manners, offered coffee, but he declined, and it appeared he just wanted to get down to business. I took him into our office, the one with the display cabinet full of game pucks, signed sticks crossed on the wall, shelves full of Stan's books, written in Russian. I gestured for him to sit on the small sofa, then pulled the desk chair out and sat opposite him.

"I don't have long," I began. I was leaving the house in an hour to get to the airport. I wanted to be there long before the flight landed so I could get my head around what I was going to do and say when Stan, Eva, and Pavel landed.

"I know. That is why I have turned up unannounced right now. Layton has hired me to be your liaison today and for as long as you need me, and he wanted to explain it all, but we don't really have time."

"Liaison?"

Sacha handed over a glossy card, the kind of thing people just didn't seem to carry anymore. The company name was SI, but other than that and Sacha's name, it didn't help much.

"This situation is not new," he began. "Russian children coming to the US to join family, but it is fraught with issues, not least of which is the moment the plane touches US soil. There will be immigration to pass through, TSA issues, passport issues maybe, paperwork, everything is official and needs to be handled the right way. So far, and God knows how he's done it, your partner has passed over years of red tape to get Eva and Pavel onto the plane."

"He knows people," I said weakly. That was a joke now—that my big bad Russian lover was in possession of friends who could help in the weirdest situations. But it seemed as though this was no joke. How did I even think it would be easy?

"He certainly does," Sacha said and leaned forward in his chair. "But this is what we need to do now…"

THE AIRPORT LOUNGE for the Aeroflot flight was quieter than I'd expected. The plane was due in ten minutes, and I was mesmerized watching the arrivals screen, desperately needing to see Stan and the children. I knew that both Galina and her mom had wanted to be there, but Sacha had said that the welcome party should just be me. And him, of course. Somehow he'd won them over, and they'd agreed to stay at home for Noah's sake.

He'd also found a room for us, a private space for us to meet, away from cameras, from any person who might've recognized me or Stan. He'd thought of everything and had had several heated conversations with an immigration officer and at least two TSA representatives. I don't know what he was doing or saying, but somehow he'd smoothed things, signed papers, had me sign papers, and finally when the plane landed, Stan and the children were to be ushered privately and separately through a VIP access.

Not that this would be make the process they had to undergo any easier, but they would at least arrive away from the public gaze.

Who cares what two hockey players do with their lives?

"Plenty of people," Sacha replied, and I realized I must have said that out loud. "Tensions are high."

He didn't have to say anything else, and then he left

me in the room and said he'd be back, and that I was to wait.

So I waited, and it was exactly forty-two minutes from him leaving until the second door in the room opened, and I scrambled to stand, my gaze heading right for Stan, who was as serious and focused as Sacha had been.

"Stan," I murmured, and I could see some of the tension slip from his shoulders at the simple mention of his name. I wanted to hug him, kiss him, hold him there, and never, ever let him go back to Russia or even out of the damn state. Sacha ushered everyone in and shut the door.

I crouched in front of the children and held out a hand. "I'm Erik," I said, keeping it simple. Pavel was having none of it. He hid behind his sister. She kept a protective hand on his shoulder. At least she was looking at me, and I smiled.

"Hello Erik," she said and held out a hand. I could see her trembling, see the fear in her beautiful gray eyes, and I took the offered hand gently. "My name is Eva," she added, and I squeezed her hand and let it drop. That might have been the extent of her English. Who knew?

"Dobro pozhalovat' v Ameriku," I said, just as I had practiced with Stan before he left. "Welcome to America."

She gave me a shy smile but didn't move away from Stan's leg against which she leaned. "We are most happy to be making for America," Eva added, and my heart melted. She sounded like a mini-Stan, and I knew in that moment I could love Eva.

"Pavel?" I asked, and he peeked out from behind his sister, his eyes so similar to his sister's, wide with fear or shock? I didn't know, but Sacha joined me on bended knee and spoke gently in Russian. I heard my name, and then shyly Pavel extended a hand.

"Hello," he murmured, and I quickly took his hand before he retreated.

"Pavel does not make good English," Eva said. "I teached some little bit." She launched into Russian and tapped her brother on the head; Pavel's expression lightened.

"Big Mac," Pavel announced and made a show of rubbing his belly. "Hungry." He appeared so proud that he'd said those words, and all I wanted to do was reach over and ruffle his dark hair. I didn't though. I just smiled as hard as I could. After all, smiling is a universal language.

"Happy Meal and toy," I corrected, thinking that a Big Mac might be something we could work up to.

"Much happy," Eva said and nodded at me.

I expected there to be tears, grief, and shock, and maybe that would come when the journey was done, and we were back home. I stood, and leaned over to kiss Stan, just a quick brush of lips and a quiet promise of a better hello later. I wanted to hug him, keep him close, and never let him go.

He was pale with bags under his eyes; I'm not sure he'd slept much since he'd left me, and he needed to be cared for. So did the children, and I did what I do best. I channeled my dad-skills and held out a hand for Eva to take as Stan picked up Pavel.

"Okay, guys, ready to go?" Sacha asked. He had his hand on the door, the final barrier between us and home. I meant to ask about bags, but the feel of Eva's hand in mine and the way Pavel looked at me over Stan's shoulder meant all I could think about was that we were the luckiest men alive to be adding them to our family.

The bags were in the car, I didn't even ask, although Stan thanked Sacha, so I assumed the fixer had had something to do with it. He didn't come in the car with us. He patted the roof, said he had things to do, and that he'd visit in the morning. I shook his hand through the open window and thanked him.

Then it was just the four of us, the kids belted in, Stan in the passenger seat where I could see him. We exchanged glances, and I could see his eyes were bright with emotion; this meant so much to him. He cleared his throat and squeezed my hand and then took a breath.

"McDonald's!" he announced.

We made our way home, stopping for lunch, the kids fascinated with the staff, the food, the sauce dispenser, the bathroom signs, and most of all, the Happy Meal toys.

I don't think I will ever forget Pavel taking his toy and holding it close to his chest, looking as if he'd won the lottery. The little figurine of a dinosaur was precious to him, and he wasn't letting it go. Eva gave him her toy as well, a tiny figure dressed in safari gear, with a big butterfly net. I'm not sure what film tie-in this was, but it didn't matter to Pavel. He carefully took the other toy and seemed uncertain, looking to Stan for confirmation of whether he could have both.

Stan said something soft and low, and my heart expanded when Pavel smiled shyly and held both his toys right next to his heart.

And just like that, Pavel was part of my family, my

heart, and he was our new son. And right now I would buy every single Happy Meal toy in the world for him, just to keep seeing that smile.

Stan

THERE HAD NEVER BEEN ANYTHING THAT FELT AS GOOD AS sinking into our bed the night we'd brought our new children home. The day had been frantic, filled with excitement that had made all the children edgy. So many people talking at Eva and Pavel, not enough people fussing over Noah, three languages flying through the air, and food. My God, but Mama had cooked herself into a state, making every dish she could think of to entice the new arrivals to eat. She too had seen their images. Galina had shown her. We'd all agreed that good nutrition, medical care, and schooling was our top priority, but surely we couldn't make them gain all the weight in one sitting? I chuckled as I sprawled over our large bed, face into the pillows, smelling fresh spring scent and Erik, as it was his pillow I was nuzzling.

"What's so funny?" he asked, pattering around our bedroom, picking up the clothes I'd shed and let fall to the floor.

"Mama making so many food dishes," I mumbled into

the pillow, then turned my head to speak more clearly. "She'll not have to cook for a week," I said, then softly chortled, rolling a bit to try to work out the kinks of two international flights. My lower back knotted up, and I hissed in pain.

"What's wrong?" Erik asked, sliding into the bed, worry thick in his voice. He was always so concerned. A worrier, much like Mama. "I told you not to give Pavel a ride through the house on your shoulders."

"Is not my shoulders; it is my back. Even with big seats, I am cramped like sardine in can."

"Let me see if I can work the knots out." I peeked at him as he shucked off his clothes and joined me in bed, the brush of his warm flesh over my naked ass was pleasant. He settled on my thighs, his weight pressing me deeper into the mattress. Then he put his hands to my back and began kneading. My eyes rolled back into my skull, and I moaned long and low.

"So good," I purred as my mind and muscles began to unwind. Such a long day for all of us. "Door is locked, yes?"

"Yes, the door is locked," he assured me, his strong fingers digging deep into the tight muscles. His cock lay between my thighs, growing longer and firmer with each passing moment. "I love your back," he softly said, rolling and working. "And your shoulders." He moved upward, massaging as he went, his prick now resting on my ass. He covered me for a moment, his chest to my back, and rained small kisses along the shoulders he so admired. My cock was plump now. I thrust into the bedding, the soft friction quite enjoyable.

"Take my ass," I growled after several long moments

had passed with him nibbling my spine and shoulder blades while humping my backside. He paused, his breath hot little puffs on the nape of my neck. "Do it, Erik."

"But the kids…"

"Are sleeping, sound good. Do you not wish to fuck me?"

"Of course I do. I want to I just…"

I closed my eyes and let him waver a bit. Such a worrywart, my beloved.

"We will be quiet. The door is locked. Take my ass."

"Yes, okay," he whispered, wiggling around to locate the lube in the drawer of the nightstand. "I love doing this."

I grunted and rolled my hips, working to give him a little room to get his cock between my ass cheeks. Thighs tight, ass canted upward, back loose now and bowed, I gave him a treat that he always relished. Usually I was on top, but sometimes, I wanted to feel him inside me. And Erik was always willing, eager even, to slip deep into me. The round head of his cock moved over my hole, seeking entry.

"There, push hard there." I snarled, my fingers curling around the headboard, gripping the thin iron posts in preparation for a sound fucking. "Hard, push hard into me…yes. Yes!"

"Shh," Erik hissed, working his hips, sliding deeper with each hard thrust until he was in me as far as he could go in this position. "Quiet, Stan, the kids…"

"Yes, fuck, shit." I needed more. "More. I need faster fucking now, Erik." He grabbed my ass cheeks and spread them wider, slamming into me with force. I buried my face into his pillow, moaning in pleasure, my cock rubbing over the rumpled covers, the wadded-up coverlet caressing the underside of my cock. *"Mm, ah da, khorosho. Da, da, bystro, bystro!"*

"Faster, huh?" He panted and pounded me with increased speed. He came first, his spunk filling me as he held on to my ass, his grip tight and painful. We had tossed away the condoms months ago after being tested together, and now I reveled in the rush of heat deep inside me. With each pulse, his cock spewed more cum into me. He squeezed my ass cheeks together and then spread them, soft beautiful words in his language joining my grunts and pleas in Russian. "Stan, oh, hell," he gasped, pulling out in a hurry, then yanking my hip. I rolled over, and he fell on my cock, sucking me down his throat. He slid his hand between my legs, his long fingers finding my slick hole, then pushing inside. With my cock filling his mouth and his fingers bumping my prostate, I bucked wildly as my orgasm fired off. Erik swallowed every drop. I cried out once and then pawed for a pillow to bite down on. Wave after beautiful wave washed over me. His cum leaked out of me, coating his fingers as he milked that knot of nerves. I finally had to beg him to stop so I could find my breath.

He did, shimmying up over me, removing the pillow from my teeth and licking his way into my mouth, his slippery fingers plucking at my left nipple as he lapped at me.

"I am for making good words, but…brain has gone on big trip…to maybe Florida for fun and…sun times," I huffed, my chest working like a bellows, Erik lying over me, his strong limbs soft and rubbery.

"God." My sweet man sighed, his curls damp and sticking to my neck. "I love your ass."

"Heh, and I am in love with yours." I pressed a kiss to his tangled hair and cinched him close. "Life is so good perfect.... now, dreams are true, and I am quite happy fucked... senseless by my true best love."

"Sweet talker," he whispered before lifting his head to kiss me sloppily. "I'm not sure I can move."

"Stay putted then." I held him even closer. "I am good bed for you. Safe. Keep you comfy and warm."

"Love you so much," he murmured, his breathing slowing as he drifted off.

"I love you so much too," I told him, then dropped off as well, sleep not even sneaking up on me. It ran up and hit me in the face with a dream bat.

It was sometime after three when I heard crying, soft, like a sad puppy. It was not Noah. His cries I knew. I slid out from under Erik, who never twitched, his nerves having worn him out perhaps as bad as my two flights to and from Russia had me. I pulled on some sleep pants with unicorns on them—a gift from Adler on my birthday—and stepped out into the hallway. The whimpering was coming from Pavel's room, which was beside Eva's and across from Noah's, all three children having their own rooms at the end of the hall.

I padded down the hallway and pushed the door to Pavel's room open. There was not much in the rooms for either child. The walls were bare, and the closets sadly barren. We would fix this soon, very soon, with new clothes and bright things on the wall.

Both of my newest children looked up at me, the cold winter moon shining strong and white in the window. Eva sat up straight, her face damp with tears, as was Pavel's, but her chin coming up stubbornly. As if me seeing her cry was an unwanted thing for her.

"What's wrong, little ones?" I asked in Russian. Pavel burrowed into his sister's side, his sniffles pronounced. Eva held her brother close. Both were in spiffy new pajamas that were slightly too big. Clothes shopping with Mama and Galina was moving up to tomorrow.

"Pavel had a bad dream," Eva replied, also in our native tongue. I walked over and sat on the edge of the twin bed, the mattress dipping under my weight. "He says he sees Anatoli at the window."

She pointed at the window with a shaking finger.

"Anatoli looked bad, like our dog in the road." Pavel coughed, then started weeping again. I shimmied back onto the bed and pulled both trembling children to me. Had they seen their guardian's body after the accident? I prayed not.

"Your guardian is with God now, at his right-hand side, and he is perfectly beautiful, just like your Mama and Pappa," I told the two dark-haired cherubs clinging to me. Both were shaking strongly. "When we die, we go to heaven, yes?"

Two heads bobbed. I rubbed Pavel's back gently. He was lean. Far too lean. Mama would fatten them up quickly, but what of the other children in my village? Who would put meat on their bones?

"They said he was smashed bad like our dog last year," Eva said so softly I could barely hear her.

"That was just his earthly body, little ones. When we join God, our sins are washed away, and we are then in a state of glory."

"State of glory?" Pavel enquired, his sobbing slowing to mere snivels.

"Yes, we're as beautiful as the archangels, we glow with God's love, and our souls are rich and golden. The light of glory makes us whole and young and healthy."

"Even dogs?" Eva asked.

I nodded. "and cats especially are silky and spry once they reach heaven. God loves animals and gives them toys and treats. So see, the vision that you dreamed of your guardian, that wasn't him, you know that, yes?" I took Pavel's round chin in my hand and tipped his gaze up to me. He nodded and hiccuped. I glanced at Eva. She inclined her head. "Good. Know that your guardian is with God and that he is filled with golden love. What you saw was a bad dream made by sadness. I know you are sad, little ones, and I know this is confusing." I waved a hand, because it was a lot easier to speak the truth in my native tongue. "But with time, life here in America, with Erik and me, will be so good. And you will have so many opportunities: college, good jobs, loving and marrying who you wish. America is the land of dreams for immigrants like us. You will grow up big and strong and so happy." I smiled at them. They worked at smiling back, but they failed. "Is there something I can get you before you go back to bed? Cookies? Milk?"

"Can the dogs sleep with us?" Pavel asked, his chin still resting in my palm.

"Yes, of course, if you wish. But they take up a lot of room in the bed," I explained, but neither child seemed to mind.

Ten minutes later, both children were in their beds, curled up with our dogs. I checked on Noah, who was on his belly, and I mourned the loss of his gold curls. I ran a finger over his smooth cheek, pulled up his bunny blanket, and sneaked back to my bedroom.

Erik was lying on his side in bed, watching me, his head propped up on his hand. "Dogs in the bed, huh?"

I shrugged and closed the door quietly behind me. "Pavel had a dark dream. Dogs are good for keeping evils at bay."

"So they are. You handled that well."

I shucked off my pants and wiggled under the covers he was holding up for me. His skin was toasty warm when he nestled into my side. I loved the smell of him. Rich, masculine, a touch of the manly soap and shampoo he used still lingering on his heated skin.

"Pavel had bad dreams of his pappa. I think maybe they hear peoples talking and it sticks in the scary parts of their minds," I explained.

Erik sighed sadly before resting his head on my chest. "I heard." He waved at the two baby monitors on his nightstand. We had not gotten one for Eva as she was too old and required privacy. Or so Galina had informed us. "They're lucky that you're their father."

"*We* are their fathers." I turned my head and buried my nose into his hair. He cooed softly, melting into my embrace, and I drifted off. The rest of the night passed peacefully. Due to dogs guarding innocent sleep, I am sure.

Erik

I WAS UP AT FIVE A.M. IT WASN'T SO MUCH THAT I couldn't turn over and go back to sleep, but that I woke and then my head was full of what-ifs and maybes. My first thought was Noah; he'd been quiet yesterday, overwhelmed by the noise, and probably wondering who those two strange kids were in the house with him.

I tried to explain as best I could, but how much could a toddler actually understand? I couldn't help that, even though Eva and Pavel were a permanent addition to our family, my instinct was to shelter Noah. I untangled myself from Stan, who rolled away and buried his face in the pillow, muttering something in Russian that I had no hope of translating. I pressed a kiss to his shoulder blade as I pulled up the covers, then padded into the kitchen. This was my favorite part of the day—that softly lit early morning as dawn sketched the sky with blue, and there was complete peace. It wouldn't last long, Noah would be up soon, the dogs would want to be let out and walked, Stan's mama would make breakfast, Stan himself would wander into the kitchen looking all kinds of sleepy, and he would kiss me good morning and demand coffee. Now, add in two more children, and our house would be full.

But for now, it was just me, coffee, dawn, and silence. I walked the hallway, opening the door to Pavel's room carefully. Both dogs lifted their heads, BB immediately lying back down in his lazy way, but Wolfie seemed like maybe he wanted to go out, and I held the door a little wider so he could slip past. Eva was fast asleep, her arms wrapped around Pavel, who had his face buried into his sister's neck. Everything had to be so hard for them, and we shouldn't have tried to have them sleep in separate rooms. They were in a new country, with people they didn't know. Of course they would want to be together. I made a note to check with Stan about whether they wanted to share a bedroom for a while. If that was okay. I mean, they could share a room couldn't they? I didn't know the rules, and even if there were any.

I pulled the door closed, let Wolfie outside in the huge sprawling yard, and then went directly to Noah's room. This was another part of my morning ritual, spending a little time watching Noah sleep, and there was a chair in his room just for me. Stan had put it in there, so I would have somewhere to sit when Noah needed me.

Only Noah wasn't asleep. He was sitting up in his toddler bed, holding his blue rabbit and the purple teddy that Adler had bought him close to his chest.

"Hey, Noah," I said quietly and crossed to him, then placed my coffee on the small table.

"Dadda," he said, but he sounded sad, not his usual bouncy self. I held out my hands to pick him up, and he looked down at his rabbit and teddy, finally deciding both had to come with him and clambered into my arms until I had a hold of one small boy, the huge rabbit, and the purple teddy. The whole pile of us sat in my chair, and we cuddled.

"Who dem?" he asked, right near my ear.

"You mean Eva and Pavel? The children in the spare rooms?"

Noah wriggled in my hold, the teddy stuck under him, and I helped him until we were cozy again. I couldn't reach my coffee, but none of that mattered when I had an armful of my baby boy.

"Who dem?" he repeated.

"They are Pappa's cousins, and they are here to live with us."

"Mmm," Noah said.

I stroked his head, missing the curls, but seeing the way the short length was already kinking at the ends. Soon, he'd be back to normal, and I hoped to hell he never touched the shaver again. I wasn't sure Noah really understood, but how the hell was I going to explain in a way that made sense?

"You love rabbit and bear. They are your bestest favorites, right?"

Noah nodded, gripping teddy close and kissing him soundly on the top of his furry purple head.

"What about Choochie?" Choochie was the proposed new Railers mascot. A big-headed bear wearing the uniform of a steam train driver, with the Railers logo front and center. He had the classic big eyes and wide mouth of many a mascot, and I think Noah was disconcerted by the five-foot version that Stan had brought home. It stood in the corner of Noah's room, along with twenty other cuddly toys. "Is he your favorite, too?"

"Nuh-uh," he said.

"What if Choochie was sad right now, and needed a little boy to love him? What would you do?"

Noah wrinkled his nose in thought, then tugged at teddy's ear. "Hug him."

"I think Eva and Pavel are like a sad Choochie," I explained, realizing as I did that I was probably making no sense. I just knew that Noah had a big heart and so much love to give. "They will stay here forever, like Choochie will, and they need hugs because they are sad."

He nodded, his eyes wide as he processed, and then he clambered down off my lap.

"Juice," he announced.

My baby was up, Stan nearly mowed me down as he darted out of our bedroom, and Wolfie was scratching at the door to be let in.

And so my peace was finished.

It didn't get any better, Stan's mama was up and cooking, the dogs both milled around, Noah was singing *The Wheels on the Bus*, over and over, and Stan was pacing outside Eva and Pavel's room, waiting for them to get up.

"Knock on the door and go in," I encouraged.

He side-eyed me as if I'd suggested he blow open the door with explosives, but he didn't have to actually do anything when it opened a little and two sets of gray eyes peered out.

Eva whispered something in Russian. Stan went to an immediate crouch and answered, and there was nothing I could do to help. My Russian lessons were going okay, and hell, I knew how to ask for a burrito in Moscow if I needed one, if there even were burrito places in Moscow. The really emotional stuff, other than I love you—that was harder to learn.

Luckily for me, the doorbell rang, and I was the only one free to answer, so I didn't have to get involved in whatever Stan was handling. *Coward.* I opened the door to Arvy, Galina, and, more surprisingly, Sacha. Seeing him made my chest tighten. Why was he here so early? Was some government agency going to take Eva and Pavel back? *Over my dead body will they take away our children.* I let them all in because three more wasn't going to make the morning any more chaotic.

Arvy fist-bumped me. "Riding with you to the arena," he announced.

"Cool." I liked Arvy, and he and Galina were made for each other. Galina hugged me, and the two of them went into the kitchen.

"Is everything okay?" I asked Sacha immediately.

"Absolutely," he said and took off his coat. "I'm here to do a welfare check, write reports, assess finances and risk, and make recommendations."

"What? I thought we were done here? We assumed Eva and Pavel were here to stay. Stan knew people."

Sacha smiled and nodded. "They are here to stay, but it doesn't matter who Stan knows now, it won't stop people having something to say. Two Russian children, two gay dads, mother country, and so on. What I do here is cover every eventuality, tick all the boxes, make sure everything is as legally watertight as we are able. I'll be spending some time here with you and the children, starting today."

That was when I noticed the briefcase in his hand,

packed full of something that made it nearly burst at the seams. A laptop, no doubt, but my imagination had me picturing reams of official forms.

"Erik? Earth to Erik?"

I snapped back to glance at him, and he was still smiling. "This is my job, Erik, it's what the Railers hired me to do. Stop worrying, and we'll make this work. Okay?"

"Okay. Uhm, do you need a space to... I mean... we have an office you can use..."

"I'm cool with a dining table. I will need to speak to everyone at some point, but it's all chatting, nothing that needs an office." He pushed back his dark hair and reseated his glasses. "Okay?"

I gestured for him to go through, and he went immediately to the large oak table in the wood-paneled dining room. Galina's touches were everywhere in there, soft furnishings on a sofa in the corner, the table holding large candles in an ornate brass candelabrum that would have seemed crazy in a room smaller than this.

"That's one thing," he announced as he spread out paperwork and plugged in his laptop. "You pull in what, something like seven or eight million a year between you; money isn't an issue."

No, money wasn't an issue, but finding a nanny was, and actually playing the game we were being paid the millions for? That was an issue. Stan was due at practice this morning; the same as I obviously was. We couldn't miss any more. The Railers had been understanding enough.

"The only issue I can see is that the two of you aren't married, which might give me better peace of mind. Still, it's no biggie as I assume you both have wills and trusts in place?"

I backed slowly out of the room. "Okay," I said, although everything was actually far from okay. I didn't need any doubts or worries in my head. I needed to know that for sure no one could take Eva and Pavel from us. "Make it work," I demanded, then softened my tone. "Please."

Sacha smiled at me. "Everything is okay."

I went to find Stan then, who was supervising all three children, providing towels for Pavel and Eva, showing them how the shower worked and rocking a clingy Noah in his arms.

How could we leave all this today?

"Everything will be okay," Galina said from my left, taking me by surprise.

"I wish people wouldn't keep saying that," I snapped and was instantly remorseful. "Shit," I muttered and pulled her in for a hug. "I know it will. I'm sorry."

"Go to practice, take my brother with you, let Arvy drive your car. I'll be here with Mama and the children."

I looked into her eyes, so similar to Stan's. "But—"

"No buts, go play, come back home. Everything will be fine, and I also have a line on a Russian nanny through Sacha, okay? We are here to help."

"I love you, Galina," I said dramatically, and we hugged again. This time I felt a little lighter.

When we left the house, wrangling over who was driving my car, Sacha and Galina were talking at the table, all three children were in the kitchen with Stan's mama, and there was a certain amount of order to the chaos. Still,

I felt as if everything was going to go wrong without warning.

"Frowny face is bad thing," Stan announced, bumping elbows with me as we walked into the arena.

I knew my frowny face was a bad thing. I *knew.* So for Stan, I smiled. For the team, I smiled, but inside, fear still gripped me, and I just wanted everything to be done. I wanted to paint Eva's room with as much girly glitter as we could buy, or if she wanted black with navy stripes, we could do that. Hell, she could have whatever she wanted. I refused to impose gender expectations on her, but I was the first to admit that I was kind of excited about the concept of pink and glitter. I wanted to make a den for Pavel, full of cushions and games, and give him a place to hide away if he needed it.

Most of all, I just wanted us to all be able to live in peace.

Stan

A WEEK HAD PASSED SINCE EVA AND PAVEL HAD COME TO us. Parenting three children was much different than parenting one. Pavel woke up every night with bad dreams, which meant that Eva and Noah also woke up because Pavel was crying so loudly. Erik would comfort Noah, Mama would counsel Eva, and I would try to calm Pavel. Seven days of such fractured sleep did not do wonders for our performance on the ice. Erik had taken to falling asleep in the whirlpool after practice. Coach Madsen found me once napping at my cubicle, my pads and skates on, just lacking my sweater. I'd been in the process of wrapping my wrists with tape, the tape dangling from my left wrist when Coach had tapped me on the shoulder.

I snapped awake, shouted something to my mother in Russian, and then blinked when my teammates all laughed at me. A blush crept into my cheeks.

"Go home and sit on celery," I told the chuckling baboons. They only laughed harder.

So yes, three children were much harder than one at night. Also, now that Eva and Pavel were beginning to settle in, they'd started bickering. It had been nothing big at first, but then simple things would set them off, or more honestly set Eva off. One moment she was carrying her baby brother through the house, singing to him in Russian; the next she was slamming her door in his face and calling him a crusty butthole, which made him cry. I planned to speak with Galina about Eva's up-and-down moods before we ran to the new counselor Sacha had set up for the family. He explained that part of the process was to ensure the children were adapting well. Then there was schooling to set up, but we needed a nanny first. How we wished Noah's old babysitter was available, but she had gone back to college. Even though she'd not spoken Russian, her help would have been valuable, and Noah knew her. Our sweet rabbit was not his usual self with so many strangers in his house. One who cried often, and the other who slammed doors and called people crusty buttholes.

A puck slapped me in the helmet, right above my eyes. It startled me but didn't hurt too much. I snapped back to our morning skate, eyeing the men at center ice.

"Who hit me in the forehead with a puck? I am not ready yet for making star saves. I have not had talk with pipes yet, and my brain is slippery slow. Who shoot this at my face?!" I yelled because now my head was aching a little, and I was mad at myself for thinking of nanny things when I was in net. "Tell me! I am no making jokes. I will find who shoot me in the head, and I will sit on your face until you pass out from bad goalie pants on nose!"

The large huddle of men parted, and there, in a white no-contact jersey, was Ten.

"Yeah, that was maybe kind of me," Ten called.

I threw the puck aside and skated from the net, arms open, and grabbed my best friend up from his skates. He made a squeaking sound. I kissed both his cheeks, patted his face with my glove, and rubbed his head gently with my blocker.

"Is so good for you coming back! Is head good?" I left my catching mitt on his head as I spoke.

"Dude, my head is really extra good." Tennant laughed, reaching up to move my mitt from his helmet. I stared at him, into his eyes, and poked him in the belly. He gasped at the poke.

"Okay, is just making sure doctors are making right call." I patted his back, then pointed my blocker at the rest of the Railers. "No one makes hits on Tennant."

"We know what the no-contact jersey means, Stan. We're not assholes," Dieter said, shoving at me playfully, then skating back to the bench.

"Well, you kind of are D," Adler threw out.

The men chortled and nudged each other with shoulders and elbows as they all returned to the bench for a drink. I held on to Tennant's arm for a moment.

He turned big green eyes up to me. "What's up, bruh?"

"I have two new children now. They are here, in America. Eva and Pavel Lyamin. I would be much honored if you and Jared would come over for dinner soon, so to meet your godchildren."

The happy-go-lucky smile on Ten's face slipped. He cleared his throat and held out a gloved fist. "It would be an incredible privilege to come meet Eva and Pavel, but, dude, are you sure you want me as their godfather? Don't you want someone older? Like with more kid experience? Someone like Jared?"

"No," I said as I rapped his gloved fist with mine. "You are my dearest best friend. You take me into wing when English was bad and teach me groovy cool words. You join me into the Pokémon group, make me feel like member of team. You are brother I never have. And I would only ever ask a family member to be godfather of my most precious possessions."

Ten blinked, then dragged the back of his glove across his eyes. "You honor me, my man. I am totally there for you and those kids." He hugged me hard, kissed me on the cheeks, just as we did in Russia, and then skated off, his arm dropping around Erik, to chat and joke.

God blessed me many times over by bringing my Erik back to me, then giving me a wonderful, inclusive team and adding three beautiful children to my bounty. Oh, and Mama and Galina of course, and even Arvy, who was a good brother-in-law. He had better be. The first time my sister comes to me crying, his liver will be plucked out by vultures in hot desert. I know people who can make liver plucking happen.

THE FOLLOWING Sunday we had an afternoon game, a matinee, which was good because Erik and I could be home for the nighttime routine before we left for a five-game Canadian road trip. Tonight, we would sit down with the children for spaghetti and meatballs and tell them that we were going away but only for a short time. We also had to explain to Eva that Sacha had found us a tutor and a nanny. The nanny, Anna Sanarov was a smiling woman with red hair who would begin the morning we left for Toronto. I wanted to call her Red, like the Russian redhead in the woman's prison show, but Erik vehemently objected. I liked Anna, and so did Erik. Also, Mama approved. That was most important, for Mama ruled the house. We two men thought we did, but no, Mama did.

Sacha was still working with us, but we saw less of him now. That wasn't a bad thing for me as he was very handsome and manly, and I worried Erik's head might be taken with him.

The tutor, a slim Russian/American man by the name of Professor Peter Minkoff, who was retired, would start tomorrow. He would ease the children into a school-like routine while teaching them English so they could go to public schools. Pavel was having trouble learning any new words, and I wondered if he were even trying. I suspected he clung to Russian, as it kept him close to his guardian and all he had left behind. Or perhaps I was far off base. I was no child psychiatrist. I was only a man who played hockey.

Which was what I should be thinking on now. The current game against Philadelphia had been a slow one. Philly had been traveling and had come into our city late last night. They were tired and not nearly as gritty as usual. Our team was well rested but sluggish. Maybe the lethargy of the Philly team had infected the Railers. I couldn't say, but neither goalie was working too hard. Weak shots on goal, no net front presence, and a tight defense left me standing there thinking about meatballs. Then the tide turned quickly when one of the Philadelphia forwards skated into our zone after an icing had been whistled the other end of the ice. He slapped the puck into the net.

"Hey, fish-face asshole, what is with that shit dick move?" I shouted at the man in orange, then spun to fish the puck out of my net. My teammates took offense, as they should have. That was an unwritten rule of the game. There were many, such as take off your gloves before a fight, don't ice the goalie, never turtle during a fight, always try to get your teammate that third goal, heavyweights fight heavyweights, and you never shoot the puck on the net after the whistle blows. There are more, but those are a few. And fish-face asshole had shot the puck on the net after the whistle.

Dieter got right up into fish-face's space, shoving him into the boards while reminding him that his behavior had been tacky. I think his exact words were, "Yo, shit for brains, what the fuck was that bullshit?!" but the fans at home were making so much noise I might have misheard.

The knot of players to my right spiced things up like hot chili peppers. The next ten minutes were lively, and we managed to grab a win with a sloppy goal that Adler deflected into the Philly net with less than forty-seconds left on the clock. I got many head pats and forehead bonks on the ice. Erik rubbed my helmet in a special way that meant something romantic just between us.

We hurried home to Hershey two hours later. I opened the front door, and the smell of garlic and the sound of children talking filled our home. I looked over at Erik as we stripped off our coats in the foyer.

"Listen to that. That is the sound of a happy house," I said and then stole a kiss, a good one too; one that left him pink in the cheeks and short of breath. "Come, let us do dinner time!"

I led him past the living room—which was covered in toys and dogs—to the kitchen. Lucy, my cat, was the first to see me, and she ran over to rub on my legs. Noah spotted us from the floor, where he and Pavel were seated with blocks. Eva was chattering at Mama while they worked on a tossed salad.

"Da! Pa!" Noah shrieked and threw himself at Erik. I got a loud kiss from Noah, then he padded over to kneel beside Pavel. "Blocks for dagoons fall over! We make towers for dagoons, Da. Da, cat throw up mouse head. Gam say Rush words at Lucy. I say Rush words for Lucy. Meatballs! Meatballs! Meatballs!"

"What are we making here?" I asked in Russian.

He placed a block on top of the wobbly stack he and Noah had built. "Tall towers for dragons to sit on," the boy replied, peeking up at me through unruly dark bangs.

I ruffled his hair and placed a tiny plastic purple dragon on the top of the tower. Pavel gave me a shy little smile that made my heart expand. I then stood, smiling at Eva, who smiled back. Mama barked at me to set the table, and I snapped to attention, giving her a salute that made Eva giggle.

Once we were all seated—Noah strapped into his booster seat—Mama made a fast prayer, and then we started eating.

"Meatball! Da, me like meatballs," Noah announced after getting his dish readied by Erik and placed before him.

"Children, we have things to tell you," I shouted over

the chitter-chatter of three kids and my mother, who seemed to talk steadily now that she had three children and two men to keep in line. She was always telling someone something.

Eva and Pavel looked up, Pavel with spaghetti strands dangling from his lips that he sucked up with a slurp, making Noah laugh. Noah then sucked a strand, and Pavel giggled. That went on for a few moments, with Eva even getting in on the slurping fun until Mama gently chided them not to be rude.

"Erik and I are going to Canada for a long trip for hockey." I said it in Russian for the two oldest. Noah was too busy slurping and smashing meatballs with his fingers. Also, he was used to us traveling. Eva blinked. Pavel stopped eating and stared at me as if he'd been struck. "Long, like eleven days, little ones," I quickly said.

Some of the panic left their faces. "You come back?" Pavel asked in terribly fractured English, his eyes darting from me to Erik.

"Yes, of course," Erik said, reaching over the table to pat Pavel's thin arm tenderly. "You'll *always* have someone here who loves and protects you. We promise that. Your new *babushka* will be here all the time and Aunt Galina in the evening. And the new nanny, Anna, and Professor Pete. You'll never be left alone ever again."

I translated for the wary young boy with the trembling lower lip. Once he understood, he relaxed and went back to slurping Mama's zesty spaghetti. I reached under the table and gave my man's thick thigh a squeeze.

I loved my Erik so much at that moment. Just when I thought I could not love him more, he did something so wonderful that my affection for him tripled yet again. Such a wonderful family we had. Life was nearly perfect. I just wanted one small little thing to happen, and then all would be magical.

Erik

THE CANADIAN ROAD TRIP WAS AN EYE-OPENER. IT WASN'T just that we were lined up against Vancouver, Winnipeg, and Toronto, Calgary, and Montreal, all in the space of eleven nights, but also there was the whole team bonding session in the middle.

Banff was stunning, and the team had what seemed like an entire hotel to ourselves. This was where we were supposed to bond, make friends, find out each other's secrets, but it was also where bad things happened.

Like me and Stan in separate rooms, with the agreement we wouldn't be crossing the hall at midnight. Or Ten getting on the ice on day one at the practice rink and then mutually deciding with the coach that he needed to sit things out a little longer. Then there was missing the children. Both Stan and I FaceTimed all three of them; Noah enthusiastically chatted away, sat on Galina's knee, explaining about meatballs and bagetti, which was his super cute way of saying spaghetti. I missed my little man with a fierceness that stole my breath, but he was fine, used to our absences, and he actually seemed to be having fun in our house full of people.

Pavel was quiet; he didn't really talk to me much, but Stan got a response every time he asked something in their native tongue. At one point Pavel was animated, and Stan explained they'd been discussing hockey. Apparently, Pavel was a huge fan and had messed around on a frozen pond, as most Russian kids did, alongside Canadians, and of course Swedes like me.

"Why didn't we know he liked hockey?" I asked as we waited for Eva to come to the iPad to talk to us.

"I'm never ask him." Stan was thoughtful. "We can put a rink in our garden."

Privately, I wondered if that was overkill, but wisely I said nothing. Stan would think about this and conclude that maybe we should just be taking Pavel to the Railers' practice rink and messing about there.

"With most big lights for playing in dark," he added. I wasn't sure our neighbors would be cool with floodlights. They may not have been close—after all Stan's acreage was on the big side—but the lights would spread a long way if they were as big as Stan's waving hands suggested.

"We need round thing on it," Stan said as if a lightbulb had gone off in his head. "Big circles."

I spoke Stan, most of the time, but I wasn't entirely following this one.

"A circle?" Did he mean the lines and circles in the ice?

He gestured with his hands, this huge expansive wave of something that looked a little like…

"A dome? You want to build an ice rink in our yard, with lighting, and cover it in a dome."

"A dome," Stan repeated. "Much big, with popcorn maker and place for pucks and sticks. And seats for Mama and Galina to watch and a teeny tiny Jumbotron."

I leaned over and kissed him. "You realize you are describing the Capital Ice Complex in Rutherford, our practice rink, right?"

He wrinkled his nose and then brightened. "We take him there," he announced as if he'd thought that through and come to the right conclusion. I didn't argue but was quietly pleased we weren't going to alienate all the neighbors in our district with a brightly lit ice rink in our yard.

"Good call," I said, and he was so proud of himself that my heart expanded just a tiny bit more with the love I had for him.

Eva sat in the chair at the table and peered at the screen but didn't say anything. Not an enthusiastic hello or even the hint of missing us or even a smile. In fact, she seemed miserable and tired and pale. Was she ill? Stan began to talk to her, and I fired a quick text to Galina, asking what was wrong with Eva. Was it a reaction to food? Was our house too hot? Too cold? Was she ill from something she'd brought from Russia? Did she need to see a doctor? I couldn't even concentrate on Eva and Stan talking while I conjured up all manner of horrible things in my head.

<Women's problems.> Galina answered simply and to the point. I felt my face heat and pushed back the instinctive panic. Periods didn't scare me. I could handle that; it was the fact that this was our new daughter who was struggling and was so sad.

I placed the cell facedown on the table.

"How are you?" I asked Eva during the next break in her and Stan's rapid-fire Russian.

"Okay," she said and nodded. I thought she looked like she was going to cry, but no wonder she was. Her thin body was not only having to deal with America, the flight, losing her guardian, but was also being ravaged by hormones. I knew Galina would be helping her, but I needed desperately to say something that might make her smile.

"I miss you," I said, which was the truth. Apart from the mini-tantrums and rudeness, I saw something of Stan in Eva, a love for life, a willingness to focus on the bright side of things. "I saw a beautiful flower today on the mountain, and it reminded me of you."

Wow. Way to come off with the overkill vibe. Everyone stopped. Stan looked at me. I could see him openmouthed, and Eva's eyes widened.

Fuck.

"What kind of flower?" she asked.

"I don't know what it's called, but even in the snow, it was growing and seemed like it was as strong as you are."

"Oh," she said and then gave a cautious smile. Maybe I'd connected with her inner teenage angst. Maybe I'd fucked up completely, and she was laughing at me, but I didn't care. I'd made Eva smile. Me. With flower analogies and a willingness to open my heart. She shuffled in her chair. "Professor Pete is making us do math," she said, but her smile didn't drop. She leaned into the screen to tell us a secret, and I realized I mirrored her movement. "Pavel hates it, but I think I want to do math when I am older."

"We can give much math to you," Stan said eagerly. I

didn't ask how he was going to do that. After the whole domed-rink-in-the-garden thing, I imagined him coming up with the idea of building a math room just for her.

"Thank you," she said a little shyly.

"We miss you much, our flower," Stan said, and my chest tightened. That could either be complete overkill, or Eva could think it was the best thing ever.

"We miss you, too," she said with no hint of embarrassment. "Come home soon."

We said our goodbyes, blew kisses to Noah, and ended the call. It was six in the evening. I was tired from practice and would have liked nothing more than to cuddle with Stan in our bed at home and watch movies.

"Yo," Adler shouted from the main door, "you ready or what?"

Tonight was dinner out. I wasn't allowed to sit with Stan. I had to buddy up with someone I wouldn't ordinarily sit with. That was the rule, and even though we all knew each other quite well, I decided that I would sit with Gids, the kid brought up from the Rush to fill the space with everyone moving lines to fill Ten's shoes. I called him a kid, but I was only a few years older than him, but in hockey years I was like Old Father Time to his baby.

I was envious that somehow Stan had finagled it so he was sitting with Ten. I mean, come on, Stan and Ten are best friends. How had they managed that? I guess no one wanted to go toe-to-toe with the big man over where he sat and whom he sat with. Then, I realized as the evening progressed, that Stan had deliberately sat forward to give Ten a space to hide if it all became too much. Ten looked bright tonight, not at all angry that he'd had to leave the ice. He'd actually put in thirty minutes of slow drills, working on balance, which he hadn't appeared to have lost, and practicing his wicked slap shot. We missed that slap shot, we missed Ten, but right now I had Gids next to me, and that was whom I needed to focus on.

"How are you?" I asked because that was the only question I could think of.

"Good. You?" he asked and half turned in his seat. He likely had a list of things that he thought we should talk about—mostly based around hockey, I guessed. I knew what his hockey was like. He'd make it to the Railers permanently one day. He was fast, focused, and reminded me of me at times. He was a good kid, earnest, and so damn smiley.

"Tell me about your family," I said.

He paused a moment. "My family? I thought we were supposed to discuss hockey." He glanced over at Coach, who sat at the head of the table with a serene expression on his face.

"Nah, I know you're excellent at that, so tell me about your family. Who is Gideon Levesque?"

I found out he was the youngest of three brothers, the same as Ten, that no one in his family played hockey except him, that he loved his home city of Winnipeg, and that he *really* loved playing NHL hockey.

By the time the evening was done and we were heading back to the hotel, I'd bonded with Gids in a big way, invited him to the house, found out he loved reading, and that he was in awe of Ten. It was a good night, and we fist-bumped in the foyer before he left to go to his room. I sat in the bar, waited for Stan, wasn't surprised when he and Ten, along with Jared, all sat with me. I wanted to ask how Ten felt, but that was probably the last thing he needed to be asked, so I asked him about the wedding.

"Small," Jared said.

"But with family and friends," Ten countered.

"At a hotel, end of June."

"At our house, in the gardens, July."

They grinned at each other as if this was maybe an ongoing argument.

"With the Stanley Cup in attendance," Jared said.

Ten laughed. "Well, that's one thing we agree on."

I wasn't sure the Railers would get the cup this year. We were languishing at fifth out of eight and overall were about nineteenth out of all teams. We missed Ten. That much was clear. His accident had rocked us to the core, and we'd taken a long time to get our shit together and fight back. We were putting some solid points up now, but too many of them were overtime or shootout wins where we relied heavily on Stan and Bryan. Thank God we had two good net-minders. Maybe this year wasn't going to be our year. It was more than possible we wouldn't get to the very end and lift the cup, because miracles aside, we had a lot of catching up to do. Ten laced his fingers with Jared's, and Jared nodded as if he was answering an unspoken question.

"Stan, I wanted to ask you something," Ten began.

"Yes, yes. I'm stop all goals and lifting cup with you," Stan interjected.

Ten reached over and patted his knee. "No, this isn't about hockey. I wanted to ask you if you would be part of our wedding. Be a groomsman. It just means you show people to seats, and you stand next to me and my brothers and Ryker."

Stan tensed, and I heard the soft sound he made. The one that meant he didn't know what to say and that he was choked with emotion.

"Yes," he said and stood, extending his hand to Ten. They hugged a while, and just when I considered breaking them up, they sat, grinning at each other like idiots.

Then Stan frowned and patted his heavy thighs. "I will write most excellent words to say."

Jared began to talk. "You won't need to do a speech or—"

"I'm need custom suit, like Elvis," Stan interrupted.

I snorted a laugh. I couldn't help it—the thought of my man in a flashy white suit with sequins was funny.

But Ten didn't flinch at all. "Anything you want, big man. Anything at all."

Stan

NOTHING WAS MORE WONDERFUL THAN COMING HOME. THE children were all happy to see us. Even Pavel clambered up to sit on Erik's lap to watch a movie the night we returned. Noah took some offense to that, and a small shoving match broke out until I swooped the jealous little rabbit up and cuddled with him on my lap. I felt Pavel and Erik needed time to bond, as the difficulty with communicating was perhaps making my beloved feel left out. Noah settled down after a soft but firm whisper, and we all enjoyed *Milo and Otis* a great deal. That night, after the children were asleep, I made love to Erik, quietly, in the shower of our master bath. His cries of passion were buried in my shoulder. We tumbled into bed, exhausted but sated, our underwear clinging to our still damp skin.

The following morning, Sunday, Mama rapped on our door strongly at six in the morning.

"Make for to wear Sunday best clothes," she shouted, and then went down the hall, waking the children for church.

"Muffle donuts," Erik said into his pillow.

I rolled to my side, pulled him close, and dozed off. Five minutes later, Mama was hammering at the door again, startling us both badly.

"Church time. Get up or find foot in lazybone ass!"

"Her grasp of English cursing is improving by leaps and bounds," Erik grumbled, sitting up and rubbing at his eyes with the heels of his hands.

"Oh, yes, we Russians are experts at making cussing," I replied around a yawn. I lay there watching the flow of his muscles as he stretched his arms over his head. He was so beautiful, so toned, and so marked as mine. I touched the love bite on his side. He jerked and snorted and rolled out of bed. "You are the most beautiful man on this world. I love you so much. My love is so big."

He smiled sweetly down at me. "My love for you is big as well," he said, just as three children thundered past our bedroom door, shouting about who got the purple spoon for their oatmeal. "And my love for them is big, too."

"As is mine. How do they wake up running? This is quite a question that I needs reply to." I sighed, kicking off the covers and planting my feet on the floor.

Erik laughed. Then we went down to have oatmeal and toast. Galina and Arvy were meeting us at the Rose of Beulah Baptist Church, so they got to avoid the madcap meal. It seemed all meals were loud now. I loved it.

I was wiping the mess off of Noah's face when someone knocked on the door. Knowing it was not my sister and her husband, I gave Erik a confused glance, handed him the wet washcloth, and stood, pulling the sash of my winter robe tight around my waist. At the door stood a slim woman, dark-skinned, with short black hair and an air of authority. She looked familiar.

"Hello, Mr. Lyamin. Do you remember me?"

"I think I should, but no. Sorry for that."

She smiled up at me. "That's fine. I know your life has been hectic since the children arrived. I'm Clarice Rose, from the Pennsylvania Department of Children, Youth, and Family Services. I've been assigned to assist and advocate for you and your partner in any post-adoption manners that you may need assistance with. Your final hearing isn't until the end of the year, but I'm here to do an unscheduled placement visit. May I come in?"

"Oh, yes, Miss Clarice Rose, I remember now. Come in. We are just eating breakfast before church. You come with us to church!" I was happy to show Miss Rose our church. And our house and anything else she needed to see. Erik meandered out, hair rumpled, whiskery, with Noah on his hip. So beautiful my man and son were it took my breath away sometimes. When he saw Miss Rose, his blue eyes rounded. "Erik, Miss Rose from the Children Office of Family Planning is here for visit! She is going to church with us. There we will all sing and make good with God. Mama! Miss Rose from Family Planning is here! Get her bowl of oatmeal!"

"Stan, it's not family planning," Erik whispered as I tugged Miss Rose into the kitchen to see the children. "It's child services, or something."

I led her to a seat beside Eva. She seemed as if she were winded from running when she sat down. Mama placed a bowl of oatmeal in front of our guest and directed Miss Rose to eat, in Russian. I nodded and smiled. And Miss Rose had a hearty breakfast and then went with us to church, even though she was not so sure at first, but I talked her into it. She sat next to me looking very tiny.

A lot of singing and dancing took place, as did serious praying and asking God to bless those who are sick, hungry, and hurting. Again, the prickle of my family back in Russia nipped at me. Here I sat, in a fancy suit, with my sweet Erik, our beautiful children, Mama, my sister and her husband, and Miss Rose, without a care in the world. We had so much. I needed to find a way to help poor children in my homeland but had no idea how. I decided, as the chorus jumped into *When I Get in Glory* and Noah and I began to wiggle in our seats, that I would talk with Erik and then Layton Foxx. Perhaps the Railers would wish to set up something. Maybe a hockey tournament or a charitable foundation of some sort. The music was taking over my soul, so I stopped thinking and let the Holy Spirit make me sing and dance with Miss Rose.

And when Miss Rose left, she was happy and said we were doing much good things.

———

THE FOLLOWING DAY, a Monday morning, I burst into Layton's office, smiling, with a large cup of decaf coffee in hand. Layton stared up from the laptop he was tapping away on, his slim eyebrows drawing down.

"Are you bringing me coffee?" He sounded shocked.

"Ah, yes, but it is not bad jittery coffee. It is decaf coffee. Fools mind into being energetic." I sat the jumbo decaf on his desk. It was a tidy desk. It fit Layton, who was also tidy. He sat back, crossed his arms over his dark blue suit jacket, and gave me a long look.

"What did you do?" he asked with resignation in his voice.

"Me?" I pointed to myself. He nodded. "I do nothing. Well, I mean I do many things. Today I wake up, suck on Erik's—"

"Whoa, hold up." He threw a hand into the air. "I don't need a play-by-play of your morning. I mean what did you do wrong that I'm going to have to fix on social media? You must have done something, since you brought me coffee, and you're always hounding me to give it up."

"No, I say give up bad jitter coffee. This is good no jitter coffee, and I have done no bad." He raised an eyebrow. "Is true. Crossing my heart." I made an "X" over my chest. "I bring you coffee gift to make you happy."

"Uh-huh. Adler does the same thing."

"Well, Adler is making to spoil you so he can nibble on your nuts." Layton's smooth cheeks flamed red. "I am not wishing to nibble your nuts. I nibbled on Erik's this morning."

"Stan, can we just get to the reason that you're here?" His whole face was rosy now, even his ears.

I closed the door and sat across from him, shoving the coffee cup in his direction. "I wish to make a charity to help poor children. Mostly, I am thinking for Russian children, but I know America and Russia are not making nice right now. So for maybe poor children in Europe for more general help. I read online that one hockey player has big charity game for his child foundation. Invites many big names during summer. This player is from Norway, but I think maybe we could do this in Sweden? Erik knows many people there. We all do. I wish to make good life for poor babies. Can you help me do this?"

He blinked at me, grabbed my gift, and took a long swig. I could hear the other players, arriving for morning skate, walking past the closed door. Erik was coming in later. Our nanny's car broke down, and so he had to go pick her up. Always something with children.

"I'm not sure that I'm the person to talk to about this, but I'd be happy to do what I can to get you headed in the right direction."

I smiled and stood, shoving my hand at him. "Yes! You are miracle worker. I see how many bacons you save for the team, and I know, deep in heart, that you are man for the job. I leave you to make foundation big and good. Oh! Name it after my cousin who dies and leaves his children to Anatoli and then me. Call it the Lyamin Foundation for Children. Yes, I like this." I pumped his hand hard.

"Stan, I'm not the one who'll be setting this up. I'm just—"

"Yes, yes, making good for poor children." I shook and shook his hand. "Find good peoples for me and the foundation. We make summer hockey game and give all monies to the children."

"Stan, it's not going to be as easy as—"

I released his hand and went for the door. "Oh, yes, I know is not easy. But you are bacon saver, so you will pull my crispy fat pork meat from hot pan too. Many thanks!"

"Stan, I just…" I paused in the hall to check back with him. His eyes met mine, and he smiled just a little. "I'll get things started for the Anatoli Lyamin Foundation."

"You are good man, Layton Foxx." I saluted him before heading down the hall into the dressing room. "Listen up, I have bigly news!"

Everyone dressing for morning skate quieted and

looked my way. Tennant gave me a grin. It was so good to have my best friend back. Even if he wasn't playing just yet, he would be soon, and then all would be right with the world. "I make big hockey game for summer, play for new charity for poor children in Europe. Who will sign up to do this with me?"

Every hand in the dressing room went up.

Erik

I'D NEVER SEEN PINK THAT WAS QUITE SO... ROSY. THINK flamingo. Actually, think a whole flamboyance of flamingos in some kind of personal fight with strawberries and candy floss all in one place, and there was Eva's newly painted room.

"I love it," she said. She wasn't squealing or smiling or dancing around in glee, but the way she stood in the middle of the rosy room, in awe even, made me all warm and glowy inside. When we'd picked out the colors, I wasn't sure. I mean, I like pink, but this was... a lot. Galina had then put herself in charge, telling Eva that men knew nothing, and now she and Eva stood together in the center of the space, eyeing the walls thoughtfully.

"A space for posters," Galina suggested.

Eva smiled then and looked over at me and Stan briefly. "Ten."

"Ten posters," Galina murmured, "Okay, wow, that's a big space."

Eva dipped her head and flushed the same color as her room. "No, can I have a poster of Ten?"

Stan huffed a laugh next to me. "And ones of goalie and winger," he whispered, loud enough for Eva to hear.

"But you're like... my pappa's," she finished after the pause. "And Ten's so cute."

Well, I couldn't argue with that. Ten was cute, and if I was a teenage girl, or hell, if Ten had been playing when I was a teenager, then I'd have had a poster of him on my wall as well. No argument. Of course it would be right next to my Stan poster, but who said you can't have two up there?

"I'm getting much bigly posters for you," Stan said and vanished, probably to call the Railers and get posters, jerseys, pucks, and an array of sticks all signed by Ten. I followed him to stop him before he bought out the entire shop of Ten-related merchandise, and found him on the phone.

"Three, much big ones," I heard him say, and I took the phone off him quickly.

"Hello?"

"Erik, that you?" Ten asked. Seemed like my man had bypassed the team shop and gone directly to the source.

"Ten, don't listen to Stan. One poster is good and maybe a jersey in her size."

"I can do that. Jared has a whole supply I need to sign for the next auction. Does she want it in one of those glass cabinets? I can get her a display case for pucks as well. Would she like that? What about a Tennant Rowe stick. We have some of those, and she'd grow into it."

Oh my God, Stan and Ten were as bad as each other. "One poster, and a jersey she can wear is good." It seemed to be down to me to stop them from spoiling Eva, who had an entire closet of stuffed elephants after she'd casually mentioned she liked them. Four of them from Stan and six from Ten, in varying sizes. Ten was certainly taking his godparent duties seriously. Of course, the six elephants he'd bought were matched by a collection of remote-controlled cars for Pavel and a mystery box of books and teddies for Noah.

Pavel's cars were still in their boxes. He seemed happiest with his books and watching hockey games, but he had thanked Ten with some enthusiasm. His bedroom used a much more sedate palette of greens and blues, along with clouds, that Galina had painted, and we'd erected a bed in there with a huge tent over it, so it was like a den.

Eva and Pavel had been here four weeks now. We'd settled into a routine, and we couldn't overwhelm the kids with too much of everything at the same time. Stan and I had actually covered this concept of not spoiling them last night. Again.

I handed the phone back to Stan. "One poster. One jersey." I warned him.

"Cross hearts to die," he promised and took the phone into the study. God knew what he and Ten were planning.

"Erik, can you help move this cabinet?" Galina called, and steeling myself, I went back into the flamingo palace and felt my eyes water. I lifted the cabinet they wanted moved, and then stood back, ready for my next order.

"Right there," Eva said and pointed to the space. She held out a photo, and Galina studied it for a moment before rolling her shoulders and tacking the photo to the wall where she could see it.

"Okay then."

In a few deft strokes of chalk, she'd drawn the outline of a house, sketched in some trees, and added windows, a door, and made the merest suggestion of a yard. I sat on the edge of Eva's bed, always fascinated when Galina began to draw, and Eva sat next to me.

"What is she drawing?" I asked. Although I could see it was a house, it had to be more than *just* a house

"My home in Leskovo, where Pavel was born."

Galina began to fill in details, building layers with the different paints she had on a glass sheet. The structure, the clouds, trees, and the garden took shape, greens with splashes of red. It shouldn't have worked on the pink wall, but it did. Eva leaned against me, and I put my arm over her shoulder.

"Tell me all about your home," I asked her as we watched.

"It was old and warm, and Mama was always cooking. I remember she always smelled so nice," she began, "and that she was very ill when Pavel was only two. I miss her."

I squeezed a little, just to let her know I was there. We'd seen a counselor the previous week after a recommendation from Miss Rose at family services. Just Stan and I. We'd listened as they'd spoken about the children and their grief, both of us choking back emotion at what we needed to do. Both Eva and Pavel would benefit from help, and we would get everything they needed. From mental health support all the way up to a pink bedroom and books.

"And then we had a new pappa... and we didn't like him much. I don't think he liked us either. But we were sad when he died."

Galina turned to face us. "Okay then, which window, Eva?"

Eva shrunk into my hold and gripped my free hand, holding on tight. "The top one, the left there."

"This one?" Galina checked and pointed at the window. When Eva nodded, Galina loaded her brush with a dark color, and in the top left window, she drew a shape. I couldn't make out what it was until she added some white, and then it made sense. Two people in the window in a close embrace—a hug—a man and a woman.

"That's Mama and Pappa, like a picture we have of them in our old home," Eva murmured, and then she began to cry. I held her for a long time. Stan came in and sat on the bed as well. Eva sat on his lap, burying her face in his chest. I wondered if she remembered her parents at all, or was everything she had of them only in photos?

Pavel stood in the doorway, stricken, and asked something in Russian. Stan extended an arm, and he clambered up to sit on my knee.

"What did he ask?" I needed to know.

Stan's eyes were so bright. "He wants know, is it Eva's turn for leaving him," Stan said after swallowing a couple of times. "I'm say no."

Galina slipped out of the room, and the four of us left stared at the painting with its purples and blues, which blended amazingly well into the pink walls, and at the couple in the window. Noah joined us, wanting in on the hug, and I held my little boy close, desperately wanting to promise him that I could stop time and spare him any pain of losing parents. One day he would know this kind of pain, but I hoped he would be a very old man by then.

Then the five of us sat in a huddle, and we didn't move

until Ten and Jared appeared at the bedroom door. It was actually Eva, who moved first, untangling herself from Stan's hug and helping Pavel down, smoothing her top and smiling shyly at Ten.

"Hello," she said and looked at the floor.

"Hello gorgeous girl," Ten said, always the smooth one. "Your dads said you wanted some stuff for your room." He hefted a box, and I noticed Jared had one as well. I caught Jared's eye and saw him shake his head in exasperation. I'd bet *anything* that the boxes were packed with more than just one jersey. I wasn't wrong. Jerseys, plural, pucks signed by Ten, and a couple from Jared, bags, cups, signs, and poking out of the box, a huge rolled poster. The second box was for Pavel and contained more of the same. Then there was the bag in the hall that Noah had clearly rummaged through, which held smaller versions of the new mascot, with various team numbers on the back, along with a selection of bobbleheads. I caught Noah trying to bury Adler's figure in a plant pot, and as much as all of the team wanted to do that to Adler at times, I didn't want to encourage it.

"And now we go skating," Stan announced.

"We are?" This was the first I'd heard. I thought today was decorating, family time, and chilling on our day off. Clearly not.

We had the Railers' practice arena to ourselves, but I noticed that the locker room had been set up for us, along with Ten and Jared, so I assumed Stan or Ten had organized this during that phone call.

"I love you." I kissed the tip of Stan's nose.

"Love you," Stan said and then scooped up a squealing Noah. Our son had on his tiny skates and a jersey with the word *Daddy* on the back. The space was way too small to fit Lyamin-Gunnarsson or Gunnarsson-Lyamin, and *Daddy* covered us both. Ten offered a hand to Eva, and they headed out. That left me with Pavel, who was visibly shaking with excitement, his mouth stretched in a big grin.

I held out a hand, and he took it, but as soon as his blades touched ice he was away, not exactly gliding smoothly at first, but our little man had some skills on ice. I kept my eye on him, on Eva, who was showing Ten how she could skate backward, and on Noah, who was being carted around the ice on a small sled by Jared. Stan skated slowly toward me. I loved him so much it hurt. Seeing him with Noah, and now Eva and Pavel, being with him, it was all I ever wanted for the rest of my life. For all of it, the messy, the sad, the happy, and the love. I wanted us to be together forever. I wanted to marry my man. Seeing Ten and Jared sporting their rings, engaged, planning a wedding, I wanted that. Maybe not all the planning, but to be tied to Stan in a way that was forever? Yes, that was what I wanted. Now.

"I'm love family skating," Stan murmured, and I gripped his hands.

"We should get the kids new jerseys, with our names on," I began, then stopped. That wasn't what I meant to say, even though it had sounded clever in my head. "Gunnarsson-Lyamin, or Lyamin-Gunnarsson," I added.

"Is big words for little jerseys," Stan murmured and appeared thoughtful, as if he was considering how he could fit all of that in a small space. But that wasn't what I was trying to say, and trying to be cute was failing me. "Teeny tiny letters—"

"Marry me, Stan."

His mouth fell open, his grip on my hand tightened, and I could see that he was lost for words. Then he pulled me close, bent me backward, and kissed me like we hadn't kissed for years.

"Yes, yes, much Elvis things, and red with ruffles or blue," he said, a mix of Russian in there as well. "We do now." He pulled back and checked our surroundings, as if he was searching for a priest right there.

"We have to plan—"

"Vegas baby." He snapped his fingers. "For much sin and valentine kisses, when game in Vegas."

We were playing Vegas on or around February 14, which was only a week away. A Vegas wedding. The Team. Family. Stan.

"Yeah," I agreed, "perfect."

Stan

"DID YOU SEE ME MAKE SUCH BIG SINGING?" I ASKED breathlessly, dropping to the seat of the limo, the warm Las Vegas night air whipping through the open sunroof. Mama clapped, as did the children. Erik smiled at me as he does sometimes at Noah. "I did not miss one word of *Viva Las Vegas,* even when a bug flew into my mouth. Elvis is being most proud!"

"Pappa," Pavel moaned, tugging at the red bow tie of his scarlet tuxedo. I reached around Galina to fix his tie. "What is Elvis?"

My mouth fell open. I glanced at Erik holding Noah on his lap, both in bright red tuxes with sequined lapels just like mine and Pavel's. Elvis would be so proud.

"We have failed big for parenting. I will teach you much about Elvis Presley, the greatest rock and roll singer in all of American history. Is this not right, Mama?"

"Engelbert Humperdinck is greatest," Mama replied flatly as she fussed with Eva's bright red sequined dress. All the ladies had pretty red sequined dresses to match the lapels of our tuxedoes. Mama hated hers, saying it make her look like an old *prostitutka*. Galina and Eva liked the dresses I had bought. Erik and the other Railers in the wedding party loved the bright red suits we'd rented. Mama always had words to say about everything. I loved her. I would not buy a fallen angel dress for my Mama, sister, or my beautiful daughter.

"Mama, no, is not so. Why must you be so mule-faced?"

"You mean mulish," Erik said, bouncing Noah, who also was not happy with his bow tie. He too kept pulling at it and frowning.

"Yes, mulish. We are making wedding vows in Las Vegas after winning big game yesterday!" I waved a hand at the open sunroof, the bright lights of the Las Vegas strip flashing brilliantly inside the limo as we drove to our chapel. "People here in America make fancy dressing for coming to Las Vegas. Elvis, who is god here in city of blackjack and Russian roulette wheels..." Erik made a sound that made me pause, but he just sighed and waved me on to continue teaching Mama and the children about proper ways to dress in the United States and Las Vegas. "He wears flashy pantsuits, so pretty! Some with colored birds on the back, glittering in sequins, with big diamond rings and shiny boots and belt buckles set with a million rubies."

The children all stared at me wide-eyed, soaking up my American wisdom. I'd learned a lot studying for my citizenship test. I was going to be the best American ever.

"Saggy boobs in fancy dress like *prostitutka*," Mama grumbled in broken English. Galina snorted while braiding Eva's long, dark hair.

I rolled my eyes. "Mama, your boobs are not so much saggy. And the dress makes you look like Ann-Margaret, who makes shimmy dance with Elvis, also in *Viva Las Vegas*."

"Pfft. My boobs no like Ann-Margaret boobs." Mama chuckled and slapped my biceps.

"Is it okay to mention that I'm really uncomfortable talking about your mother's boobs?" Arvy asked from the corner of the limo he'd been shoved into.

Galina laughed out loud at her husband, then patted his head as if he were no older than Pavel, who had again untied his bow tie. Arvy looked handsome in his red tux. I couldn't wait to get to the King of the Strip Wedding Chapel that I'd booked and see the rest of wedding party. Erik had been so nice to let me plan the wedding, even when I had shown him the tuxedoes I'd rented for the wedding party, and he choked and spit coffee all over his lap. He never said a bad word.

"Saggy boobs." Pavel snickered behind a dirty hand. How he had gotten dirty when he'd been clean when we'd gotten into the limo was a mystery. Boys did that. Mystery dirt just appeared on them.

"So, onto another subject," Erik quickly said as the children tittered. "Are you two sure you'll be able to handle all three of them overnight?"

"Sure, it's good. We have a luxury suite," Arvy replied, ruffling Pavel's hair as he spoke. "We've got video games and treats all lined up. You two can go do newlywed stuff, wink nudge, and leave the babysitting to us, right, babe?"

"Right, we'll keep them busy while you two smooch, and Mama loses all her quarters in the slot machines,"

Galina teased, whirling Eva's thin braids into a fancy knot atop her head.

"Big money and no whammies!" Mama shouted and pumped the air with her fist.

I grinned at my family as the limo pulled up in front of the King of the Strip Wedding Chapel. Our driver hurried around to open the door and help the ladies out before we men exited. The chapel was big and white and had a forty-foot statue of the King outside. The statue had a real cape that fluttered in the dry desert wind.

"Is most beautiful thing I ever see," I murmured and walked over to put a stick of gum at the foot of the King, as Adler had told me to do with any Elvis sighting I might have. "The King loved gum!" my teammate had told me back at the hotel as he handed me ten packs of peppermint gum. I had not known of this custom, but I was thankful to Adler for filling me in.

Taking my groom by the hand, I then led the party inside. The chapel was small, but it was magnificent. Draped with red curtains of crushed velvet, the walls were covered with images of Elvis from his youthful days to his days here in the city of dreams. I left Erik to place a stick of gum under every portrait. At the last picture—one of the King in an army uniform—my best man called to me from behind the row of pews.

"Dude, what are you doing?" Ten shouted.

I placed my gum in homage and then stood, smiling at my best friend, who was dashing in his red tuxedo. As were Dieter, Adler, Max, and Bryan.

"I'm paying peppermint homage to the King," I told them, hurrying to them to shake their hands soundly. Adler snorted. I gave him a confused look.

"I'm allergic to desert dust," Adler replied.

"Oh no, that is most bad. This city has much desert dust," I said and clapped Adler on the shoulder. "Do not blow nose on lapels. They are scratchy and rental company is not for refunding cash when nose dribble is found."

The guys all smiled tightly. I wondered if their bow ties were too itchy like Pavel said his was. I walked through the small gathering of my teammates and their beloveds, Erik at my side, thanking newcomers for flying out to join us and the team. Trent flitted around the chapel, tossing glitter into the air because it was lacking the wonderful queer touch that he felt glitter gave everything, such as his eyelids, his lips, his hair, and the shoulders of his plum-and-yellow suit.

"We're so not doing red tuxes at our wedding," I heard Tennant whisper to Jared.

"Can you not find red for your nuptials?" I asked. Ten's green eyes flared. "I can recommend rental place in Carlisle where I find these." I tugged on my sparkly lapels.

"Oh, wow, that's awesome and all, but…uhm…Mads is allergic to red material, big guy," Ten said with a faulty smile.

I looked at Jared. "Yes. Severe allergy to red material," Mads quickly agreed.

"What a pity shame. So many allergies to things people have." I sighed, while Erik mumbled something to Ten and led me to stand between the pews. Eva walked down the aisle throwing glitter on the thick carpeting. Pavel followed, his bow tie missing, hand in hand with Noah, both carrying a small pillow with our bands fastened to them. Then the best man and the wedding boys walked down. We had no handmaidens to march with Ten and the others down the aisle to the preacher, just my sister, who was the matron of honor. But this was not a regular boring wedding. It was a Vegas wedding, and so who cared if we didn't follow all the rules?

With Erik on my arm, I walked down the glitter path. Trent stood and threw more on us as we passed, then sat and sniffled into a purple hankie. I patted Mama's smooth cheek as we walked by. She too was crying into a hankie. Galina stood across from Tennant, the matron of honor and the best man, facing each other. The children had taken their seats by Mama and Mads in the front row. The rest of the team filled the other pews, all very glittery. I waved at my guests. They chuckled and waved back. Then the officiant appeared from behind two golden curtains.

He was a fine man, tall but pudgy, with a thick, black pompadour wig, sunglasses, and a tight white jumpsuit with gold wedding bells all over it. The bells were sequins and caught the flashing lights that were now rolling. I felt as if I were on stage with my idol. A grin broke out over my face that I couldn't stop. Erik smiled up at me, his pretty eyes shiny with emotion as the preacher began to sing his part of the ceremony. He sang about how he was thrilled to be the voice of conviction that every relationship between two human beings is a celebration and public affirmation. Then he sang about silent, unspeakable memories and how two souls joined in love will share with each other in gladness and sorrows.

"Are you two ready to speak your vows?" Judge Elvis asked. We both nodded, turned to face each other, and linked our hands.

"Stan, I know we're keeping this short because what more could we say to each other here that we haven't said to each other in the past? I love you, our children, and our life, and I will honor our vows and our love for each other until death do us part. You're my light, my life, and my soul mate."

I kissed him.

"We're not at that part yet," Judge Elvis whispered, which made everyone in attendance giggle.

"But his lips are so pretty, and his words moved me," I explained but leaned away from Erik for a bit. "My words are not so refined as yours, my beloved. I only know that in my heart my adoration for you beats like a steady drum. I shall make you happy all the days of my lives and search for tomorrow with you at my side. With all our children, we shall stay young and restless. I now will marry you and kiss you many time while we drink champagne."

Again, everyone laughed. I smiled as well. My vows were wonderful. I could see how much Erik had enjoyed them. I'd watched hours of American daytime soap operas —which are famous for romancing housewives and lost twins appearing out of the fog—to hone my words into perfection.

Ten handed the rings to Judge Elvis, who I later learned was not really named Elvis. His name was His Honor Avery, and he was a real retired judge/minister who traveled the country making dream weddings for Elvis fans come true. Just like mine. I slid a band onto Erik's finger, and he did the same for me. Judge Elvis blessed our rings, our union, and our new marriage.

"*Now* you can kiss your husband." Judge Elvis laughed.

And so I did. I took Erik in my arms, bent him back

into a big dip, and covered his mouth with mine, kissing him breathless as everyone clapped and threw more glitter.

We got our license signed, paid Judge Elvis His Honor Avery, and went back to the Venetian Hotel, where we all drank lots of bubbly, ate shrimp the size of water bottles, played blackjack, danced with a showgirl with feathers on her butt, and left the children with my sister and her husband. Mama had already taken root by a slot machine with a bucket of quarters and a bottle of champagne and could be heard yelling, "No whammies!" at the top of her lungs clear across the lobby.

I pulled Erik into our room. It was the newlywed suite, and it was sinfully luxurious. It had a view of the Strip and a big round bed that vibrated and moved. Our fingers were entwined, our bow ties in our pockets, and our rings shiny and new. I gently tugged my husband to the window, spun him to face me, and captured his glittery face between my hands. He looked up and into my soul.

"I love you so much right now," I whispered, my fingertips resting on his jaw, the rub of his new gold whiskers lighting a fire in my belly.

"Just right now?" His hands lighted on my hips.

"Mm, no, not just right now. Always. Always and forever."

I led his mouth to mine and kissed him deeply to seal the vows that we'd just made in front of Mama, our children, our teammates, God, and Elvis.

Epilogue

Erik

I DIDN'T KNOW WHETHER TO BE EXCITED OR TERRIFIED AS we waited to hit the ice against Ottawa. The excitement of getting out there was all-consuming normally, but I was in the starting lineup, and right next to me was Ten. That was what scared me. Who thought it was a good idea to move me to the first line and to be Ten's winger along with Lee Addison on his other side?

What if I fuck up?

What if I leave him exposed to a whole push of stampeding defensemen who decided he was fragile and vulnerable? Or worse, what if I hurt him? What if I slap shot a puck right into his head?

Not that he shouldn't have been on the ice. He'd been cleared to play, had passed every test, was fit and ready, and visibly vibrating with excitement to get out.

"Watch him," I mouthed to Arvy, our starting

defenseman, there to keep people away from Ten. Well, that wasn't his job completely, but we'd already talked about how to protect Ten, what not to do, what we should do, and I think he was on the same page as me. I moved from side to side on my skates, looking up at the big figure of Stan, who always led us onto the ice. What I wouldn't give for one last Stan'ism about how Ten was fine and that he was ready to get back on the ice.

"Stop," Ten snapped at me, and I blinked up at him.

"What?"

"And you," he said and pointed right at Arvy, who pasted an innocent expression on his face.

"Me?" Arvy asked and tapped his chest with his glove.

"I'm cleared to skate. I'm okay."

He wasn't entirely okay. Yes, he'd been cleared to go back on the ice, and he was one hundred percent fit, but there was that lingering inability to get some of his words right. It didn't happen often, only when he tried to use a long word, and only when he wasn't skating. The docs said that might stay with him, but he would learn how to handle it. I waited for the vulnerability to show tonight, but as soon as he strapped on skates, he became before-the-accident-Ten.

"We're not doing anything," I lied.

Ten tapped his stick on my calf. "Play the game, okay?"

Cheers grew in volume around the arena. Ten's first game back was on home ice, and eighteen thousand Railers fans were out there waiting to witness his return, and then the line began to move through the tunnel, and finally, Ten was on the ice, skating to the center, where our line would stand for the national anthem. The fans had already seen him in uniform tonight, in our warmups, but this? Everyone on their feet, a hundred *Welcome Back, Ten* signs, cheering, shouting, and I moved a little closer to Ten, bumping shoulders with him. I didn't have to use words. I could see a tear on his face and the way he held himself, so strong and certain. He raised his stick in salute, and the cheers were impossibly louder. Stan skated around us, stopping in front of Ten, and they touched helmets before Stan skated backward to his net and stood silent for the anthem.

And then we played.

At first, I was nervous. It was me who turned over the puck. It was me who gave our rivals the first chance at shooting on Stan, an attempted goal that he stopped with ease.

I need to get my head in the game. Shake this off.

The Ottawa side was pushing hard, our line on the defensive, and I knew that wasn't sitting right with Ten; he was pissed. I could see it in the way he threw himself onto the bench. Hell, it wasn't sitting right with me either.

"What the fuck," Ten snapped. He wasn't talking to anyone, just to himself, his expression one of fixed determination. Ten needed to play. He needed to push forward, score goals—it was what he was made for. And what was I doing to help him? Nothing. All I was doing was fucking things up on his wing. This had to change. When we went over the boards the second time, it was different. It had to be, and I could feel the purpose in Ten, and Addison and I were there, and it was beautiful. Addison collected the puck on an Ottawa turnover, passed to me. I avoided a big D-man, pushing hard, finding Ten, shoveling the puck to him. He collected it outside the blue paint, one of the Ottawa D's on his ass, and he passed it to an empty space, finding me. I could feel this goal; somehow I *knew*. Their biggest D checked me, but he was too late. The puck was off my stick, heading to Ten.

Ten corralled the puck with his skate, then steering one hand, using his body to keep off the D who crowded him, he redirected the puck on his backhand, shot hard. His angle was off, the puck hitting the pipes, and I skated hard to collect the rebound, but Ten was there already, dancing around the defense. He batted it out of midair, his stick low, on the backhand, and he tipped the puck in, right over the stick of the out-of-place goalie. The celebration for that goal was intense. We hugged so damn hard, and when he skated to the rest of the team for fist bumps, he was grinning from ear to ear. The crowd went mad, the shouting and clapping and whistling so loud, and hell, it seemed to last forever.

Ten was back, and he was on fire.

We won the game five goals to nothing. Stan with a shutout. Ten with two goals. Celebration was a given, and we piled into the locker rooms with smiles and laughter, everyone on a high. I found a space next to Stan, who was grinning so wide I thought it must've hurt.

"Ten is God," he announced.

"He is."

"Afraid of nothing, like good Russian skater." We bumped elbows. "Except for bears," Stan added and frowned. "All Russians must be big afraid of growly black bears. This is much good thing."

That was my Stan, and I loved him for all his words and his kisses and his big Russian heart.

"You play like hockey hero tonight also," Stan pointed out and leaned into me. "Noah, Eva, and Pavel will be much proud."

"They'll be proud of your shutout as well," I murmured and kissed his cheek.

He turned his head and captured a quick kiss from me. "Love you."

"I love you, too, big man."

Stan

February in Pennsylvania could be very wintery. A big snowstorm had blown in earlier, leaving Hershey, Harrisburg, and all of the state covered with sixteen inches of snow. The game against Pittsburgh had been canceled so that meant a night at home with my family. My favorite kind of night.

We were all gathered in the playroom, a large area on the first floor that used to be a formal dining room. What need did we have of a formal dining room? We always ate in the big kitchen, warmed by the oven and the glow of Mama's home cooking. The playroom was really just a room filled with toys and a small child's table with matching chairs. There was a rocking chair in the corner, which was Mama's. Tonight she was rocking and knitting, humming *Kalinka*, an old Russian folk song she always returned to when she was content. I loved that song as well and started singing it softly, getting smiles from Eva and Pavel, who were seated at the small table with me. We were doing homework. Noah was seated with us, but he was making scribbles on his paper. Eva was doing math problems, and Pavel was working on English. Professor Pete was doing amazing things with them both, and we were confident they would be able to go to American schools come fall.

"Little snowberry, snowberry, snowberry of mine," I cooed to Noah. His eyes lit up, and I touched his button nose. Then I sang it in Russian again, and our little rabbit sang it back to me in my native tongue. "You are such smart children!"

"Stan, are you singing when you're supposed to be studying?" Erik asked, walking into the room after loading the dishwasher and wiping down the table. We took turns. Mama cooked, so Mama shouldn't have to clean up.

"I am waiting for you to flash me," I said, wishing the tiny plastic chair I was sitting on was larger. My legs were splayed out to the sides and my back bowed as I tried to write answers to my test questions on my paper.

"You mean you want me to use the flash cards," Erik said, with a chuckle. "I don't think Mama wants anyone flashing."

Mama smiled and rocked, her sweater for Pavel taking shape slowly. She might have it done by summertime.

"Yes, use the flash cards. Flash card me. I have studied most hard." I sat back and folded my arms over my chest. Eva and Pavel wiggled in their seats, obviously bored with their lessons and looking for any diversion. "You listen to me, close with sharp ears," I told the three children. "And see how smart your pappa is for citizenship test when he can take it in summer."

Erik pulled a beanbag chair over to the table and fell

back into it, making all the little ones laugh. When he was settled and had his phone, I cleared my throat and nodded at my beloved to begin.

"What is the supreme law of the land?" His sky-blue eyes flickered from his phone to me.

"The Constitution," I replied quickly.

Erik bobbed his head. Everyone clapped, even Noah, although he wasn't sure why he was clapping. He was just a happy bunny and liked to clap.

"Very good. And what does the Constitution do?" Erik asked. His cheeks were pink and his eyes bright. His curls were especially bouncy. Thinking of his curls made me want to run my fingers through them as he sucked on my — "Stan? What does the Constitution do?"

"Oh, sorry, my mind was picking wools. The Constitution sets up the government, defines the government, and protects basic rights of all Americans."

"That's right." Erik smiled at me. I lowered my head in recognition of all the applause. "What is one reason colonists came to America?"

"There are many such as religious freedom, political liberty, economic opportunity, and to escape persecution."

"Right again. You've really been studying hard. Uhm," He flicked through the online questions. "Okay, how many justices are on the Supreme Court?"

"Nine."

"Man, you're hard to stump," Erik said as I bowed to the clapping from my family. "Name the U. S. war between the North and the South."

"Too much easy. The Civil War. Is fought over slavery, which is most bad, little ones." They all nodded, even Noah and Pavel, who, I am sure, did not quite understand the horrors of slavery. "Hit me for one more, and then we must wrap up homework and get baths."

Pavel made a face. Noah drew a circle on the table with a purple crayon, and Eva giggled at the face her brother made. How wonderful it was that the only worry my sweet ones had now was how much a certain young man hated his bath or which color lip gloss to buy.

"Right, we're going to watch the Elvis Aloha show," Erik said as a reminder to the children.

"*Elvis Aloha from Hawaii*," I gently corrected. My husband made a face at me that Noah found extremely amusing. "Hit me for one more question."

"When was the Declaration of Independence adopted?"

"July 4th, 1776!"

"Yes!" Erik hooted with glee. I leaped to my feet to celebrate, but the chair stuck to my butt, and I couldn't shake it free. The children and Mama roared with laughter as I wiggled my backside to try to shake the blue plastic chair off. Finally Erik, who was crying from laughing so hard, stood and grabbed the chair. With a firm yank, my butt popped free.

"I have free butt now!" I shouted and threw my arms into the air. The children all jumped up as well and began dancing and singing a new song, the *Pappa Has a Free Butt* song, which was quite clever, if I did say so myself, but I am biased. They ran at me, and I gathered them all into a bear hug, down on one knee, my arms filled with the wonderful hat trick of children that now filled my life.

"Come here. Family hugs are not family hugs without whole family," I called to Erik and Mama. Mama wiggled between her grandchildren, kissing each head. Erik slid under my arm on the left, gathered Pavel to his side, and tipped his face up to smile at me. I couldn't help myself. I pressed my lips to his, just for a tiny kiss, but the love I had for him was anything but small. It was huge, just like the hug and happy home we were all sharing.

THE END

A RAILERS NOVELLA

SAVE *the* Date

RJ SCOTT &
V.L. LOCEY

Tennant

I DIPPED MY HAND INTO THE BAG OF PEANUTS AND nodded. I'd been nodding at a steady rate for about twenty minutes now. I'd tried to speak a few times, but my attempts to slide into the conversation had been trucked, but in the prettiest and sweetest ways possible.

"… added that picture of that triple-layer fudge cake to the food board. Did you see it?" That was Mom, high priestess of the Tennant & Jared Pinterest wedding boards. Noting the "S" on the end of that word board made me sigh.

I cracked the peanut shell and bobbed my head. "Uhm, no, I haven't been to Pinterest for a few days…"

All three women participating in this FaceTime morning meeting gaped at me.

"*Tennant*," Mom sighed and gave me her I'm-slightly-put-out-with-you stare.

"Maybe we could just pick out our top three choices for the cake patterns and send them to you? Would that work, Ten?" Brady's Lisa, the lovely blonde legal aide, asked.

"Uhm…"

"Oh! We could make a vision board and send him that when we whittle down the choices! My girlfriend Penny did that for her wedding, and it really helped us figure out what to buy as a gift," Jamie's Lisa, or Lisa #2, the tall brunette who worked as a dental assistant, chimed in. My niece Sylvia sat on her lap chewing on her fingers, her green Rowe eyes wide and happy.

"That's a great idea!" Mom and Lisa #1 exclaimed.

I took a swig of chocolate milk to wash down the peanut and dipped a toe into the rapid-fire conversation. "What's a vision board?" I inquired.

Six slim eyebrows flew up three smooth brows.

"*Tennant*," Mom said in that voice again.

"Sorry, what? I don't do a lot of pinning or vision-boarding. Help a guy out here," I begged, giving the women a piteous look. It worked on my sisters-in-law but not so much on my mother. She was far too used to seeing my puppy dog face.

"Well— Girls no! No, do not feed that to Bourque! I'll be right back. The oldest twins are trying to medicate the dog with their doctor's kit. I think they've gotten into the liquid stool softener I had to take after Leah and Lanie were born. No! Do *not* give that to the dog! Bourque, no!"

Wow, okay. That was information about after-birth stuff I did not need to know.

Then mom joined in. "Ugh, I remember being so constipated after I had Tennant. I strained so hard I tore a few of my episiotomy stitches and had to—"

"Mom! Please, give a dude a break here, would you?" I

pleaded just as Jared walked into the living room, all freshly showered and shaved.

"Oh for goodness sake, Tennant. Your fiancé puts his wang into your butt, and you're getting squicked out about a little discussion about hootchie stitches?"

"*Mom*! Oh. My. *God.*" I slapped my hands over my hot cheeks. Jared raced into the kitchen, the coward. Lisa #2 was laughing so hard she was crying. Lisa #1 was heard in the distance yelling at her first set of twin girls. The second set were too young to feed the dog stool softener yet. "Can we not discuss what Jared and I do in bed? How do you even know about anal sex?"

"Tennant, for the love of Pete, I've been around the block a few times. Your father and I were quite adventurous when we were younger. One time before Brady was born we found some flavored lube and—"

"And no, nope, no way!" I shot to my feet, peanut shells tumbling from my lap to the carpet Jared had just vacuumed last night. Oops. "Mom, can we go back to talking about wedding boards?"

"Well, you looked bored so I thought we could talk about things that were important to you," she said innocently.

I rolled my eyes, sat down, and spent another fifteen minutes with all the Rowe gals, being talked at and around. Finally, when Mom called an end to the meeting to go to her tai chi class, I slapped the lid on my Dell shut and whimpered.

"Is it safe?" Jared called, peeking around the doorframe.

I waved him in. "Chicken," I huffed as he rounded the couch, then glanced down at the mess on the floor. "I'll clean that up. Come sit down with me. I have a headache."

That wiped the humor from his face. He dropped down next to me, his light blue eyes filled with worry.

"Are you okay?" he asked, taking the bottle of chocolate milk from my hand. "I still say that hit Peterson gave you during the finals should've been—"

I leaned over and put my lips on his. He chilled a bit then. But just a bit.

"It's stress. Nothing more, my brain is good. Ninety-seven percent normal, which is a twenty percent improvement from how I had been before the injury, according to Brady," I teased, dropping little smooches along his smooth jawline, then nibbling his ear. "Wedding stress."

"Ah, the women."

I kind of melted into him like a candy bar on a dashboard. "The women. Oh my God, you'd think they've never planned a wedding before."

"Well, they've never planned a wedding for two men before. They want everything to be perfect. And you *are* the baby so..."

"Mm," I murmured as I wiggled a bit so I was curled under his arm, my cheek on his shoulder. I inhaled the scent of his Dior Homme shower gel and felt the tension ease from my neck. "I don't care about cake toppers or the color of the flower girls' barrettes or the proper spices for the grilled trout. I just want to marry you and go away for a few weeks so we can fuck ourselves into comas."

"Such a simple man," he said with a chuckle, his fingers slipping through my hair.

"Simple man, simple needs. What the hell is tulle

anyway, and why would they think I'd have an opinion on it?"

That made him laugh out loud. I felt my bones softening as we cuddled on the couch. "They mean well," he said as he continued to play with my hair. "And we do need to make some final calls on things. We have three weeks."

"Right, yeah, I know. I have no clue about any of it. Should we hire a wedding planner?"

"We could, I guess. Do you know any?"

"Me? Uhm, no." I chortled and reached for my phone. "I can hit up the guys in the group chat. Lots of them are married. Maybe they know someone?"

"Okay, go for it. Perhaps if we call in a professional, she or he can rein in the Rowe women a bit." He tipped my head back by pulling gently on my hair. I wriggled up just an inch for the long, wet kiss. He fisted my hair when I rolled my hips, a low growly sound rumbling out. Hungry for more, I slid around until I was on top, my hips grinding against his, my phone slipping to the floor, wedding planners forgotten.

Then my stupid phone rang. I moaned at the Elvis song played, the one set by my best buddy so I'd know it was him.

"Ignore it," Jared said, sliding his hands down the back of my shorts to cup my ass. Elvis sang on and on and on and on.I rocked my dick into his, trying to block out *That's All Right Mama* but failing miserably.

"Let me just... ugh, sorry, watch your balls." I shifted around on the couch, picked up my phone, and slapped it to my ear. "Stan, my man, what is it?"

"Why is phone ringing seventy-two times? Is brain

being bad? I call police at eighty rings, so worry is making my fingers find other phone to send police over for checking on your head."

"Dude, my head is fine. I didn't pick up because Jared and I were getting into it."

Jared made a sound of impatience. I was with him on that sentiment.

"Getting into what?"

"You know… *getting into it?*"

"Getting into car?"

"No, Stan, we weren't getting into the car. We were about to go heels to Jesus."

Jared snickered.

"But is not Sunday, is only Friday. Is new thing for Jesus on Friday?"

That one made me snort loudly. "Dude, no, we were going to fuck."

"Ah fucking, yes, now *this* I know! Well, you can go fuck boots for Jesus in but minute. I am working on speech for wedding dinner as is fitting best friend. My words are good, but I am not sure if this is correct phrase. You will help me? Erik is burning out, and his words are not good right now."

"He's burning out?" I asked, glancing at Jared with confusion.

Jared just shrugged.

"Has been much bad day with kids. Eva is making womanly time and cried because Pavel ate all the butterscotch ice cream. Pavel and Noah painted the shower stall. I am not sure how they get paint from garage or open can or carry pink paint to Mama's shower, but they are now seeming like Pepto-Bismol hatchlings. Even hair is pink. So Erik and I wash boys while Eva cries and Mama makes good soup that no child will eat because it is beet soup. Much screaming and tears, and now Erik is burning out, and I am searching for good word help for best friend's wedding speech."

"Okay, just give me a minute," I said, then looked down at Jared. "Erik's burned out, and the kids are hellions. Can we do this in, like, ten minutes?"

"Sure. Grab the strawberries when you come to bed." He kissed me with fiery promise, then slid off the sofa, his dick tenting his lounge pants.

I wet my lips, palmed my own stiff cock, and focused on Stan and his wedding words. Forty minutes later, I was able to hang up. My head throbbed. Trying to untangle mangled English on top of working to figure out what it was that Stan was trying to get on paper had been like trying to work out some sort of advanced algebraic equation. The math would have been less taxing. We'd not gotten very far.

I sent a quick note to our Pokémon group that I was not going to be training tonight, rolled my eyes at the snarky comment from Adler about being an old married fuddy-duddy, and tossed out the wedding planner question before I chucked my phone to the coffee table and put my bare feet down on the carpet. Finally, I spent ten minutes picking up, then vacuuming peanut dander off the floor with that little handheld Dirt Devil vacuum Jared was so fond of.

Close to an hour after Jared had gone to bed to wait for me, I raced into the bedroom, container of juicy red berries in hand, dick throbbing, to find my fiancé snoring softly, his glasses on his nose, the book written by a gay Indiana mayor facedown on his chest.

A drawn-out exhalation emptied my lungs. Padding to my side, I placed the berries on my nightstand, peeled off my shorts, and slipped under the soft print sheets. The lure of him drew me to the middle of the bed after I turned off the light on my nightstand. His nightstand lamp still glowed soft white. Lying there staring at him, I felt a hundred thousand things all at once. Love, of course, tons of love, but also things like pride, desire, happiness, joy, hope, inspiration, satisfaction, amusement, and awe. It still blew me away that a man like Jared Madsen would love a guy like me. Aside from having some minor skills with a stick and puck, I couldn't see what it was that he found so alluring about me and my not fully normal brain cells.

"Always liked a Studebaker," Jared mumbled, then blinked awake, his gaze flying to me spread out beside him. "Ah, shit, that made no sense, did it?"

"Not much, no." I chuckled as he closed his book.

"This book takes place in South Bend where they used to make Studebakers. My grandfather had an old Studebaker truck. Black and white it was, with a manual transmission and AM radio." He yawned widely, his eyelids droopy. "I learned how to drive in that old truck. I was twelve. How boring am I?"

"Not boring at all."

He pulled me into his side, then drifted off. After he was sound asleep, I wiggled out from under his heavy arm, removed his DILF glasses, and put them and his current read on my nightstand, my fingers bumping the plastic tub of strawberries. I smiled when he spooned up behind me a moment later, his chest to my back, one arm flung over my hip. The light on his side was still on, but with a clap—yeah, we were that kind of couple—his light dimmed. I fell asleep wondering if I should refrigerate the berries or not, but as it turned out, Jared woke up with some tasty ideas for those warm berries. After he wrung a mind-blowing orgasm out of me with only strawberries, his fingers, and the tip of his tongue, I fell back to sleep sated and sticky.

Jared shook me awake sometime after the berry love fest. "Trent is on the phone. He's slightly... uhm, well, how do you describe it?"

"Slightly Trent?" I said, my voice thick and slurred with sleep.

"That works." He handed me his phone. I sat up, berry bits glued to my balls and back, and rolled my head in a circle. Things in my neck cracked and popped.

"Is he just slightly Trent or totally Trent?" I asked, phone jammed under my armpit to mute my conversation with Jared.

"Bordering on totally," he whispered, rose from the messy bed, and walked to the bathroom, a small green strawberry cap stuck to his sweet ass. That made me smile to myself. Good thing, because the figure skater on the other end of the phone was in full Trent mode, which is something that really should only be dealt with after a shower and some coffee.

"Hey, Trent, what's up?" I croaked.

"You're asking for a wedding planner three weeks before the big day?!"

"We thought we could do it ourselves?"

"Oh my sweet gods!"

Yeah, coffee was *so* needed for this.

Jared

I found Ten exactly where I expected to find him. Hiding.

"I swear if you leave me alone with him," I warned my fiancé, who at least had the grace to act ashamed.

"Jared, please don't make me," he whined and pushed himself a little farther back into our bathroom, pocketing his cell phone as he did so. "I can't take any more."

I shut and locked the bathroom door, then crossed my arms over my chest and gave him my patented coach stare. He couldn't meet my gaze, and instead he stared at the floor and scuffed his toe on the cream tiles.

"You told us you were going to the bathroom," I pointed out.

Ten sent me a smile and then gestured at the room around him. "And here I am."

"No, you implied you were using the bathroom and then coming straight back."

That made him wrinkle his nose, which I normally

found adorable, but which at this moment in time, stressed to hell, I found annoying.

"I said I was going to the bathroom. I never said anything about coming back."

"Tennant Rowe, you will get your ass back out into our living room, and you will listen to Trent, and you will nod your head at Trent, and you will not leave my side for the next hour."

"An hour!" Ten had gone back to that low whine, with added slumped shoulders. "Who even has green roses?" he was so forlorn I almost backed down.

"Green goes with your eyes. Trent said so."

"But he spent twenty minutes talking about different varieties, twenty long soul-destroying minutes where I swear my brain leaked out of my ears." He pressed his fingers to his temples and then sent me a calculating glance. "Maybe it'd be bad for my brain," he suggested and almost seemed happy at the idea that he had come up with some kind of excuse.

"Oh no, you are not pulling the brain damage defense."

A knock on the door made us both jump.

"Let me in," someone whispered. Well, not someone exactly, we both knew who it was, and cautiously I opened the door in case it was a trap. There was no sign of Trent, so I let a pathetic, grateful Dieter Lehmann into the bathroom and then shut and locked the door. We had a big bathroom, big enough for Ten and me to get our sexy on, with a large walk-in shower and a corner bath. But add in another hockey player, one who seemed just a little agitated, and things started to get tight.

"You need to save me," he implored. "Send me out for

food or something. I can get us Chinese or go to that Italian place, and I promise to come straight back."

I saw him exchange a look with Ten. Dieter was the only one who could help us to get Trent to leave.

Another knock on the door and we all turned to face it guiltily.

"Boys, unless you're having a three-way, in which case I want in, you all need to get your asses out here *now*." Trent sounded determined.

"I can't," Ten said in a low whisper.

"I can't either." Dieter had a small whimpering note to his voice.

"Please don't make me," Ten added.

Dieter crossed to the window. "What are we here? Two stories? I can jump that."

Ten joined him, and the two of them peered at the patio below.

This was getting out of hand, and even though I wanted to find it amusing, I was kind of tense and headachy, and just wanted to snuggle up with Ten on our sofa and watch some crappy film on Netflix. I threw the door open with dramatic flair, and Trent nearly fell in. As it was, I had to catch him when he toppled where he'd been leaning on the door, and got an armful of silk and satin for my efforts. Ten and Dieter were frozen by the window, and I had Trent in my arms, and we all stood there staring at each other.

"What are you doing?" Trent righted himself, then brushed glitter from my Railers' hoodie, looking around, wondering what to do with the flecks of silver, then tapping them back onto his top.

Ten said nothing. Dieter said nothing. Which left me.

"I came to find Ten," I said. "He was hiding."

"I have a headache—"

"I needed to use the toilet—"

Dieter and Ten spoke at the same time, and I left the three of them to it, heading back out to the place that used to be our living room with its cozy sofas and widescreen television. Now it was wedding central, or at least that is what Trent called it. He'd installed whiteboards. Three of them right in front of the television, one for the venue, one for guests, and the other for what he liked to call incidentals. One of which was green roses to match Ten's eyes. Or something.

I bypassed the room and headed for the kitchen, grabbing as much beer as I could, plus a healthy supply of non-healthy snacks, and sat on the sofa.

Ten came back first, slinking into the room, and sat next to me.

"You left me," he accused and pushed his hand into the pack of Cheetos, coming out with a messy handful that he shoved into his mouth.

"Do you really think you'd have gotten away with staying in the bathroom for that long?"

He did this cute Cheeto pout. "I managed ten minutes; it was going well."

"Eleven minutes and thirty-two seconds." I pointed at my watch, which showed the numbers in neon. "I timed you from the minute you left the sofa."

"I might hate you," he muttered.

I had a witty answer all ready to go, but it was Dieter's turn to pad back into the room, and on his way past me, he took half the beer and snacks and carried the single chair near the window.

"If I die of boredom, I want to be drunk when I'm doing it," he said and swallowed nearly an entire bottle down. Thank god it was the off-season—that was all I thought as I watched him drink.

Finally, Trent was back, and with steely-eyed determination, he felt it was important to summarize what we had so far.

I stopped listening after the ninety-seventh mention of the roses.

Next thing I knew an earthquake interrupted my beautiful dream of sitting on a beach somewhere hot, and I startled awake, only to realize it was Ten shaking me.

"What do you think of that?" he asked.

I blinked at him, then focused on Trent. "Can you uhmm… summarize?"

"Cake tasting is Thursday. I'd like to slot that in with getting you fitted for your tuxes."

"Wait. I have a tuxedo. The one I wore to the casino night." I turned my head to check Ten, whose eyes had widened as if he was warning me about something. "Remember, babe? You loved that tux."

"A secondhand tux for your wedding?" Trent's voice was deceptively quiet. "Next you'll be telling me that you want me to buy a cake from Walmart and then scrape happy birthday from it for the big day."

"Of course not," I backpedaled. "The cake thing now… and… uhm… A new tux. Obviously. I mean, I was only joking."

Trent looked down at his wrist as if he was checking a watch, which he wasn't, because he didn't have one, but it was a very pointed glance. "Two weeks and six days, Jared, there is no time for joking."

"No, sir," I deadpanned, and he raised a single perfect eyebrow. I'd faced down some of the best in the league, but that single eyebrow thing from Trent was enough to have me subsiding and doing a good show of pretending it was vital I select exactly the right Cheeto from the bag.

"So we're okay on the date for the cake and the tux. I'll add it to the planner and send you the password."

Passworded planners? I'd clearly missed something big here and only hoped Ten had been taking notes.

When Trent left, or rather when Dieter finally managed to persuade him that Ten and I needed time to consider options, the silence in the room was deafening.

"I don't know… what… yeah…" I managed.

"It gets worse," Ten muttered and showed me his phone. The page showed some kind of chat group, and I read the heading of it out loud.

"Sex, Drugs, Groupies, etc., what is that?"

"It's a chat for our bachelor party."

"That doesn't sound ominous at all."

"Yeah, well, the guys decided on the person organizing the bachelor weekend."

"What bachelor weekend?" I had no memory of a weekend. The last I'd heard, our bachelor party was to consist of a nice meal, with wine and beer of course, at a local restaurant. Well, at least that was *my* idea. We would probably push the boat out and book a room, but that was it.

"Stan wanted it to be in Vegas—," Ten scrolled up— "but Connor pointed out that if any of the Vegas team were still in town and they spotted us…" He left the rest unsaid, and I could fill in the blanks. "So then, this happened." He scrolled some more and handed me the phone. I read the comment.

Then I read it again.

On the Railers team, there is one person who can be guaranteed to cause chaos, to mess things up, to speak inappropriately, and just in general be a pain in everyone's ass.

"No," I groaned.

"Yeah," Ten said.

"Please don't tell me Adler *freaking* Lockhart is organizing our bachelor party."

"He volunteered, and no one stopped him," Ten pointed out.

I groaned and scrubbed my hands over my eyes. Then something hit me. "When did it become an entire weekend?"

"I don't know. Call him and tell him you want just the one night, somewhere close and friends only, private."

"You tell him," I countered because I actively went out of my way to avoid Adler socially, for fear of being the next victim of one of his stupid-ass pranks.

"You have my phone," Ten said and sunk lower into the sofa, sitting on his hands, then closing his eyes with a loud sigh. "You do it."

I was going to push, but Ten looked tired, and there was still that nagging worry at the back of my mind all the time where he was concerned.

"Okay," I said and typed a quick message. *One night, no negotiation, no weekends, no drugs, sex, or groupies.* I signed it as Jared, so they'd know it wasn't Ten, but at the last minute, I added Ten's name as well. After all, we were in this together.

The group chat blew up immediately. Stan harping on about Vegas, Adler stating we were spoiling his fun, Layton attempting to rein Adler in, Erik countering Vegas with Toronto, Ben suggesting we have it at the dog rescue place, Max agreeing with Erik and also Ben. I turned off notifications on the chat and shoved the phone down between the cushions then slumped next to Ten.

"What the hell are we doing?"

In a smooth move, Ten straddled my lap, looking suspiciously perkier than he had a few moments ago. He cradled my face and kissed me, but I was stressed and tired and overwhelmed.

He sat back on my knees and tilted his head. "Just let them all get on with it. As long as it's you and me, saying our vows, being *us*, then the rest is just noise," he said, then leaned back down for another kiss.

This time I joined in, shuffling a little so that he fit on my lap perfectly. "Imagine eloping to that beach, though. With the ocean and the endless sky and hammocks."

"The sky would be the same color as your eyes," Ten murmured and kissed me again. "And I can see us drinking fruity cocktails with tiny umbrellas."

"We could still do that."

Ten chuckled low in his throat. "My family would be heartbroken, Ryker would murder me, Trent would contact the FBI, and anyway, all of this, it's not *that* bad. Together we can deal with all of this, and our day will be special and perfect."

Another kiss, and this time I was hard, he was hard, and I could see this going the way of sex on the couch.

His cell vibrated deep down in the cushions, and it couldn't be the chat group after I'd muted that mess of a conversation. He reached for the cell on instinct, glancing at the screen and wincing.

"Who is it?" I asked as he connected the call. He shook his head.

"What, Brady?" I could hear some of Brady's words, but not enough to make sense of them. Ten shut his eyes tight and let out a noisy exhalation. "No, I want both of you. Yes, Adler is in charge of the bachelor party, and no, we're not doing an entire weekend. Was that it?" He sighed some more; whatever Brady was saying was likely the usual big brother stuff, and Ten was used to it now. "What?" Ten asked and then sat upright on my lap, sliding off to the side and shooting me a look that screamed "what the fuck"?

"What?" I mouthed.

"Seriously, Brady?" Ten said into the phone and then put it on handsfree so I could hear.

"… and they said the interview would be informal, wanted the three of us, to do a profile, and I said I was sure you'd be cool with it being the gay hockey phenom you are." Brady snorted a laugh at his own joke.

"You know it will end up being you and Jamie ganging up on me and making me look stupid."

"Well, duh," Brady said. "That's our job. And if you back out after saying yes, then you'll just come across as a spoiled and whiny little brother."

"Fuck you, Brady," Ten said without heat.

"They want you as the headline. Why I don't know. After all, I'm the one playing for an original six team…" He chuckled because that was his standard go-to line when it came to Ten playing for the Railers.

Ten stared at the phone. "An original six team who can't beat the Railers."

Brady didn't rise to the goading, "Good, then it's agreed. Saturday, Mom's place."

"What if we're busy Saturday?"

Ten looked at me hopefully, but I had nothing. This weekend was free apart from working hard to avoid Trent.

"Yeah, right, like two childless guys would be doing anything except lazing in bed," Brady said. "I'll text you details, and we'll see you there. Bye, loser."

Ten stared at his phone after the call ended, and then placed it carefully onto the coffee table. "*Harrisburg Hockey Now* wants an interview with the Rowe brothers." He didn't need to explain, as I'd already put two and two together.

"Okay, that doesn't sound too bad. We can call Layton, and he can guide us through pointers for when you talk about the wedding."

Ten climbed in my lap again.

"After," he said and kissed me. "We can talk to Layton. After."

Kissing Ten was way more entertaining than wedding planning, interviews, and bachelor parties.

Infinitely more fun.

Tennant

"... ASKING FOR INPUT ON THE NAPKINS. SHOULD THE edging be silver or blue, or should we simply have the edges end with white stitching? I mean, who thinks of these things?"

"Someone planning a wedding?" Gatlin deadpanned.

"Ah, well, okay, I'll give you that one, but not me. You ever debated over napkin edging?"

"There are days that I'm lucky I remember to *use* a napkin."

I snorted in amusement. "Seriously."

"You okay here?"

"Yeah, I'm good. Nice to be able to chill here and just talk about stuff."

"Shout if you need to stretch." I gave him a thumbs-up, then let my eyes flutter open. Gatlin smiled down at me— tattoo gun freshly dipped into a beautiful rich gold color. "We're looking at another two hours or so, and I have orders that I'm not to let your neck stiffen up."

I rolled my eyes, the wild metal strains of Metallica's

Master of Puppets rocking and rolling through Gat's inking room.

"He's worse than my mother. Never tell him I said that," I muttered, sprawling out a bit on the well-padded tattoo table. Using the break that finishing up the outline of my lion had delivered, I stretched a bit, arms over my head, legs out. My neck was tender, but that was okay. It was time to cover that scar and bury all evidence of the night that had nearly ended my career.

"Ah, Jared loves you. I worry over Bryan all the time. You kids all think you're bulletproof." He adjusted his glasses on his nose with a pinkie finger covered with violet latex. I loved that a dude who looked like Gatlin—all tatted up head to toe—stocked rainbow medical gloves. "You need a drink? Bathroom break?"

"Nope. Give me an hour of fill-in, then we'll take five."

"Okay, but if this gets too intense…"

"Dude, it's fine. It's healed. You saw the note the surgeon gave me for you."

"Yeah, yeah, I know. Still, if it gets to be too much, speak up."

"Will do."

I closed my eyes, pressed the side of my head back to the small pillow, and offered Gatlin my neck. He rolled closer and began coloring in the golden lion. The Rowe coat of arms' regal beast would be forever inked into my skin, standing on its back legs holding a silver sword with a sleek gold crown sitting atop his head. It was a symbol not only of the Rowe family's English roots but of my courage, bravery, and strength in fighting back from my brain injury. Those flowery words had been Gatlin's, not mine. I wanted the ugly-ass scar covered so it would quit reminding me and everyone else who saw it just how close it had been.

The hum of the tattoo gun was steady, and yeah, there were a few times during the whole over-three-hour process that I winced and cursed, but when it was done, that small amount of discomfort had been totally worth it.

"So, you like?" Gatlin asked, walking up behind me, glasses on the top of his head as I admired the stunning old English lion he'd inked on the side of my neck.

"Dude, that is fucking *bestial!*" I tipped my chin up and to the side. The Rowe lion moved with me, its mouth opening into a wide roar.

"Yeah, it turned out even better than I'd anticipated." He grinned at me over my shoulder. The shop phone jingled. "Meet me at the register for your after-care papers." He slapped my shoulder, then jogged off to answer the phone.

I stood there for a minute or two longer, admiring the artwork, even if the skin under and near it was still red and puffy. The lion looked ready to rumble. I knew I was. There was a certain Raptor whose number was permanently tatted in my mind, not unlike the big cat was inked into my flesh. We'd play Arizona again. I'd be whole and healthy and searching for a little retribution for that three percent of my brain function that'd been stolen from me.

"Ten, you still admiring your pretty face?" Gatlin shouted.

I snickered, grabbed my Railers' cap from under the table, and hustled out to pay the man for getting me that much closer to putting that dark time behind me once and for all.

THE NEXT DAY, a sunny Friday, my family gathered at my parents' kitchen table around noon. Jared sat at the island, sipping coffee and trying to stay out of the range of the camera. Brady and Jamie had insisted he be a part of this, even though their wives were in their respective cities. Not that I minded the company on the flight down. A couple of hours holding hands with my man without a frenetic figure skater flitting around was a relief.

"If you're ready?" Joy Pak asked. She was the only Asian female reporter from the wide pool of media requests for interviews with the Rowe family. Layton had handpicked her for her social awareness and the fact that she tended to get shoved to the side by the white male sports journalists. I nodded at her as a sound man fiddled with the mic attached to my tank top.

Once the crew was out of camera range, it was all lights, camera, and action. Joy sat beside my father and to Brady's left.

"Hello, and welcome to *Harrisburg Hockey Now's* special interview with the royal family of hockey, the Rowes," Joy said with a smile for the camera. "Tell us what it was like growing up here in Myrtle Beach. People don't generally associate ice hockey with sand and palm trees."

"It's a great place to grow up," Brady said, taking the lead because... well, he was Brady. "Hockey is slowly making its way below the Mason-Dixon line with great success. There's room for skates and football cleats in the hearts of most southern sports fans."

Lots of nodding at the eldest Rowe boy took place.

"Which of you has the best shot?" Joy asked with a sweet innocence that warred with the twinkle of mischief in her eye.

"Probably Tennant," Jamie admitted.

"Well, only because we taught him how to shoot so well," Brady added quickly.

Everyone chuckled. Jared gave me a wink as I played along as expected and looked as humble as I could. I mean, it was true. I did have a better shot than either of my brothers, but boasting wasn't what hockey players did. Ever.

"How did you all feel when Tennant came out?" Joy inquired, pulling the jocular mood down into a rather serious place.

"Proud. Incredibly proud," my father stated.

My brothers bobbed their heads. Mom sat there with her tea mug, eyes a little dewy, silently staring at my neck.

"Who will score the most goals this year?" Joy then asked, expertly taking us away from the deep stuff so we didn't wallow in the politics of equality that so many fans complained about.

"Oh, me for sure," Brady boasted.

Jamie choked on his coffee. Jared snorted into his mug, and I gave the big D-man a raised eyebrow.

"Dude, you scored six goals last year," I pointed out.

Jamie then recited Brady's points stats for the past four years. He was dead last in the Rowe brothers goals tally.

"Defensemen don't have time to score goals. We're doing the hard work of keeping you superstars from being

trucked every time your skates touch ice. Right, Jared?"
Brady turned to stare at my fiancé.

Jared raised a hand as the camera panned to him.
"Don't bring me into this. I'm just a soon-to-be in-law."

"How are the wedding plans going, Ten?" Joy asked. I
smiled at the camera and made up some fluffy stuff about
how things were coming together. It wasn't like I could say
the wedding plans were a dumpster fire of chaos. "Are you
and Jared planning on having kids one day?"

The kitchen grew horribly quiet. This was a topic that
Mom hadn't dared broach with me, although she had
expressed some concern to the Lisas, who had then told
me on the sly.

"Well, I'll be getting a son in Ryker, when I say 'I do,'
so that's kind of handy," I quipped, and the mood
brightened a bit. We talked a bit about Ryker and college
hockey. Then Joy brought us around to another less than
fluffy query.

"So this is a question for Brady and Jamie. What was it
like to watch Tennant win the cup?"

I looked at Brady, and he stared right at me. "Probably
one of the most exciting moments of my life."

A thing happened, and I saw the love in his eyes that I
sometimes forgot about. Brady could be one of the biggest
asses I had ever known, but he also had been one of my
biggest supporters.

Mom sniffled into her tea. Dad slapped Brady on the
shoulder. Jamie gave me a side-saddle sort of hug.

"Which one of you is the scariest on the breakaway?"
Joy asked next, and that got us all out of emo-land and
back into competitive brothers world.

"Jamie," I said.

He puffed up. "True, but Ten has some moves. Brady is too old and slow to dazzle anyone on a breakaway," Jamie tossed out and got a playful slug in the arm from Brady.

After that, it was some loose hockey talk, thoughts on next season for our teams. Joy thanked us after the lights had been packed up, and we were saying goodbye in the yard.

"You have no idea how much being picked for this means to me." She shook my hand firmly, her smile wide, the hot winds whipping around my parents' tidy house ruffling her long, black hair. "Thank you again."

"Anytime." I leaned into Jared and gave a wave to the van that carried the crew off down our lovely little middle-class street. "She was nice."

"Pretty too," Jared tacked on. I gave him a quick sort of oh-really-now glance. He kissed the side of my head. "Not as pretty as you, though."

"Pfft, yeah, right." I laughed, took him by the hand, and led him back into the air-conditioning. The gang was still in the kitchen, cleaning up the coffee mugs and coffee cake crumbs that were all over the table.

"I have to head to the store." Dad gave me a shoulder squeeze and shook Jared's hand. "I'll see you two for the big day. Try not to be too nervous. If you pick the right one, marriage is a joy."

"Nicely done, dear," Mom said as she placed mugs into the dishwasher.

Dad gave us a wink, then left for work. Jamie and Brady needed to run to the corner store for something, and so it was me wiping the kitchen table and Jared sneaking off to call the florist as Trent was *"Utterly too inundated to possibly call about the flowers!"*

"Don't brush the crumbs on the floor, Tennant," Mom called from across the room. How did she know?

"The Roomba will get them," I tossed out. She gasped, then started crying. My brain slewed off the rails a bit. Had the Roomba died? Why would that upset her so? "Mom?" I chucked the dishrag into the sink and hurried over to her. "What's wrong? I promise I won't wipe the crumbs to the floor anymore."

"Oh, baby." She coughed, reaching up to take my face in her tiny hands. "It's not the crumbs; it's... oh, that damn lion."

"You don't like the tat?"

"Tennant, I love that it covers up the scar. I know how much you hated it. It's just that when I look at that lion, I see you lying on the ice... all that blood..."

"Ah Mom, shhhhh." I held her closer. "Don't think about that now. I'm here, I'm fine, and you're going to get your first grandson soon in Ryker."

She coughed and snorted into my chest. "We nearly lost you."

"It wasn't that close," I whispered, trying to reassure her.

"You are a terrible liar, Tennant. You always have been, but thank you." She pulled back, patted my cheeks, and wiggled free so she could turn on the tap and splash some cold water on her face. I yanked some paper towels off the holder and handed them to her. "I'm sorry. I'm just an old silly goose. Weddings do this to me."

"Yeah, I know." I chuckled at the memory of how emotional she had been at her other sons' weddings.

"Yours is more special, though. It has… it has more meaning because you had to fight hard to have it. You've had to battle so ferociously for the right to wed the person they love. Brady, Jamie, and your dad and I just took that right for granted."

"I love that you're like the biggest PFLAG mom in the neighborhood," I teased.

She chuckled into her paper towel wad. "Neighborhood, hell! In the whole damn county!"

"Love you," I whispered.

"I love you too, Tennant. Gosh, I'm such a mess." She dabbed at her eyes. Jared walked into the room, phone to his ear, eyes widening in worry. "Wedding tears," Mom quickly explained, and his brows eased downward. "So do you want meatloaf or rigatoni for dinner?"

We never got to reply to that question, because at that moment my brothers returned and kidnapped us. With our bags in hand, Brady and Jamie muscled Jared and me out of my parents' house and into a nondescript rental car.

"If you're taking me out to kill me because I of that comment about being more menacing on the breakaway…"

Brady laughed as palm trees passed by. We pulled into Myrtle Beach International. Jared and I exchanged worried looks.

"Uhm," Jared said but was then hustled along into the airport. Within five minutes, we were being pushed outside again, the sun baking the top of my head as Jamie shoved me toward a streamlined personal jet.

"What the fuck is going on?" I shouted at my middle brother.

He just herded me forward. Brady was in charge of

getting Jared onto the jet, and since they were already inside, I had no option but to climb into all that luxury. A dozen white seats and four lovely flight attendants awaited us.

"Welcome aboard Lockhart Avionics newest personal jet, the Lockhart Legion CX 400. Please sit down and buckle your seat belts. We're cleared for immediate departure," a slim, blonde, fashion model of a woman said, waving at the plush leather seats as if she were Vanna White motioning at a vowel.

"Uhm, departure for *where?*" Jared asked as he dropped into a seat.

"Nowhere you need to worry about," Brady said and shoved our bags into the hands of a flight attendant. "Just have a drink, enjoy the flight, and stop being so uptight."

"Can you just tell me one thing?" I asked while I buckled my belt. No sooner had the seat belt light turned on than the jet began to roll to the runway. My personal flight attendant, a beautiful woman with red hair and a Rubenesque figure nodded while handing me a pillow. "You said Lockhart Avionics. As in Adler Lockhart?"

"Yes, Mister Adler has personally arranged everything," she replied, her accent soft and British. "Just relax, and as soon as we're at cruising altitude, we'll serve drinks and lunch."

Uh-huh. *"Just relax"* she said. Jared and I had just been hijacked and bullied into a plane headed God knows where, and Adler Lockhart was behind it all. Right. Relax. Sure.

Not.

Jared

"CHARLESTON?" I SAID AS SOON AS IT BECAME OBVIOUS where we were going, not quite putting Charleston up there with Vegas as the bachelor party hell that I'd imagined.

Was that a good thing? Wasn't Charleston genteel, with southern manners and beaches, and quite dignified in an old-fashioned South Carolina kind of way? Did that mean our bachelor party was going to be a tasteful, dignified affair?

Remember, it's Adler organizing this.

"I've never been to Charleston," Ten mused and stared out of the window.

I couldn't get my head around that, given it was no more than two hours from Myrtle Beach, home of the Rowe dynasty.

"Yes, you have," Brady said and smirked as he exchanged glances with Jamie. "You were two, and I specifically remember you sitting on the ground wailing because candy floss does not go well when it comes back up."

"Oh god, yeah," Jamie piped up, "he got sick at the fair."

"All kids can get sick at the fair," I defended, but Ten shook his head, warning me to stay quiet. Sometimes with the brothers, it was best to stay out of things.

"He was sick because I hung him upside down," Brady smirked again as if that was something to be proud of. "Little shit had stolen my candy. Dad pulled me to one side and explained how holding my little brother upside down to get the missing candy out was *not* a good thing. Then I had to stay with Ten the rest of the visit." He sighed. "That was a good day." He looked out the window, and the teasing smirk became more of a fond smile as he glanced back at Ten. "You forgave me so quickly. You didn't care. You just followed me around."

There was a moment's silence as we all took in the fact that Brady had said something thoughtful, bordering on nice. Then Jamie made gagging noises and pretended to faint, Ten snorted a laugh, and Brady hit Jamie upside the head.

Normal Rowe-service was resumed.

We landed at a private airfield, a largely empty space with hangars, and there was a limousine waiting for the group, which whisked us away to the Ellis Oaks Subdivision of James Island, or at least that is what the driver called it as he slowed down and pulled into a gated residence, pausing to type in a code before parking in a drive outside a huge contemporary house, which sprawled this way and that, screened by bushes that hid us from the road.

"Wow," Jamie murmured. None of us here were short of money, but this place was something special. Not shiny steel or blocks of brick, it was a gorgeous wood-clad building.

"Surprise!" Adler shouted from the door. Just behind him, Layton was grinning, standing next to Stan, who for some inexplicable reason was only wrapped in a towel, and Erik who was on the phone facing away from us.

"Syurpriz! Syurpriz!" Stan shouted and threw his hands in the air, his towel slipping. At the last minute, he seemed to realize, but that didn't stop him from hugging me tight when we moved into the blessedly cool house.

Jamie backed away. "If you're thinking I'm hugging a naked Russian goalie—" He didn't get a chance to finish as Stan hugged him anyway. Erik finished his call, and something passed between him and Stan, and I guessed it had something to do with the children. Stan picked Ten up and whirled him around, lifting him right off his feet. How that towel stayed in place, I don't know.

"It's one of our smallest homes, not the biggest place for twenty guys. Some of you will have to share," Adler said and laced his hands together, agitated. "But it was the only vacant Lockhart property that—"

Layton moved right in front of him and clapped him on the shoulders. "Ads."

Adler went from troubled to calm in an instant. "My bad," he said. Then he grabbed Ten's hand, which was not something he would do on the ice. It seemed that because it was our bachelor weekend, it meant all bets were off. He dragged Ten down a corridor, and I followed, trying to listen as he explained the house. I only caught a few words, and Adler didn't have to explain what was here. I could see it. The kitchen was stunning, the furniture expensive-looking, soft furnishing muted and tasteful; it was a show home. No, not a home. A show house. I knew that the Lockhart family had money, but I had to wonder if Adler had ever had a *home* until he met Layton.

Great, now I'm getting way too deep for someone on their bachelor weekend.

We ended up in a cavernous room with doors that opened to a landscaped garden, complete with pool and patio with lounge chairs and a grill. "This is your room," Adler announced and waved at the room. "There's a bathroom, and it's got this really cool bath, and you need to try that. It's big enough for two, and I put condoms and lube in the cabinet because Layton and I have—"

"Ads!" Layton interrupted.

"My bad," Ads said brightly, not at all disturbed that Layton had stopped him in mid-flow. I guess he was used to it—a lot of people stopped Adler in mid-flow.

I had to step to one side as Stan unceremoniously dumped Ten onto the enormous bed, and then it was Layton who ushered everyone to the door. He almost had it shut, but Adler kept on talking.

"We'll give you fifteen, guys, Connor texted to say he's almost here. So if there's anything you need, you only have to—"

Layton shut the door. I don't think it was to keep us in but to stop Adler's verbal diarrhea.

I turned to check on Ten, not entirely happy with the way Stan had dropped him, but he didn't look hurt. In fact he was grinning up at me, and I couldn't help myself. I *had* to kiss him. I clambered onto the bed and bracketed him with my arms, then kissed him, allowing myself to be tugged down until I was sprawled over him.

"How many of the team do you think will be coming?" he asked between kisses.

I shook my head. "This is Adler we're talking about. It could be the entire NHL for all we know."

"Do you think he arranged for Ryker to be here?"

"He wouldn't be able to make it. I know he's volunteering with Jacob. It's the farm's busiest time, and he wanted to help and there's no way he would've known about a surprise party. It's okay." I was only half lying when I said it was okay. I wish he was here but I understood our lives had different directions to take.

Ten kissed me and rolled us so he was on top, propping himself up to stare down at me.

"He'll be at the wedding," he reassured with another kiss.

"Put your pants on. I'm coming in!" someone called, and the door banged open, revealing Connor. "Hey!" Our captain wore the brightest pink T-shirt I'd ever seen, and right behind him was Adler, followed by other new arrivals Max, Ben, Bryan, and Gatlin. With what seemed like the entire team in our room and Ten and I sitting on the bed, Ads took charge again.

"We have an itinerary," he began and counted off each item on his fingers. "Golf, food, beach, followed by drinking with food, a bar, dancing in a club, maybe a strip bar, then back here swimming, with a catering company bringing in food."

I groaned internally at a lot of that, most of the food references and the whole strip club thing. However, none of it fazed the team, all of them leaving to collect what they were going to wear, which didn't sound ominous at all. Then it was just us and Adler, with a long-suffering Layton hovering by his side.

"These are for you," Adler announced and tossed a plastic bag to me. "Put them on, ten minutes, and the cars are waiting."

Finally alone, I unpacked the T-shirts Adler had thrown at us, and held one up. An eye-watering mix of cerise and purple, with accents of lime, the rainbow and unicorn were luminous, and one said *Groom 1*, the other *Groom 2*, emblazoned in neon orange across the center.

"I'm blind!" Ten covered his eyes in faux shock, then peered out from behind his hand. "He seriously wants us to wear those?"

I tossed him one. "Suck it up, Groom 2."

"Hang on a minute. Why am I Groom 2? Is it because you're so old now?" Ten tried for innocent but couldn't hold it together.

"Asshole," I muttered as I smoothed down my Groom 1 shirt. "Says the man who's heading for thirty."

"Yeah, in, like a million years."

He stripped off his classy blue shirt and pulled on the monstrosity that was the official bachelor shirt, turning this way and that in front of the mirror and wincing.

I came up behind him, put my arms around his waist, and held on. "I've never seen you look so sexy," I teased.

But I wasn't lying. His hair was silky, falling in soft layers over his eyebrows, his lips plump from kissing, and I was so damn happy, so at peace.

"I can't put into words how much I love you," I said.

He caught my eye in the mirror and turned in my hold, lacing his hands behind my head. "Same here."

"I hope we fix that before we exchange vows," I teased.

He kissed me then. "All we need is kisses."

In shorts and the tees, we headed for the front door, and that was when it hit us in all its Technicolor glory. Stan was in scarlet, standing to the left, Erik in orange, and all the way to Ben, who wore purple, the guys were a rainbow, and their T-shirts had the message *Groom Squad* written on them.

"You're missing yellow," I said because I didn't know what else to say.

Then the guys moved apart, right between orange and green, and Ryker stepped forward. I reacted instantly, grabbing him and holding him close, pulling a confused Jacob into the same hug, then Ten, who wanted in on the action. This bachelor event hadn't even started, but with Ryker here now, it was one of the best days ever.

We headed to the Ocean Golf Course on Kiawah Island, where it seemed Adler had booked a private afternoon for us, which was good because we were loud. Very loud. I swear golf was the funniest damn thing I've ever done, but most of that was because we were painfully bad.

"The hole is that way," Erik explained patiently to Stan, whose concept of golf seemed to be whacking the ball as if he was shooting a puck. Of course, this meant that there were divots in the grass, twenty-two lost balls at last count, and the rest of us bent over laughing so hard that Connor said he was going to be sick.

I thought that was more to do with the giant pizzas we'd all consumed in the limos on the way over.

"No much me laugh-ting," Stan said, with

concentration on his face, assumed the correct stance, and then at the last minute buried his club in the dirt, the ball rolling maybe an inch.

That was it, cue the entire group on the grass laughing so hard that a manager came over.

"Gentleman, I'd like to suggest you stop drinking."

"Not drink much," Stan boomed. Given he was chopping at the hedge with his golf club, I'm not sure the manager believed him.

"We've had a few complaints."

I could see the headlines, *Gay hockey superstar with gay fiancé and gay team having a gay time on a straight golf course and getting gay drunk.* I think Layton could see the same thing and stepped in to calm the situation. None of us had actually drunk a thing. We were just happy; all of us, laughing, shoving, teasing, in the South Carolina sunshine.

Layton tried to smooth it over with an apology, box tickets the next time that the Railers played Carolina, and the promise of paying to have turf re-laid. The manager wasn't impressed and folded his arms over his chest.

"I'm wondering if maybe you'd like to move this away from Ocean Course," he said in a level tone.

By mutual decision, we left around the tenth hole of the eighteen because Layton was insistent we take the hint. Ten had won the golf. At least I think he had because we'd all lost count, and most of us agreed that as he was a hockey phenom, he had to be better than us all. With pride, I realized Ryker had apparently come in a close second. *That's my boy.* I chose to ignore the fact that I'd been almost as shit as Stan had been. I used to play hockey. I was good at it. I'd never played golf in my entire life.

We headed for the beach as the evening drew in, and ended up in a private area, no doubt owned by the Lockhart family. It was decorated with tiki torches, and there was music. The food was endless, the laughter just as much, and I got to dance with Ten in the dark, holding him close.

Apparently, there had been bar action planned for after the beach, but after some heated discussion focusing on the fact that we were all partied out for tonight, we ended up heading home. Only, when the limo drove down Bay Street, Ten and I were bundled out for nightcaps and more dancing. It was two a.m. before we made it back to the house, and I fretted for a while about where Ryker and Jacob were going to sleep. In the end, they took one of the smaller bedrooms in the pool house, which was a lot better than the bedroom that Brady and Jamie were sharing.

"Bunk beds."

"I get top!" Brady pushed his way past the middle Rowe brother, but in some complicated move involving knees and elbows, it was Jamie who clambered triumphantly onto the top bunk.

I swear those two were worse than kids.

As for Ten and me, we opened the doors to the private patio and sat out under the stars, holding hands.

"I love our friends," Ten murmured after a little while.

"Me too. Even Adler. I love that Ryker is here."

Ten stood and stretched tall, his bright T-shirt riding up, the fluorescent colors twinkling in the dark. He held out a hand, and I took it, falling naturally into him and burying my face in his neck.

"Are you tired?" he whispered.

I yawned on order. "Yeah, do you think I'm too old for this?"

Ten nibbled a trail from my ear down my jawline, cradling my face in his hands. "No, I don't. Now, be honest with me, old man. Are you *too* tired to let me make love to you?"

Tiredness vanished in an instant. "When I say old, I mean, I'm not *that* old."

Tennant

HE WAS THE SEXIEST OLD MAN ON THE PLANET, AND HE had to be naked and hard in my hand, like yesterday.

"Let me get you out of this ugly thing," I said, easing out of his hold and taking the bottom of the tie-dye catastrophe in my hands.

He raised his arms when needed. I tossed the shirt somewhere behind me, then claimed his soft lips. Our tongues tangled gently, the taste of the fruity drinks we'd had lingering. He gave me the lead, groaning softly into my mouth when my hand slid between his hard stomach and the band of his shorts. Soft cotton brushed my knuckles as I wiggled my fingers into his briefs.

"Tennant," he said, my name a groaned exhalation when I fisted his stiff dick.

"Mm," I replied, kissing the corner of his mouth, then rubbing my cheek along his like a love-starved cat. His dick pulsed in my palm. I stroked him as the way he liked it, firm with a slow twist over the tip. The soft rasp of his whiskers drove me mad. I began to push on him, angling him toward the big bed, his cock hot and hard in my hand. "Did you want to say something before I swallow your dick?"

"Christ," he huffed. That made me smile. As did how eagerly he shoved his shorts and briefs to his ankles once his calves touched the mattress.

"Sit down. Spread your legs. Let me love you." I nipped at his chin, pinching his stiff nipples. He kind of did this dead drop thing to the bed, his ass just catching the edge of the firm mattress. "Dude, don't fall on the floor. We don't want a broken hip to mar our bachelor getaway."

"Wiseass." He chuckled, grabbing my shoulders, then pulling me to him with firm pressure. I went willingly, greedily even. The fact that I was fully dressed and he was naked made me twitchy. "I want to come on your lips. Right here." He ran his thumb over my lower lip, pulling it, then releasing it. My dick throbbed. I pushed on my erection with the heel of my hand, hoping to ease the ache.

"Hey, old man, I'm in charge here. You'll come where I tell you to come."

His pupils blew out, obscuring the beautiful sky blue that I loved so much. "You're starting to sound like a typical pushy spouse already."

"And you love it," I countered, kneeling between his strong legs, my hands resting on the top of his thighs, my gaze falling to his cock. A thick bead of precum hung off the tip. I leaned in to catch it, but it fell to the sheet.

"God, yes, I do," he confessed, then arched up.

His prick bumped my cheek, leaving a damp smear. I turned my head enough to latch on to his fat cockhead. Jared rolled his hips; a low grumbly sound followed his confession. He locked his arms behind his head and watched, his hot gaze never leaving the sight of me sliding the length of him down my throat. "Fuck, Tennant, you look good with my dick in your mouth."

I hummed in agreement. His eyes rolled back in his head, so I kept it up, humming and sucking, cupping his soft sac, fondling the orbs, then pressing a finger against his hole. He wiggled back and got a heel on the bed, giving me an access that I was quick to accept. Nothing made the man blow apart faster than a couple of fingers bumping his prostate while getting head. Well, he was kind of fond of a dick ramming that knot of nerves, but we'd made this stupid no-penetration-until-the-honeymoon vow eight days, seven hours, and twenty-four minutes ago. Not that I was keeping track or anything. Like, my ass was not in any way needing his dick in it. Nope. Stupid vows. I should have known better than to listen to my two sisters-in-law. Sure, it sounded romantic, but any time without making love was *brutal.*

"Tennant." Jared coughed, and I pressed a spit-slick finger into him, licking a sloppy path along the crease of his leg, then back to his glorious cock. "Ah, perfect. Shit! So fucking perfect…" The big man shuddered. Spittle coated my chin, my lips, his balls, and his ass. He began mumbling something, raspy grunts mixed with how sweet my mouth was. "Ten, please… close now."

I popped off, slid my finger out of him, and then stood. Jared, resting on his elbows, his eyes hooded and his skin coated with a fine sheen of sweat, stared at me in confusion.

"We come together," I said, ripping at my clothes, then throwing them to the four winds. He smiled as his arms folded, dropping his back to the mattress. A soft, warm wind rustled the sheers on the sliding doors, the smell of a southern night blowing in, the heady lemony-candy scent of magnolia mingling with the scent of man and sex. I straddled him, then caged him with my hands, dropping my mouth to his, lapping inside, tonguing his teeth as he pumped upward wantonly, coating my hip with streaks of his salty-sweet precum.

"Get the lube," he groaned, grabbing my hips.

"No," I gasped as he bucked up, his cock slipping over my hole. "Oh fuck," I moaned and leaned back, squeezing his dick between my sweaty ass cheeks. Jared bit my shoulder, a surefire way to get me on the cusp. "The vow…"

"Stupid," he panted, grinding into me, his cockhead moving back and forth, back and forth, back and forth over my ass. "Stupid damn vow."

"Yeah, totes," I huffed, finding a small thread of sanity and grabbing it. I slid back a bit until his cock was lying next to mine, both trapped between our damp bellies. "I want you so bad," I said, my voice thick with lust. "I love this so much." I took both our dicks in one hand. He spread his larger hand over mine, sliding it around until our cocks were in a vise of sticky, rough fingers.

"Harder," Jared snarled, then began thrusting. A small part of my brain slipped off the rails, plunging me into the world of sensation. Nothing else mattered but the feeling of our dicks slipping in and out of our hands.

"Shit, shit, shit," I cried out and blew apart, coating our fingers. Jared released us and pushed me to my back. I went willingly. "Get up here," I huffed, pulling on him with greedy hands until his prick rested on my nose.

Two hard pumps was all it took. He came hard, coating

my cheeks, chin, and lips with pearly ribbons. I licked off my lips, and he shot again, a gravelly groan of pleasure the only sound he made. Spunk flew from him, thick ropes hitting my brow and hair, my nose, my ear, and my mouth. He laid his dick on my lower lip, semen oozing from him, and I lapped up each spurt.

"You're a mess." He chuckled when he could speak again. "A beautiful mess but a mess just the same."

"They say cum is good for your skin," I murmured, working his spunk into my hair, then tasting my fingers. "Yours is delicious," I said around a cum-coated finger.

He eased away, careful not to bump my head with a knee. Then he stood beside the bed, cock hanging down his thigh, and offered me his hand. I slapped my palm across his and was pulled to my feet and into his arms. He slanted his mouth over mine, stealing the breath from me. I grabbed at his short blond hair, smearing our tastes into our mouths.

"Want to check out the shower? I hear it's man-sized," he whispered over my salty lips.

The shower was big enough for four hockey players and a polar bear. When we fell into bed later, beyond sated from the hand jobs in the shower, I yawned so wide my jaw popped.

"You want to shut the sliding door?" Jared asked sleepily. I snuggled up to his back and said something, but the door never did get closed.

I woke up on my side, facing the sliding door. Jared was behind me, his ass pressed to mine, snoring lightly. I heard someone speaking outside and reached for my phone. It was a little after seven in the morning. Who the hell would be up so early after a night like we'd all had last night?

Curiosity got the better of me, and I slipped from the bed, grabbed the shorts I'd worn yesterday from the floor, and pulled them up over my bare ass. Stepping out into the new day, I winced at the sun peeking through the trees, then checked out the grounds. There, on the patio surrounding the Olympic-sized in-ground pool, sat a man in a bright green robe and pink sunglasses. Apollo Vasquez looked at me, lifted his drink in the air, and motioned to the massive table weighted down with food. My stomach snarled, so I pulled on one of Jared's old Sabres shirts, then scribbled out a note for my sleeping fiancé before going outside.

"Morning," I heard as I stepped outside. I smiled at Apollo. The slim young man who was Adler's best friend seemed rested and refreshed. "Have you been here long?"

"I just got here an hour ago. It was my mother's birthday yesterday. Figures I'd miss all the fun." He smiled into his drink. "You look debauched."

He sipped on a raspberry mimosa and kicked his tiny bare foot up and back as I blushed to the roots of my hair.

"I think I need something to drink," I muttered and padded around the pool to the drink table. Stainless steel coffee urns stood at the ready. Creamers and sugars, tea bags, and silver flatware awaited the guests.

"The hot food is on the way," Apollo called as I made myself a cup of hot chocolate. "So, tell me, did anyone have hot sex? Besides you, of course." He tapped my shoulder after I sat down beside him, the bite mark from Jared a touch sore this morning. "Was there an orgy? God, I so need a hockey player to make love marks on me."

He was a very pretty man, lean, kind of feminine, and a little bit of a queen. Trent made him seem like a nun in comparison, but yeah, Apollo was a beautiful Latino gay man who should've been able to grab any guy's eye, be it a jock or not.

"I think our rainbow members are all spoken for, but if I hear of anyone…"

He flashed me a bright smile. "Send him my way. I do love a big jock. So, marriage. Are you nervous?"

"Mm, yeah, a little." I took a sip of cocoa. It was rich and thick, sweet enough to send a person into a diabetic shock and just perfect for a lazy Sunday morning with a friend. "You're coming, right? To the wedding?"

"If I can find a date," he replied, reaching up to lower his sunglasses a bit when Erik came stumbling out, his curls knotted. "Another married one," Apollo sighed dramatically, then glanced at me over the top of his pink sunglasses. "What is it with this team? Do you all drink happily-ever-after bottled water or something? I mean, leave some crumbs for the rest of us, will you?"

He snorted at his own teasing, and I laughed along. Erik waved sleepily. He had a hickey on his ribs that stood out plainly against his fair skin.

"Big man up yet?" I yelled at Erik over the soft splashing of the pool's filter and the familiar song of a Carolina wren.

"He's in the shower," Erik replied, dropping down beside Apollo, coffee in hand, then promptly dozing off in the soft rays of golden sun falling on him.

Apollo snickered and removed the mug from Erik's fingers. "Maybe I need to start watching baseball…"

I was about to reply that we had a team in Carlisle that

he could check out when the high priest of wedding planning arrived. Trent gave me a sour glance, then marched over, his head wrapped in a purple turban that matched his flowing silk robe.

"Hello, peanut," Trent said to Apollo, and they bussed cheeks. "You look refreshed." Apollo nodded, sipping on his raspberry mimosa as Trent turned his attention to me. "You, on the other hand, look as bad as him." He waved a hand at Erik splayed out in his chair, snoring. "I rapped on your door to speak with you both as we are now in crisis mode! God, I need a mimosa too." Apollo handed Trent his. A great fussy thank you took place, followed by a theatrical sip. "So, your betrothed told me to wait down here while Nero fiddles!" Another small sip. "Honestly, how you two can be so nonchalant about the venue being shut down is beyond me!" Another small sip.

Wait. The venue? "What?" I asked. Trent huffed, then finished Apollo's mimosa. "What do you mean the venue was shut down?"

"Something about being a fire hazard. That was the last place big enough to house all the guests that was willing to take us on such short notice. And now it's gone. *Gone!*"

He swooned gracefully into the chair on my right, turban staying in place and the mimosa glass held between his long, thin fingers.

"Where will we have the wedding and reception, then?" I inquired, because that seemed like a pretty big need-to-know thing. "We've got, like, ten days left."

"Eleven, but who's counting?" Trent murmured, then returned to swooning over the side of the tasteful patio furniture.

"You will have big wedding at my house!" Stan

announced from the double doors that hung open. Erik startled awake. Trent sat up, his swoon forgotten. Apollo arched an eyebrow at the big Russian, then sighed sadly when the sun glinted off Stan's wedding ring.

"Dude, we can't impose on you like that," I said.

Trent waved a hand in front of my face. "Hush you. Of course we can. When you say big wedding, how big is your yard?"

"Hmm, is big grass. Maybe ten acres?" Stan walked over to stand behind Trent. "I have much room. Big yards with soft grass. And fountain!"

"Oooh, a fountain! Do you have gardeners?" Trent asked.

Apollo sat up, the sad look on his pouty lips gone. I tried to speak but was plowed aside like last winter's snow.

"Many gardeners. Make flower beds pretty. We have wedding at our home. Erik is making happy good sounds for beloved friends. Or we go to Vegas and have Elvis wedding like mine!"

"*No!*" Trent and I shouted at the same time.

"Then is settled. We have big wedding on my lawns!" Stan clapped me on the shoulders so hard my fillings rattled.

"Sure, yeah, sounds good," I muttered and pasted on a smile that fell from my face when I saw Jared sneaking past the double doors. He was *so* going to catch hell for feeding me to the wedding wolves.

Jared

THE SCHEDULE WAS TIGHT, AND IN MY MIND, IT WAS THE wrong way around. We had cake tasting at ten, followed by tux fittings at one. Surely tuxes should come before cake. I've seen Ten eat cake, and he can eat a *lot* of the sticky sweet concoctions.

"And remind me, this is…?"

Ten had struck up an immediate rapport with Jenny of Jenny's Exclusive Cake Designs because it seemed that Jenny *loved* gay weddings. I wanted to remind her it was just a wedding, but I really think she'd bought into the 'gay-men-are-all-cute' thing, and Ten wasn't disabusing her of that fact. Probably because Trent had warned us this was the only decent cake place in the entirety of Pennsylvania that had the capacity to make the cake at all.

Also, Ten was taking this whole cake thing very seriously.

"Chocolate, with dulce de leche buttercream."

I had no clue what dulce de leche was. All I knew was that when Ten bit into the cake, he closed his eyes and let out a sinful moan, the kind that only me sucking him off normally produced.

"Taste it," he demanded and offered up a fork with the tiniest piece of dolcey whatever chocolate cake. I did as I was told, as I was doing in this whole grand buildup to our big day.

"Caramel," I said as the sweetness hit my taste buds.

Jenny looked at me patiently and exchanged a glance with Ten. "Yes, dulce de leche. Now, you can have the same buttercream in a vanilla cake. Then we can go wild and have chocolate ganache in each alternative layer."

Jesus, just how many layers is this cake?

I must have said this out loud because Jenny pouted at me, and Ten stifled a laugh.

She waved her hands in the air. "My vision is five layers at least, alternating with the different buttercreams, and then covered in exquisite fondant, with a tumble of roses down one side, curving to the front."

I knew she was talking because sounds were coming out of her mouth, but hadn't Ten and I already come up with our own *vision* for *our* cake that was going to be at *our* wedding?

"We just wanted a puck," I said when Ten stared down at his plate of nibble-sized cake samples.

Jenny stopped talking and was a hundred kinds of confused. "A puck?"

I did a swinging motion with a pretend hockey stick. "You. know, a puck, six ounces of vulcanized rubber, the things we hit into nets because Ten is a hockey player." I waited for at least one of those descriptions to hit home and watched as she shuddered.

"Pucks are black," she announced with great authority

and looked at Ten for backup. He slid lower in the chair and left me carrying the conversation. Ass. I don't think he'd forgiven me for ducking out on the Stan-Vegas-Backyard chat that he'd had to handle. This was payback. I pulled my shoulders back. Jenny was an itty bitty little thing, probably needed a stool to reach the table she worked on. I was a former NHL D-man; I could face her down. Maybe.

"We'd like it in the shape of a puck," I started off with confidence. "But we'd probably be cool with two layers as two pucks. It doesn't have to be black. It could be…" I searched for an alternative to black and recalled the one I'd received from my old team when I retired after my heart op. "Silver. It can be silver. Can you do silver?"

"Silver," she said faintly and sat in the closest chair.

"Yep," I was warming to this now. "And maybe with the logo of our team on one of the pucks. I found this place that screen prints logos onto edible discs of icing, so you wouldn't have to draw it from scratch."

I felt so damn helpful, and I think I might have even smiled at her.

"Mr. Madsen, I make *couture* cakes," she said and picked up the leaflet with the options we were supposed to tick, proceeding to fan herself with it. "I have won several design awards and catered the best society weddings other cake designers would kill to work on."

"Excellent," I offered because that all sounded fine, and it appeared to me she wouldn't have any trouble making a puck-shaped cake. I mean, pucks are round, and it would be easy. Right?

"No, you don't understand—"

The door opened, and a cute little bell tinkled discreetly.

"So sorry I'm late," Trent sashayed in, pushing red-rimmed sunglasses back into his hair and revealing full rainbow eye makeup. "Stan wants a temporary rink with deck hockey for the kids, and I had to explain that actually we needed that room for the string quartet. So I said to him—"

"Mr. Hanson," Jenny interrupted and jumped to her feet. "Mr. Madsen wants a cake shaped like a puck. A silver one."

Trent's mouth fell open. Then he shook his head. "That won't do," he said.

I looked at Ten for support, but somehow during this discussion, he'd cleared the entire plate of samples. I knew we should have done tuxes first. I wasn't going to get help from my fiancé, so it seemed like clearing up this issue was all up to me, then.

"Wait a minute, Trent—"

"Silver isn't the theme," Trent interrupted. "I'd have to change the colors, and I just found the right green roses as well." He pouted thoughtfully and then clapped his hands. "But what about Railers blue. That would work with a silver cake. Jenny, what do you think?"

I imagine she wanted to say that she thought the world had gone mad and that there was no way in hell she was going to lower her standards to make a silver cake in the shape of a puck. She didn't say any of that.

"Wonderful," she said through gritted teeth.

Now Ten decided to join in. "The bottom layer chocolate with the caramel, the top vanilla with the ganache. Silver. With the little dents all around, and on top, we want it to have crossed hockey sticks and the words Mr. and Mr."

Jenny seemed as if she was about ready to order us out of her shop, but I guess if she was free enough to make a last-minute cake for us, then she wasn't super busy at all.

"Absolutely, Mr. Rowe," she said and added something that sounded like it contained the word *fuck*, *vision*, and *whatever*.

We paid what she asked. I didn't even check the amount, and she didn't lose the smile pasted on her face until we left. When I glanced back, she was at the counter with her head tilted up as if she were praying to the god of dulce cream and chocolate ganache, asking for patience.

"You handled that really well," Ten said and brushed crumbs from his Railers' T-shirt.

I hustled him up against the nearest wall and kept him there, my eyes narrowing as he smirked at me. "You ate all the damn cake," I said with dark undertones, trying to be threatening. He burst out laughing, then pulled me in for a cakey kiss.

I decided I quite liked those and would have had more if Trent hadn't yanked us apart and warned us we had ten minutes to get to the tuxedo place.

All I could think was that they would have private changing rooms, and I could go to my knees and—

"There will be no sex in the fitting rooms of Lethe Taylors," Trent stated.

I really did my best to look innocent, but the fact that I had to adjust myself discreetly was enough to give me away.

Damn Trent Hanson.

. . .

"I SHOULDN'T HAVE EATEN ALL that cake," Ten said after the fifth tuxedo we tried on.

"Damn right," I agreed and peered at my reflection, wondering how in hell I was going to sit down in such tailored pants.

"What do you think about getting married in Railers' tracksuits?" he mused.

I elbowed him. "While I agree that is a great idea, can you imagine the nervous breakdown Trent would have, not to mention Stan, who said he's wearing something special."

Ten shook his head, "I heard it's ruffled again. Adler said we could always photoshop the photos."

"It wouldn't be Stan unless he was in the loudest, most Elvis-like suit."

"You know what?" Ten began and stopped fiddling with the jacket that fit him like a glove. "I think we look pretty sharp in these."

We weren't in matching suits; his was a beautiful pale gray, and I was in a contrasting dark navy. He'd picked it out the moment we walked in, said I should wear a blue shirt that matched my eyes. How did he know to say the very most perfect thing?

"You look so handsome," I murmured, and we learned in to kiss and almost made it.

"I'm coming in!" Trent announced loudly, then came in with a hand over his eyes. "Is it safe?" It was all for show because he dropped his hand and looked right at us. Then he lost all of his flamboyant Trent-ness, and I thought he was going to cry. His eyes were bright with emotion. "Oh my stars," he said. "You both look…" He pressed his lips together and then nodded as if he was having some kind of private discussion in his mind. "Perfect," he summarized. "Sometimes I wish Dieter would…" He trailed off, then brightened. "Onwards and upwards. We have Ryker, Jamie, and Brady here in the morning for their fittings. Now you're ticked off the list, so you're free until the rehearsal dinner tomorrow evening."

This was the first I'd heard about a rehearsal dinner, but I didn't care what we did now, because I really felt as if I'd reached that part of the whole thing where it was just about me and Ten. Something in Trent's expression had love and affection welling inside me. For him and his open generosity and emotion, for beautiful tuxes and helpful tailors, and for the puck-shaped cake. But most of all for Ten.

Trent made a note of pick-up times in a journal fat with notes, and then we went our separate ways; tonight Ryker and Jacob were staying over, and I had a whole heap of things planned from pizza to popcorn, games, films, and talking hockey.

"DAD? CAN WE TALK?" Ryker crouched next to me by the dishwasher. Games and films had been waylaid by Ten being in a cake and pizza coma on the sofa, and Jacob joining him in support. Jacob had been up all night with a cow or something like that, and to be fair, he looked exhausted. Ryker, on the other hand, was wide awake and agitated about something, and I think I knew what it was. After the wedding, he was moving to Arizona. Not only was this a *long* way from Jacob, and it was to join a team he was dreading. I knew my son, and I could see the dark cloud above his head.

I shut the dishwasher and set it running before wiping my hands on the nearest towel.

"Let's shoot some pucks."

He followed me out for the traditional post-dinner Dad/Ryker puck handling chat. From an early age, Ryker was all about hockey, and we'd settled into this routine, when we could, of shooting pucks and talking.

I didn't start the conversation, allowing my muscles to warm, aiming at the center of the net in our back yard, watching as the rhythm of Ryker's movements settled his agitation.

He finally stopped and then scooped the puck up on his stick, bouncing it there as he said what was on his mind. "Rumor has it that the Raptors are going to announce a rebuild. I heard it from Matt. Do you remember Matt Lewis?"

"Yeah. First-round pick, Calgary, shoots left," I rattled off the Lewis kid's stats from memory. I wanted to know the kind of players my son would meet on the ice, and I had hoped that the Railers could have picked up Lewis. He was a strong forward. Of course, I'd hoped we'd get Ryker, but that didn't happen.

"Matt's uncle is the assistant coach in Dallas and is friends with this guy, who is a hockey journalist…" He took a deep breath and exhaled noisily. "It's a long story, but yeah, looks like I got drafted by a team that's not only tanking but has plans to make a statement about a freaking rebuild."

I had to tread carefully here. "There's nothing wrong with a rebuild, Ry. All teams go through this at one point or another. It could be a team doesn't have the young kids coming up from their farm teams, or they lose key players in trades, or hell, it could be the place they play or the schedule they had to keep that messed with them."

Ryker stopped tossing the puck and instead flicked it high into the air, watching it curve and fall, and knocking it baseball-style into the net. My son had mad skills, if I say so myself.

"What if I get lost in that shuffle?"

He'd expressed his worries about the Raptors several times, and every time I'd explained that the worry was a waste of time, that he had to keep his head down, use his strong work ethic, and play his best. Maybe it was something to do with the wedding or the pizza or the tuxes or even the damn cake, but I was feeling different tonight. Ryker needed me to be the proudest dad I could be right now. He also deserved honesty and not just packaged words.

I leaned my stick against the net and gripped his shoulders, staring into eyes the same shade as mine.

"Ryker, son, it could be shit. You're walking into a notoriously shaky team and a locker room that won't be full of hope. But you know what? You can change that. Every single shift you put in, every practice, you can work that Ryker magic, and you can make a difference. I love you, Ryker, and I'm biased as hell, but you are going to be a star, and you will drag that team kicking and screaming into a new style of play. I know you will, and I'm so proud of you."

Ryker was thoughtful and then gave me a cautious smile. "Thanks, Dad."

"You're welcome." I picked up the stick, but Ten

walked into the space and slipped his arm around my waist.

"What are my fiancé and my favorite stepson-to-be doing out here?" Ten mused. He grinned and held out a hand for one of the sticks we had in a storage container. "Blindfolded and first to twenty?" he threw down the challenge to us both, but I stepped back and let them get on with it, content to watch the two most important people in my life from the stone bench, only shuffling over when Jacob sat with me.

"Why do they have T-shirts tied around their eyes?" Jacob asked and yawned behind his hand.

I huffed a laugh. "With them? I find it best not to ask."

Tennant

My love for you is like rivers of love running through my heart.

I stared at the line I'd written in my tablet.

"Tennant, that blows a big donker," I mumbled and deleted the hell out of that stupid sentence. The wind whipped around Reservoir Park, carrying the fine watery particles from the Wellspring of the Future fountain to my face and bare arms. I glanced up from my now blank Word page, my eyes shaded by the Railers' cap tugged down to my eyebrows, and stared at the statues of parents playing with their young children. It was a beautiful day in Harrisburg, mid-eighties, low humidity, and skies as blue as my fiancé's eyes. Jared. The man I loved and whom I was marrying in five days. Five. Days. And me with no vows written.

"Help me, statue mom. You're my only hope," I whined and shimmied down lower on the park bench.

I'd thought getting out of the house would help. I mean, our place was ground zero for wedding madness.

Trent woke us up at seven a.m. every day—how I wished he'd go back to Philly—with an insane amount of exuberance and a list as long as the filmy scarves he wore. There was no reining him in. We'd tried. We'd begged Dieter to keep his boyfriend at his place at least until eight or nine. Big D had replied that there was no keeping Trent anywhere when he had an event to plan. Which explained why, when he'd been competing, Trent had been on the ice at five in the morning every day. He was nothing if not dedicated. A little less dedication to the perfect wedding wouldn't have been frowned on, though. So yeah, I snuck out, leaving Jared with Trent and my mother to work out seating arrangements. I'd pay for that abandonment later, I was sure.

"Right," I said aloud, making myself stop daydreaming about sexual paybacks.

My love for you is like a waterfall that flows over the rocks of my heart.

I read that line again.

"That's worse than the first one," I moaned and deleted it with undue force. Great. Just great. I could see it now, me facing Jared after he read this epic romantic speech filled with words about love and commitment and saying something like, "Totes dude. Right back at you."

Someone sat down next to me, their elbow bumping mine. I tossed the guy a glance and saw that it was a kid. Young boy, maybe ten or so, and he was frowning as deeply as I was, only his glum was directed at his phone and not a tablet.

"Sorry," the kid said, then stared right at me. His dark eyes widened. "You're Tennant Rowe," he gushed, his grumpy mood vanishing.

"Yeah, that's me," I replied, offering him my hand. "And you are?"

"Kyle Reynolds." We shook, and I signed his left sneaker. "This is incredible," he said, running a finger over my signature on the side of his Converse high top. "You hang out here a lot?"

"Nah, I'm here trying to figure out my wedding vows, but between you and me"—I leaned to the side all covert-like—"I'm terrible at this kind of stuff. My mom had to tutor me through tenth grade English, and even then, I only tugged down a C."

"Bummer. Maybe your mom could help you with your vows for Coach Madsen?" He shrugged, then tossed his wild blond hair from his face.

"Probably, but I kind of wanted to do this by myself. What's got you in a grump?"

He exhaled theatrically. "I'm trying to hunt a shiny—"

My ears perked up. "A Pokémon shiny?"

"Yeah. You know about Pokémon?" Kyle asked with caution.

"Dude, *seriously?*" I shoved my tablet into the tiny backpack I'd brought and pulled out my phone. "Have you tried gym raids? I found two that way. Oh! And make sure you keep hatching the eggs."

Kyle and I then went on this massive hunt around the park for a shiny for him. Sadly, we never found one. They *were* rare, but he did capture an elekid in the wild that he'd not had before. So overall, a successful hunt for him. When we were done, we took a break in the shade under a fat old oak that overlooked the Levitt Pavilion bandshell. There was a concert scheduled there for this evening that Jared and I had talked about attending.

"This has been fun," Kyle said with a wide smile. "Can we do one more selfie?"

"Totes." I dropped an arm around his shoulder, and he snapped a few shots.

"Okay, so you helped me with finding an elekid, so maybe I can help with your vows?"

"Oh, man, I *so* wish you could. See, it's not like I don't know what's inside me." I rapped my breast with the side of my fist. A bee buzzed past, intent on checking out the flowering bushes that waved in the wind. "I have so much love inside me for him, right? He's the perfect man for me. He grounds me when I need tethering, and he lets me fly when I need freedom. He laughs with me and at me, holds me when things are bad, and dances with me when things are good. He's the world to me. I just wish I could say all that in a flowery way."

"Who says your vows have to be flowery? Just tell Coach Madsen how you feel."

I opened my mouth, closed it, and then slowly looked at the ten-year-old sipping on a box of cherry fruit juice we'd bought after our massive Pokémon Go hunt. Out of the mouths of babes.

"Kyle, my man, drop me your email. I want to hook you and your folks up with some season tickets. I think you just saved my life."

"... LISTEN UP! PEOPLE! *PEOPLE!*" The loud buzz that filled Stan's huge living room died down when Trent, standing on a chair, clapped his hands sharply. "My goodness, it's worse than trying to get a group of six-year-olds to grasp a crisp mohawk." I smiled at our wedding planner. I had no idea what he was talking about. What did Native Americans have to do with anything?

"We listen now good," Stan shouted from the rear, his son Pavel riding on his wide shoulders.

"Thank you, Stan. Now, I know we just had a rather bumpy rehearsal, but I have *great faith* that come tomorrow you'll all know where you're to *stand*. Ushers, please make sure you're here an hour before the wedding so you can seat the early birds." Several Railers mumbled a reply. Trent adjusted the maroon beret sitting jauntily on his head. "Also, we'll need to make sure the flower girl and the ring-bearer are here and tidy."

"Not an issue," Erik shouted. Jared slid an arm around my waist. I leaned into him. "Eva and Noah will be here on time and as clean as we can keep them."

"Dad!"

"Him. As clean as we can keep *him*," Erik quickly corrected, then dropped a kiss to his daughter's head.

"*Marvelous!* Also, it's been brought to my attention that those who are part of the wedding itself are to be here early for social media exposure. Layton wishes me to remind everyone that there's to be no campy or trampy news and/or images shared online. The world's going to be watching as the first openly out gay hockey player marries the man of his dreams. We're to display class, decorum, and courtliness. All eyes are going to be on Tennant and Jared waiting for them to act out in a manner that will give the bigots fuel for the fires of intolerance. So *please*, no rude Instagram comments or tasteless tweets. We've got one chance to make this wedding shine so, to quote Mama Ru, 'Good luck and don't F it up!'"

Everyone clapped. Jared reached up to give Trent a hand down from the chair. We both got kisses on our cheeks. Then Trent scurried off to snuggle with Dieter.

"Okay, so I feel *no* pressure at all from that pep talk," I said to Jared.

He chuckled a bit, then took my hand, sliding his fingers between mine, leading me out to the side lawn where caterers were setting up buffet tables. Stan was taking his role as friend-of-honor and wedding host very seriously. And so far, there had been no signs of sequins or pompadour hairstyles.

"Just when you think you're over the jitters, the wedding planner reminds you that everyone and their poodle will be watching your every move." He led me past the catering staff as they hurried around placing dishes and flatware on the tables.

"Not helping," I groaned. The sweet smell of roses from the perfectly manicured flower beds swept over me, and I breathed deeply. "I never wanted to be the poster boy for gay hockey. I just—"

"Wanted to play the game you adore and love who you want," Jared finished for me, making me chuckle as we strolled past a small fountain that splashed merrily. "How many new fountains did he buy?"

"Don't ask," Jared commented dryly, leading me down a small knoll and through the arch—also new—that we would walk through tomorrow. The flowers for the arch would be put on early in the morning by the florists. Green roses and white baby's breath or something along those lines. The details were starting to blur a bit. We stood by the arch, hand in hand, looking out at the lush green grass where, in less than twenty-four hours, he and I would become husband and husband. "He's quite the lifesaver."

"Oh, no doubt, but he didn't need to spend so much on the grounds and the food for the dinner. I mean, donating his place was enough."

"Nothing is too good for best friend Ten," Jared replied in his best baritone Stan imitation.

"Ah, man, he's the best."

We lingered there, resting against each other, the sun setting, but night still a few hours away. Bumblebees and hummingbirds flitted from one vibrantly colored flower bed to another, the low sounds of people filing out to eat floating down to where we were stealing a few moments of couple time. The past two days had been packed with appointments, drama, fittings, lost earrings, grumpy kids, family flying in, reporters tracking us around, and siblings. Far too many of those. We'd barely had time to wave at each other.

"Okay, don't think badly of me for this, because I love everyone so much for all the hard work they've put into our wedding, but I cannot wait to get on that plane tomorrow night and fly off to Greece."

"Mm, yeah. I cannot wait to make love to you under a Greek sunset as the waves of the Mediterranean lap at our toes." I turned to face him, eager to press my body tight to his as he whispered soft, sweet things about our upcoming trip. "Touring white-washed villages, then touring the ancient wonders of Athens."

"Sex in luxury villas that overlook Santorini and Delphi."

He licked at my lips, his hands sliding to my ass. "Touring the museums."

"Fucking under the stars as we cruise through the Saronic Gulf."

"Will three weeks be long enough?" He lapped into my mouth, cutting off my reply with a kiss that left me hard and breathless.

"No," I purred, grabbing his hair. "No amount of time will ever be long enough. I love you so much I just… words. Doh."

He peppered my face with tiny kisses. "I know exactly how you feel. Thinking of you as my husband leaves me speechless as well."

"Here they are, making out under the arch!" I tensed at the bellow from my eldest brother. "Not much longer now, guys. Keep them in your pants."

Brady slapped Jared so hard on the back I felt the vibrations. Then Jamie arrived, and Adler, Stan and two dogs, my father, my mother, two Lisas, and one howling baby. Guess couple time was officially over. I ached for Jared, even as I was led back up the hill by my brothers and shoved into the line for pulled pork sandwiches and potato salad.

I glanced back. Jared stood between my mother and Galina, plate in his hand, smiling as the women chatted with him. His gaze met mine. I felt the jolt of love and passion all the way to my toes. We couldn't say our vows and get on that plane fast enough.

Jared

If pacing was an Olympic sport, then I would've earned a gold medal by now.

"Dude, you're making me dizzy," Adler said from the chair by the door. He'd been sitting there since it was decided I needed to be in a separate room from Ten. I'm not sure if he'd been asked to stop me from leaving or whether it was just a super-comfy chair, but I swear at one point, he looked as if he was going to fall asleep.

"This is stupid," I muttered and executed a quick turn by the wall, pacing back across the wooden floor of Stan and Erik's dining room. It was a very nice room, a mix of old and new, paintings that I recognized to be by the boyfriend of someone who played for our feeder team adorned the walls, two huge candelabra sat at each end of the big table. Eight chairs ranged around it. Make that seven because Adler had scraped chair eight over to the door when he'd been put in charge of me.

"Bag skates." I pointed out to him when he tried to

stop me as I passed. I've never seen someone pull their hand back so damn quickly.

"You will have forgotten that threat by the time we're back on the ice," Adler said and smirked. I stopped very deliberately in front of him and glared down at him.

"I remember *everything*," I said.

He wriggled a little at that and dropped his gaze, but he didn't budge from his chair. I quite enjoyed intimidating Adler, or indeed anyone on the team, with the ultimate threat of the worst kind of practice ever imagined. A bag skate is any kind of exercise on ice where a coach pushes the team until he thinks they've had enough. I had a lot of different ideas about what I would put Adler through, and I hoped that was conveyed by my cross-armed stance.

"I'm still not letting you out," he said and tipped his chin defiantly. "Jamie said he would kill me if you got out."

I raised a single eyebrow. "Jamie is not a coach with the Railers," I reminded him.

"Yeah, but have you seen the dude follow through on his checks?" Adler shuddered visibly, but he did not move his foot from against the door, and I subsided into brooding at the window.

From here, I could see the entirety of the wedding setup. One hundred and twenty chairs in two groups of sixty, a walkway between them, and at the end, the arch where Ten and I would say our vows. I watched as a huge fluffy cat wound its way through the chairs before leaping to the top of the arch, planting its furry butt, and staring out toward one of Stan's fountains. Sunlight sparkled from the water spray, and beyond that, I knew thousands of tiny fairy lights had been twined through the trees. Stan and

Erik had gone overboard with every suggestion Trent had made, and I loved them for it. I wanted the best day for Ten, but I also wanted the celebration to start.

"Fifteen minutes still," Adler said as if he'd read my mind.

This was going to be the longest quarter-hour of my life. It was going to feel even longer than when Ryker was born with the umbilical cord wrapped around his neck. Time was damn well standing still as I watched people begin to walk in. Ryker's mom was first, with her husband and daughters in tow. Then there were the team members who didn't have a part in the ceremony, managers, hockey friends, more family, Ten's sisters-in-law. It was a kaleidoscope of color, all placed according to a plan that had been in Trent's head. I was actually surprised he didn't get people to coordinate outfits in some kind of rainbow.

The door opened. Someone cursed in Russian, and Adler nearly went flying off his chair.

"Adler, no foot for prisons," Stan declared, "time for marrying."

I was out of that room like a shot, careening into Ryker, who was walking in the opposite direction. He steadied me and grinned.

"In a hurry, Dad?"

"Maybe I am."

He looked me up and down. "Okay then, last checks. Something old, something new, something borrowed, something blue." He straightened my tie. "Blue tie, so we're good there. The suit's new." He brushed the lapels of my navy suit jacket. "Something old? You don't need that —you're old all by yourself."

"Yeah, yeah." I let out a noisy sigh. Given I'd been a

teenager when he'd made his appearance in the world, I wasn't *that* old, but he did love to say things like that.

Of course I was older than Ten, as well.

Am I too old? Why am I thinking that? What is wrong with me? Is it just me, or is it hot in here? I want to marry Ten. Can't we get this started now? Why am I—?

"Earth to Dad?" Ryker shook me, and I snapped out of my spiral. "I bet you don't have anything borrowed."

"I don't have… I didn't think…"

"Chill. Mom gave me this for you to take."

Casey gave him something for me?

He held out his hand, and sitting in his palm was a pebble. Smooth and round, it was the pebble Ryker had found on his first trip to the beach. He'd only been three, and so proud of his find, even more so when Casey affixed googly eyes to it and called it Fred. When we split, I guess it had been one of the things that had gone to her. "She wants it back, though."

I picked up the googly-eyed Fred and smiled as memories of Ryker as a little boy, all fire and fun, flooded me. I'd split amicably from Casey, or at least as harmoniously as my asshole of an ex-father-in-law had allowed it to be. All the way through, we'd wanted to give Ryker a happy, stable upbringing, and I think Casey and I had done right by him.

"Did we do okay?" I asked before my mouth caught up with my brain. Ryker looked at me with expectation "With you. Did we always let you know we loved you?"

Ryker's eyes brightened, and he swallowed hard. "Always, Dad, always." We hugged, and when he stood back, he was smiling so hard. "Come on, let's go do this thing."

We met Ten at the wide patio doors, and he reached for my hand as soon as he saw me.

"Hey," he whispered.

I pocketed googly-eyed Fred and took his hand.

"Hey, back."

We didn't kiss, but our fingers laced together so perfectly, and in a weird-ass processional way, we made our way to the start of the path to the arch.

Ten crouched down to look Pavel in the face. "You okay, little dude?"

Pavel's chest puffed up with pride. "Not to lost the rings," he announced and shook the tiny pillow they sat on. Thankfully, they were held in place with ribbon because otherwise I could've seen them ending up in the grass somewhere. Then Ten turned to Eva, who was so sweet in her bridesmaid dress.

"Wow," Ten said and let out a low whistle. "Look at you, gorgeous."

She blushed and wrinkled her nose. She adored Ten, and he adored her right back. Maybe one day we would have kids of our own, get a bigger place, build a small rink, build a whole new franchise of players.

Wow, where did that come from?

"Thank you, Uncle Ten," she murmured, and then, shoulders back, she followed Pavel down the path, throwing rose petals to the ground. Then it was just me, Ten, and the people standing up for us. Ten had his brothers, I had Ryker, and the group stood in a loose huddle. I could imagine us doing some weird handshake thing with a loud "team, let's go!" at the end. Instead of that, Brady went into big brother mode.

"Not too late to change your mind," Brady faux-whispered to Ten. "We have a fast car out front, ready to run."

"Brady, take this seriously," Jamie whispered back.

"It's brotherly advice." Brady smirked when he knew I could see him. Then he grew serious and turned to face me. "Hurt him, and I will hunt you down," he threatened and looked deadly serious.

"I will never hurt him," I promised, and we shook hands.

Then it was Jamie's turn. "Brady might hunt you down, but I'll be the one with the box and the shovel."

"Noted," I said and shook his hand.

Jamie cleared his throat, "See you at the arch."

They followed Pavel and Eva, and then it was Ryker's turn to go. He hugged me, pressed a kiss to my cheek, and did the same to Ten.

"Go get married so I can say I have two dads," he deadpanned. Then he followed Ten's brothers. Finally, it was just the two of us, and we laced fingers again. Trent had come up with all these marvelous ideas of how we were going to get to the arch, but at the end of it, both Ten and I wanted to walk together.

The short distance seemed to take forever. People smiled, there were pictures, some spoke to us as we passed, and I saw Stan holding the cat that had been sitting on the arch. The sky was the brightest sapphire, a faint breeze brought with it the scent of the flowers Trent had organized, and everything we'd been through to get there, crystallized in this one moment.

I was marrying the man I loved.

Everyone sat when we reached the end as Jamie and

Brady stood back from Ten, and Ryker took a few steps away from me. I scanned the group of people there to help us celebrate, and my eyes landed on Casey. She smiled at me and then made circles of her hands and placed them around her eyes just like googly-eyed Fred. She would always be my friend, and together we were Mom and Dad to Ryker.

Jeez, I am getting so emotional.

There were words spoken, talking of what marriage meant, and most of it was a blur, a beautiful love-filled haze, and then it was time for me to speak. We'd agreed I would go first. I hadn't thought at the time we'd talked about it that the words I wanted to give to Ten right now would be some of the hardest I'd ever spoken. I knew Ten had written things down and I knew he'd thought long and hard about what he wanted to say. I bet his vows would be full of flowery words that could express love in more poetic ways than the things I could say. But I wanted to speak from the heart, and that was where I started.

I faced him head on, and we held hands. My breathing settled, and the gentle noises of the beautiful summer day slipped away.

"When I fell to the ice, it was because my heart had broken. I fought so hard to deny that the one thing I relied on had failed me. Then, as I got better, I realized that I had Ryker in my heart alongside that broken part, and when I thought of him there, I would start to calm and feel peaceful. I could face the entire world if I could just make Ryker proud."

Ten worried at his lip with his teeth, and he watched me closely. Did any of this sound right?

"Then I met you, and the other bits of my hurting heart slowly began to heal. It didn't take me long to fall for you, and I'm the luckiest man alive that you noticed me and wanted me back. Hell, I can remember that first morning, when you were at the glass, doing an interview, all shiny-new in a Railers' sweatshirt. You were the hockey phenom, one of the best of your generation, and in the locker room, we knew that if you fit in with us, the Railers could grow as a team. That was how I was supposed to see you, as a player, as a skater. But I think that from day one, I saw you as something else, and only my stubbornness stopped me from realizing it sooner."

I paused again. This wasn't supposed to be a recounting of how well Ten fit in as a Railer. But I had to stick with the conviction that I needed him to know this.

"I fell in love so fast, so hard, and from sneaking into tree houses to getting punched by your brother, you were the best thing to happen to me. Ten, I have you in my heart right next to Ryker. You know that, right?"

He smiled at me, and his eyes were bright, and I thought I must be making some kind of sense. He didn't have to answer. I could see his smile.

"And then you fell to the ice"—I was choked, and I swallowed to clear my throat—"and every part of me hurt with you when they picked you up and took you away. I can't imagine a life without you, so please know that if you *ever* fall on the ice again, I will always be there for you, bringing you home where you belong."

I gripped his hands a little tighter; I just had one more thing I wanted to say.

"Ten, I love you, with all my heart."

The incredible happiness that curled inside me was

making me feel lightheaded, and I wanted to scoop him into my arms, hold him tight, and never let him go.

I'd found my forever person, and we had a lifetime of love to share.

Then it was his turn, and I didn't know how I was going to stop myself from crying.

Tennant

THERE ARE THINGS THAT STAND OUT IN YOUR MEMORIES.

First time on skates, first goal, first kiss, first love, first realization that the first kiss shared with Becky Addison from next door paled in comparison to the first kiss shared with Dylan Doyle, the fullback for your high school football team. First signing with a professional team. First trade. First time hoisting the Cup.

All of those "first" memories were special and important. Things that stood out and had molded me into the man I was now. But none of them could compare to the memory that this day—this *moment*—was going to be. Nothing would ever compare to knowing that I'd found my soulmate and that he and everyone else sitting here on these meticulously sculpted grounds were waiting for me to say something memorable. I squeezed the fingers meshed with mine. His gaze caressed my face.

"A week ago I was playing Pokémon Go with a kid named Kyle," I began. Jared's eyes flared a bit. Someone who sounded like Adler Lockhart hooted. Dork. Still, the shout made me smile and eased the tight band around my chest. "He'd been searching for this special kind of beast and hadn't had any luck finding one. See, they're rare." Jared nodded but was confused. I wanted to kiss the furrows on his brow away. "Sometimes you have to look a long time to find the seldom-seen treasures. Sometimes you seek and you search, you walk for miles and miles, you cross mighty oceans, and you scale killer mountains to find that remarkable and precious gem. Sometimes you dig deep into the earth or soar into the sky to find that richness. And then, sometimes, you're giving an interview, and you turn around to find that the splendor you seek is just on the other side of the glass."

He drew in a shaky breath. I heard my mother cough discreetly. A bird sang out in a nearby oak.

"I was lucky. I didn't have to cross the globe or traverse jungles to find that most sought-after trove... true love. It was right there, looking at me, and I knew right then that even if I never won a championship, or signed a billion-dollar contract, or never wore one of those big, blingy rings, I'd still be rich beyond measure because I'd found you. Our love is a treasure. It's the most precious thing in my life. How lucky am I to be able to have found your love so soon? How lucky am I to be able to wear our adoration as a king wears his crown jewels? How lucky am I to have found you, Jared Madsen? And how damn lucky am I to be able to call you my husband, my lover, and my best friend? I love you."

With that, I pressed my lips to his.

"We're not to that part of the ceremony quite yet," the officiant said with humor.

"I know, but it had to be done," I replied as my gaze rested on Jared's face.

"Always the impatient one," Jared whispered and gave my knuckles a kiss.

The rest of the ceremony went quickly, the words kind of blurring a bit until we got to the power-vested-in-me and the I-now-pronounce-you-husband-and-husband and the you-can-kiss-now bit.

Jared pulled me into his arms, lowered his head, and kissed me with such love and passion I felt it down to my toes. Applause filled the warm summer air. We were still kissing. Hoots and hollers broke out. We were still kissing. Laughter broke out, and yes, we were still kissing.

"Okay, save it for the honeymoon," I heard Brady say, and that kind of dulled the lust. A little. Pulling back an inch, I smiled at my husband. He smiled back. We were pelted with bird seed and good wishes as we dashed past our guests, hand in hand.

"We did it," I panted, yanking Jared to the nearest tree, then kissing him again. His hands roamed over my back, pinning me to him "We did it. We got married. Would it be rude to ditch the food, dancing, and drinking in favor of the honeymoon sex? I'm asking for a friend. His name is Dick."

"Ass," Jared laughed, pressing his lips to mine for another moment.

Sadly, it was just a moment because the wedding party and the planner arrived, as did the photographer. The happy couple was then made to stand here, then there, and then over here at least forty-five thousand times. I kept eyeing the massive white tents billowing in the warm wind, knowing that the food and the band were awaiting us. We'd not leave the grounds for at *least* six hours, so obsessing over getting Jared naked wasn't going to do much for me, aside from leaving me with a half-hard dick to contend with. Instead of dealing with a chub for the entire reception, I threw myself into the madness of the moment, letting Trent lead me around like a prize pug on a glittery leash.

"Mother of the groom! We need the mother of the groom over here by the azalea!" Trent shouted and clapped to be heard over the band warming up a few hundred feet away.

"Which groom?" Jared yelled back, and we all snickered.

Trent waved him off with a swirl of the black-and-white-checkered taffeta scarf hanging artfully around his neck. And here all I'd worn as a decoration for my tux was a green rose boutonnière.

I posed with my mother, my father, then my mother and father together, my brothers, my sisters-in-law, my nieces, my husband, my husband and Ryker, and my best friend. Oh, and then Jared and I posed with the team. Layton buzzed around, taking pictures for the official Railers Twitter, Facebook, and Instagram pages. Trent flitted around like a well-dressed hummingbird, sipping some sort of sweet-looking melon-colored drink from a tall skinny flute, his white sunbonnet never leaving his head despite a few good gusts of wind.

"Did he staple that hat on?" I asked Dieter as we were waiting for all the guests to find the food/bar tent—aka the Big Top—so we could be announced and Stan could give his best friend speech.

"He has tricks," Dieter replied with a shrug. "Lots of

goopy hair stuff and bobby pins, I think? I don't really know. I just kind of give all the stuff on the bathroom counter a wide berth. The last time I tried some of his pomade crap, my hair kind of cemented into a solid block that required some sort of relaxer and a pair of clippers to remedy."

"Oh damn, I remember when you went buzzed that time!"

"Yep, that was why. Of course then I got a lecture on the abuse of his expensive pomade and how only those who are skilled in the arts of the coiffure should be using such advanced hair care products," Dieter said warmly, the love he had for Trent obvious in the way he was always seeking his man out among a crowd, and how his gaze softened when he looked upon Trent.

"Okay, people, the band is ready, and the appetizers are about to be served. I need the ushers and the wedding party front and center. Oh nice, lovely. Bring on the wives and little ones!"

Jared slid up beside me, gave my neck a nuzzle, and grabbed my hand. My family and his filed into the huge tent to loud applause.

When the band began to play Beyoncé and Jay-Z's *Crazy in Love,* we were shoved forward. Everyone stood and clapped as we danced into the tent. I was glad to see that Trent had used our song list as we'd asked. He'd not done much else that we'd suggested, but the tunes had been a solid must-have for me. Also, I did have to confess that Jared could shake his ass with the best of us. Not a bad move to be seen.

After a short series of bows, we made our way to the main table, a long thing draped with white cloth that had huge glass urns of blue, silver, and white flowers every five feet or so. The other tables each had one centerpiece, as did the food tables and the bar, which was hopping still, as well as the small bandstand to the left.

Stan rose from his seat next to me. He embraced me, kissed both my cheeks, and then did the same for Jared before motioning for us to sit. We did and were given flutes of bubbly pink champagne.

Stan lifted his glass, then coughed, only once. Silence fell. I guess no one wanted to upset our gentle giant. He did *know people*, after all.

"Is for my great honor to be chosen to be best official friend for Tennant and Jared's wedding," he said, his booming voice carrying well, so he had no need for the microphone lying on the table. "My speech is good speech. Working hard with my beloved and my children Eva, Pavel, and Noah, we craft best speech ever for wedding." The kids all gathered around their fathers, Eva blushing when I glanced at her, Pavel climbing into Erik's lap, and Noah skittering under the table to join Brady's twin girls in a game of hide. No seeking was taking place yet, just lots of giggly hiding.

"In speech making, I discover many feelings come to the top of my emotion wall. Like water in big storms, my feeling run over the top and make wet messes of villages below. I think of many things to talk of and why my flood happens. Tennant was first person on team to be friend with me, true friend. We eat many Big Macs together, and he show me how to capture Pokémon. Tennant make feel not just part of team but part of team family. Not outsider Russian looking in but now insider sitting at popular table."

I got a little teary then, recalling how much Stan's friendship had meant to me as well when I'd first come to Harrisburg. Our bond had grown tighter over the years, and now he was more like a third sibling, his children my godchildren, our homes and lives tangled up in that wild, messy way families are.

"… times he tells me juicy things about romance times with Jared that I cannot say now for tiny ears are poking into speech."

I blinked. Ah man, what had I missed? Given the snickers of those under the big top, it was something pure Stan.

"I am happy to give my friend Tennant to my other friend Jared. They are handsome couple, loving and true, rising above hatred to lead way for other gay or bisexual or trans players to speak up and come out if they wish. Courage fills their hearts, and pride fills my breast. I am honored to call them my brothers. Now we drink! Lift high the glasses!" He turned to us, the sequins on the lapels of his tuxedo glittering brightly. "May stars of fate that bring together shine forever on much blessed happy union. May you and many future children have great happiness, wealth, and health. May great love carry on good times and very bad, and keep you warm on coldest of nights. Let us drink to love. Gorka! To the newlyweds!"

We smiled at our guests as they drank to our marriage.

"Ah! Is good. Now, we eat!" Stan bellowed, and the servers in their blue shirts, black slacks, and tidy white aprons began moving through the crowd to allow one table, then the next to go to the buffet tables, but only after our table had made the trip first. Our plates were piled high with braised beef tips over noodles, herbed chicken, mashed potatoes, broiled cod with lemon, and several vegetable side dishes. Rolls, butter, and a dark red soup that Stan slurped up while making deep yummy sounds. The band played as we ate, easy rock ballads mostly.

When the food was cleared away, we did something called Russian 'bread and salt' that our goalie had insisted must be part of the festivities. A huge loaf of bread was presented to Jared and me. We both ripped a hunk off the crusty, soft loaf. The person who had the biggest chunk was the boss or something along those lines.

Then the puck-shaped cake was rolled in. Jared and I both grinned at the Mr. and Mr. topper with the crossed hockey sticks. We sliced into the cake, Jared's hand on top of mine, and then things kind of slipped into chaos. All decorum was lost. I jammed my slice into his face. He crammed his slice up my nose. Everyone laughed and clapped as we wiped our faces clean, then shared a soft, sweet, icing kiss.

Dessert was served to the guests, and everyone chatted and laughed, throwing good natured insults our way. It was perfect.

"Yes!"

The voice echoed in the big tent, louder than the hubbub of talking, and I looked over to see Dieter on his knees, or one knee at least. Trent had been the one to shout yes, and the ripple of congratulations began to circle toward us.

"I think Dieter proposed," Jared murmured and gripped my hand.

"I think you're right."

Dieter stood up, and pulled Trent into a deep kiss that seemed to go on for ages. Then in one smooth move he swept Trent up in his arms and strode out of the tent, applause following them.

"You know what we should do?" Jared mused, "We should organize Trent's wedding for him."

I looked at him aghast, "You're joking?"

He snorted a laugh, "I think he'd be pissed if we booked an island wedding just for the two of them, and ordered a puck shaped cake."

After food was cleared away, the bar got busy, as did the band. Jared led me to the dance floor, a huge wooden deck that had been laid down on the lush green grass. I stepped into his arms as the lead singer slid beautifully into *Walk with Me,* one of our favorite songs by Matt Alber.

"Someone is waiting for their dance," Jared whispered beside my ear. I nodded, kissed his cheek, and walked to my mother.

Her eyes grew dewy as I held out my hand for her. "My baby boy," she said so softly no one but us could hear it. She laid her head on my shoulder, the warm flowery aroma of her perfume blanketing me with love and comfort. She hummed along to *You'll Be in My Heart* as I led her around the dance floor. "Tennant, I'm so happy that you found Jared."

I kissed her soft cheek, then glanced at my husband.

"I am too, Mom. I am too."

Jared

WE SPENT MOST OF THE FLIGHT FROM HARRISBURG TO Philly with caps pulled down over our heads. There were too many orange jerseys on the flight for our liking, well, two anyway. On this short hop, there wasn't exactly a first class where we could hide, and Ten was *the* Tennant Rowe, skating phenom, blah, blah. He was also my husband, and the wedding had made it to social media a few hours ago.

The kids in the seats in front of us kept peering over, and even though this was only a fifty-minute flight, by the end of it, the nearest seats to us were all very much aware that there was a hockey player in seat 23A. Not only that, but a skater for one of Philly's biggest rivals.

"We should have driven," I said and slid down farther down in my aisle seat. Ten had the window, and I was at least some kind of barrier between him and anyone who decided that it was entirely his fault we'd won all four matchups against Philly this season.

Which it was of course. There was something about

those statewide matchups that had tempers flaring, and Ten had been a star in all of them.

By the time we were done with that first part of our journey, Ten had signed his name to everything from the two Philly jerseys to one woman's shoulder. I was at least thankful she hadn't pulled her stretchy top even farther down and asked him to sign her boob. Seemed she was going to get the signature tattooed in place, and went away happy with a recommendation for Gatlin.

Philly airport was another exercise in staying on the down low, and we'd spent most of our three-hour wait for the first class long-haul flight to Greece in a VIP lounge.

"Mr. Rowe?"

I'd been lulled into a false sense of security when a woman stopped right in front of Ten.

Ten and I exchanged glances, and he sat up in his chair, expecting a request for a photo or an autograph. He was used to it, didn't actively seek out the attention, but also dealt with every request with good humor. He'd become an ambassador for the sport, as long as the person he was talking to wasn't one of the good ol' boys who thought being a gay hockey player meant Ten should be removed from the Railers.

"Madsen-Rowe," Ten corrected simply, and I sat up with a start. I'd always assumed we would change our surnames, meld the two into one, Rowe-Madsen or Madsen-Rowe, but to hear Ten say it was hot and moving, all at the same time.

"My apologies," she checked the sheet in her hand. "Mr. Madsen-Rowe, I wonder if you could spare me a few minutes?"

"Is there a problem?" I asked, assuming my bodyguard protector role again.

She smiled at me. "Not really a problem, but there is a young man who saw you come in here, said he was on a connecting flight from Harrisburg but didn't want to bother you himself. He is wondering if you could spare him a few moments, but he understands if you can't."

Ten didn't hesitate; he stood and followed her, and there was no way I was letting him go alone. Why was it that at the arena in front of eighteen thousand fans I knew he was safe, but the minute we stepped outside, I started to see danger everywhere.

She showed us into a small side room with a glass wall full of puffy sofas and a view over the concourse. Alone, looking lost and small, a kid of around fourteen or so, skinny, in scuffed sneakers and a Railers' hoodie, sat on the very edge of the chair near the door. He shot to his feet as soon as we entered, and then stared at Ten, his mouth dropping open.

"Hi, I'm Ten," Ten said and extended his hand.

The kid took the hand and shook it briefly. "I know, I mean, oh god, I'm... Joe. My name is Joe Reeves. Thank you for agreeing to see me."

Ten sat on a sofa, and I glanced at the clock on the wall; we had maybe an hour before we needed to board our flight to Athens.

"Everything okay?" Ten asked offhand, as if it wasn't the most important thing he needed to ask.

Joe nodded and then stopped nodding and instead shook his head. Finally he held out his hand and pulled up his sleeve, where a tattoo of the number 97 sat under the

Railers' logo. Was the kid old enough to have a tattoo? *Jeez, why am I turning into my dad?*

"Mom and Dad didn't want me to bother you, but they don't understand. They've been the best, they love me, but they want to keep me safe. They agree maybe I should stop playing." He pinched the top of his nose. "I need to start again. One day I want to play the same as you." Joe frowned. "Not the same as you, obviously. *No one* is like you, but I want to play hockey because I *can* play hockey, you know?"

There was more to this than met the eye, and I sat down on the other side of Joe.

"What position do you play?" Ten asked.

"I'm on the wing at the moment. I shoot left, but there's been some… trouble." Joe turned to face Ten. "All I need is for you to tell Coach that what the other kids say isn't right and that even if I'm different, I can play. Okay. Because Coach said maybe I should give hockey a miss, and some of the others on the team say they don't want me playing."

"Why?" Ten asked, but he didn't need to. We could both see where this was heading.

"They hate me, now they know I'm gay. Not all of them of course, but they don't listen when I tell them that Tennant Rowe is gay, and he's the best player in the world." He leaned in. "Some of them are Philly fans."

Ten dipped his head—he always did when someone said things like that about him. He had no idea how to react to that at the best of times, but this was different.

"I can help," Ten said. "You want to give me all the details, and I can come visit, talk to the team? Maybe bring some of the other Railers with me?"

I suppressed a laugh. Ten didn't even know where Joe played. It could be Alaska, Hawaii, or Europe even, but it didn't matter to the man I loved, who pulled out his phone and exchanged details with Joe.

By the time we left that room, something wonderful had happened. Joe's parents were outside waiting for him, hugged Ten and me. Then the three of them left for their Dallas flight. Ten was a little subdued until we were in our seats on the plane that would take us the ten hours or so to Greece, but by the time the plane landed and the heat of a Greek summer hit us, we had a whole new idea. An education program, something structured with Ten as the figurehead, school visits, a sponsored competition, logos, a mission statement, and of course, it would all start with a visit to Joe's school in Dallas.

THE FLIGHT from Athens to the far island of Santorini was only forty-five minutes. I think we'd both had enough of flying, so the car ride to the villa on the north of the island in a place called Oia was welcome. Our driver was chatty, but his accent was difficult to decipher for the first ten minutes or so. I think he was saying something about volcanoes and that Santorini was probably the only volcano in the world whose crater was in the sea. I hope he wasn't explaining that the volcano was about to blow, because that would've been a shitty way to spend a honeymoon.

"Cousteau looked for the lost city of Atlantis here," Ten murmured and passed me the leaflet he'd picked up at the small Santorini airport. "I can see why."

One moment we were seeing beaches, some with white

pebbles; some that looked red. The next we were passing spectacular rock formations with individual villas built into them. Everything was white and blue, and it was stunning.

Once we'd moved out of the town, we wound our way up the island, passing clusters of villas and bays with views of the bluest water. We arrived at our new home for the next three weeks just as the sun was setting on the Aegean Sea, and with the driver tipped, we dragged our bags into the wide marble hallway. I'd seen photos of this place when we'd booked it, but the photos hadn't done it justice. The rooms were high-ceilinged, the walls painted white, with accents in a sapphire shade similar to the sea. By unspoken agreement, we headed through the main hall and the kitchen and ended up on the patio with the ocean view.

"Wow," Ten said, and I agreed with him. The sun was dipping low, casting scarlet light across the sea and touching the tips of the mountains surrounding us. The island was crescent-shaped, and we faced west, and if all the sunsets were this spectacular, I couldn't wait to cuddle with Ten on one of the patio sofas and watch the colors change every evening. Ten pulled off his T-shirt and shucked off his shoes, socks, and jeans until he was just in his underwear.

"Swim?" he asked and stared at me pointedly.

I followed his stripping routine, but sue me if I did it a hell of a lot slower than he did. Anything to keep his eyes on me. We stepped into the infinity pool and sank below the surface, making our way to the side and leaning there, looking at the beach below. I could see people on the shoreline. I counted three, and a couple of dogs jumping around in the waves, but it became too dark to see much, and we still hadn't moved from the spot we'd chosen.

"I guess we should go and eat something or at least unpack," I suggested, but Ten shook his head and floated on his back. Soft lighting around the pool gave an intimate feel to where we were, but I knew we'd have to wait until tomorrow and check who could wander in unannounced before enjoying any pool sex. Shame.

"I want to stay out here all night and stare at the stars," he said, and I joined him floating in the water, lazily sculling with my hands to keep me close to him, and staring at the sky.

"There's nothing sexier than two pruned-up skaters," I joked, and he splashed me, although it wasn't enough for me to retaliate. Yet.

WE WENT INDOORS, a tray of cold food all prepared for us in the fridge, along with a bowl of plump strawberries and a container of cream.

"You remember the strawberries?" Ten asked and wet his lips with the tip of his tongue. Messy sticky sex with strawberries? That was a memory I would never lose.

"Oh yeah, I remember that."

"Wanna do it again?" Ten said suggestively. Then he smirked. "This time, there won't be any brothers beating you up after."

I winced at the memory of the day with the strawberries and Brady finding out about me and Ten and just how hard my friend had hit me.

"Your brother..." I said and left it there, picking up one of the strawberries and nibbling on it. My stomach growled, which put an end to the idea of making love right now, although I knew we'd pick it up later.

After food.

"Food," Ten announced as if he could read my mind.

Then, curled up on the sofas looking at the stars, we drank wine and ate cheese and crackers, and the juiciest grapes. Beginning tomorrow, we had a personal chef who would be available to us on demand, but the supper we ate was the most perfect food ever. Neither of us fetched the strawberries. We were exhausted, and I didn't know what time it was back in the States, but it felt as if we hadn't slept for days. Yawning, it was Ten who suggested we were old and needed a nap. We halfheartedly unpacked, between kisses, and then pushed back the white linens and climbed into the bed. I wanted to make love. I was hard, he was hard, and we kissed, but the orgasms we gave each other in the quiet room, were slow and gentle and full of love.

After, when Ten went limp with his weight half on me, I gave in, sated and happier than I'd ever been, and we slept.

Epilogue

TENNANT

WAKING TO THE SUN CREEPING UP AND TINTING THE SKY soft gold and peach is a marvelous thing. The whisper of the Aegean Sea rolled into our room, the smell of salt water drifting over our massive bed. I lay on my side for a few minutes, enjoying the view, my mind sleepy and dreamy still, my dick stiff. I stroked it a few times, sighing at the sensations, when the memory of who rested beside me slid into my drowsy mind.

I rolled over to stare at Jared sleeping on his back, his blond hair rich and golden in the first new rays of the day. He looked like a god. Apollo perhaps, the sun god, eternally beautiful, a man who glowed with solar energy. His chest rose and fell steadily, lifting his left hand as it rested on his stomach. My gaze lingered on his wedding band, an exact match to mine, just larger. Want coursed through me. My belly rumbled. I smiled to myself and slithered out of the bed, pushed the doors open wider to invite more sunshine in, and then pattered to the fridge.

Jared was still sleeping when I crawled back into bed,

the container of fat red berries in one hand and a tube of lube in the other. Oh yes, Tennant had plans. Laying the lube on my pillow, just one of about ten scattered over the bed, I then lifted the lid from the berries and began placing them around him, one every foot or so, until he was outlined with strawberries. Like a crime scene chalk outline, only fruity.

Biting into one, I groaned at the burst of sugary juice. I ran my tongue over my lips and then shimmied up and sat on his pelvis. He blinked a time or two, squinting into the rays of warm Greek sun flowing into our room.

"Ten," he said groggily. I lowered myself down, hands on his chest, and pressed my lips to his. He was slow to return the kiss, but he finally did, touching my lower lip with his tongue, then sliding into my mouth, his hand coming up to cradle the back of my head. The kiss was long and wet, his cock filling as we sucked and licked. "Mm, you taste delicious."

I smiled and sat back, rubbing my ass against the stiff length resting between my cheeks. His hand fell to the bed, and a berry met its maker. Jared's eyebrows knotted. I grabbed his hand, licked the back clean, and then placed it on my thigh.

"What's all this?" he asked after he gave the bed a quick scan.

I plucked a berry from the container, then fed it to him. "You looked like a Greek god all stretched out in our bed, hard and strong, a picture of masculinity and power, like Apollo. So, as is fitting, I have presented an offering to your godliness."

He chuckled. "I'm way too old and too scarred up to be

considered any kind of match for Apollo. Have you not seen the gray hairs popping up all over the place?"

I fed him another berry. "I have seen them, and they turn me right the fuck on. I can't wait until you're covered with silver. I dream of burying my nose in your pubes when they're all white because we'll have grown old together."

"God, I love you." He reached for me, and I let him grab a shoulder. The kiss was hot and needy, way more so than our first taste of each other. "What are you looking for, Tennant?"

I slid a berry between his teeth. He smiled wickedly, then flattened it with his tongue, red juice staining his lips and chin. I licked him clean, then fed him another and another and another, kissing him between each offering, smearing the sweet liquid over our mouths and chins. Some ran down to his throat, pooling in the divot of his neck. I drank from the small recess, using my tongue to remove the berry juice.

"You're delicious," I purred into his neck before I sat back and dumped the fleshy red berries on his chest. A seagull soared past, its cries joining in with the sea and the surf and the sun to remind me that we were far, far from Harrisburg. "And mine." I lay down on him, flesh to flesh, chest to chest, squashing the strawberries into a slick paste.

"Yes, yours," he replied, threading his fingers into my hair to guide me back to his mouth. I nipped at his bottom lip, diving deep into his mouth time and again, rolling my hips in a hard circle that pressed his dick up and back, side to side, until he was huffing like a marathon runner. "Tell me what you want, Tennant, and it's yours."

"I already have everything I want," I whispered, using

my sticky tongue in his ear. He moaned and thrust upward. "You're all I ever wanted."

"Do you want me inside you?" He bit down on my shoulder. I shuddered wantonly. "Tell me what you want, Tennant."

"I want you inside me. Deep inside me," I panted into his ear.

The big man trembled, berry-coated fingers slipping down my sides. "I want that as well," he said, and something inside me snapped like a piano wire.

I found the lube between the pillows, the pretty white pillows, and pumped my hand full. Then I coated his cock and eased myself down onto him. The burn was intense. I rocked up and back, around and around, stretching myself on him. He grabbed my hips, easing me up and down. I looked down at him and lost my breath. "Shit, but you're gorgeous."

He muttered something, then arched up with a punch of his hips. I gasped at the pressure, then melted over him, lowering my mouth to his chest, using my tongue and lips to clean the fruit mash from his nipples.

"So tight and hot," he said on a sigh, his words sending a bolt of searing need to my balls.

"Faster." God, but he was always so damn slow...

"Always the impatient one," he panted, taking my cock in his hand. "We have three weeks. I don't plan on rushing our lovemaking."

"Oh, man," I whined, nipped at his chin, and then rolled with him to my back, his dick sliding back into me with ease. Berries pressed into my spine, and I clawed at the bedding as he began that slow, thorough pace that would make me half-mad to come in no time at all. He ground into me, stealing any kind of coherent thought or semi-intelligent words. I ran my palms over his shoulders and biceps, locked my ankles behind his ass, and fell into that place that was sex and Jared, and pumping and scratching. He knew what I loved, how much stimulation my prostate could take before it became too much, how to touch my thighs to bring me down, and how to talk to ramp me up. He knew me, all of me, and I knew him.

He took me to the edge several times, then eased me back from the precipice, pulling near enough out of me when I was dangling over the cliff, then moving back. Drove me nuts, and I told him so, loudly. When he wouldn't stop, I ground berries into his neck and hair, begged him for more and for less, and then whimpered in frustration when he pulled out to lave wet kisses to my belly and balls. Time was nothing, the world outside our room another universe. There was only Jared and me. I shoved at him, pushing him to his back, his head resting on the pillows we'd kicked down to the bottom of the bed.

"Do it, Ten. Do it. Take what you want from me."

His cock kicked in my hand. I held him in place, then sat down. Hard. He grabbed my dick and gave it a tug. A yelp bubbled up from inside me, and I came right then and there. He surged upward, heels digging into the bed, eyes closed and jaw tight, and pumped with mad passion. A hot wash of cum deep inside me made my orgasm that much better. He fisted my dick. I sat still, milking him with my body, digging at his chest as wave after wave of sweet pleasure surged up and over me, the pulses of body and cock matching the roar of the sea below our balcony.

"Oh holy shits," I coughed when speech was again a working thing. Jared lay under me, splayed out, sweaty and gummy and coated with spunk, lube, and tiny berry bits and seeds. My nose rested by his armpit, and I breathed in, pulling in the scent of my husband, sex, and strawberry. "So, is married sex... always that fucking magnificent?"

"I hope so," he replied as his dick slid free of my body. My ass puckered at the loss.

"Shit, man," I murmured and slipped off him, hoping to make a run to the bathroom for a washcloth, but my wobbly legs folded, and I went to the floor, face to the bedding. "You know the sex was good when..." I said, and he laughed gruffly.

"Give me a few minutes to summon my godly powers, and I'll carry you to the shower where I shall pay homage to your earthly beauty."

"Mm, 'kay." I knelt there on the floor, face buried in the mattress until my Greek god got his legs under him. Then I let him sweep me up and tote me into the white-and-tan bathroom. The shower was big and open, easily fitting two hockey players. We soaped each other up, kissing and whispering, smiling at the stupid jokes the other would make. The soaps were rich, frothy, as were the shampoos, and the towels were heated. Neither of us shaved. Hell, we were lucky we had the energy to wash the cum and fruit from our nuts.

We pulled on shorts and tank tops and went out to lounge on the patio overlooking the Bay of Ammoudi. The Jacuzzi awaited us. I waved at it.

"Maybe later," Jared said as he settled into a softly

padded chair, then called for our chef. Pulling on some sunglasses, I sat on his lap, angling myself sideways so that my head could rest on his shoulder. "Right now, I'm happy to sit here and hold you."

I dropped a few kisses to his scruffy jaw. "Dude, we never even combed." I ran my fingers through his hair. His eyelids got droopy. "Jetlag and sex-lag are kicking your ass, eh, old man?"

"Give me some food, and I'll be running circles around you," he said, then yawned widely.

The chef arrived at our villa just as Jared had dozed off under the sun. He was a cheery man in a white coat and hat, who cooked up an amazing breakfast on the big grill tucked into a corner of the patio. Assistants in crisp white uniforms hustled around, placing dish after dish on the cloth-covered patio table.

Scrambled eggs with seasoned tomatoes and feta was the main dish. On the side were yogurt with honey and walnuts, a tray of olive and feta bread with cheese and nuts, a small goat cheese and spinach pie, Greek coffee, and cold mountain tea. The coffee was too strong. The tea, though was earthy with a hint of citrus and mint that I much preferred. Jared loved the coffee. By the time the chef and his assistants left, my husband was ready and raring to go investigate Santorini.

We walked down to the black sand beach from our villa, strolling hand in hand, snapping pictures to send back to Ryker, my family, and our friends. Time felt sluggish. We lounged by the sea, walked in the foam, talked to beautiful Greek women and men, and kissed as the sea rolled up over our calves. Sandals in hand, we then hailed a small yellow cab and rode to touristy site number one on our long list of things to see in Greece.

Visiting the prehistoric town of Akrotiri was ah-may-zing. The Bronze Age settlement rested on the southern tip of the island, and the town was incredibly well preserved.

"Did you know that this whole area was swallowed up when the volcano, Thera, erupted way back when?" I asked Jared as I read through a brochure after we'd toured the settlement and were enjoying some of that awesome mountain tea outside in the cool shade of lemon trees. He shook his head, the sun doing incredible things with that golden hair of his. "Well, it did. Oh! And check this. This town was so advanced for its time, with drainage systems and the first signs of indoor lavatories, that Plato was rumored to have used it for his inspiration for Atlantis. How cool is that?"

"That's damn cool. Are you going to be this bouncy over every old thing we see in Greece?"

I bounced over to him and kissed him right on the mouth. "I kind of have this love affair with beautiful, old things."

The corners of his lips pulled up. "Do you now? Want to go back to the villa and spend the evening in the Jacuzzi while watching the sunset?"

"You think you're up to it?" I snuggled in close, not giving one care about the other tourists walking past. The sun was hot, the breeze warm, the palm trees swaying, and I had the man I loved wrapped in my arms.

"I wager I can show you a thing or two, Mr. Madsen-Rowe." He gave me a randy wink.

"Ah, yeah, I love hearing that, Mr. Madsen-Rowe."

"Good, because I plan on showing you things for at least thirty or forty years."

"I like hearing *that* even more."

THE END

Free Reads

Please note - in all of these free stories, there will be some spoilers for the main series books.

Railers Short Stories

Volume 1 | Volume 2

LA Storm

Sparkle

The Colts - AHL Short Stories

Pucks & Percentages

Breakaway

Making the Save

Standalone

Waiting for Christmas

Harrisburg Railers

When hockey wunderkind Tennant Rowe meets his new coach, he knows he's in trouble. Jared Madsen is nine years older than Tennant, impossibly attractive, and — worst of all — his brother's off-limits best friend. Is their chemistry worth the risk?

Changing Lines (Railers 1)

Can Tennant show Jared that age is just a number, and that love is all that matters?

The Rowe Brothers are famous hockey hotshots, but as the youngest of the trio, Tennant has always had to play against his brothers' reputations. To get out of their shadows, and against their advice, he accepts a trade to the Harrisburg Railers, where he runs into Jared Madsen. Mads is an old family friend and his brother's one-time teammate. Mads is Tennant's new coach. And Mads is the sexiest thing he's ever laid eyes on.

Jared Madsen's hockey career was cut short by a fault in his heart, but coaching keeps him close to the game. When Ten is traded to the team, his carefully organized world is thrown into chaos. Nine years his junior and his best friend's brother, he knows Ten is strictly off-limits, but as soon as he sees Ten's moves, on and off the ice, he knows that his heart could get him into trouble again.

Changing Lines

Harrisburg Railers (Hockey Romance)

1. Changing Lines
2. First Season
3. Deep Edge
4. Poke Check
5. Last Defense
6. Goal Line
7. Neutral Zone
8. Hat Trick
9. Save The Date
10. Baby Makes Three
11. Rivals
12. Perfect Gifts
13. Family First

Railers Volume 1 | Railers Volume 2 | Railers Volume 3 | Railers Volume 4

Meet the men of Owatonna University's hockey team

Ryker (Owatonna U, 1)

Ryker

Ryker is hockey royalty, Jacob is a poor country boy. Can two vastly different people find common ground and become the men they want to be?

Ryker comes from a long line of championship-winning hockey players. Playing college hockey to develop his game is his only focus, and nothing will stand in the way of him working to become the best player. He has no room for relationships, people who point out his flaws, or anyone who calls him on his dreams. He certainly has no place for love, and meeting Jacob is nothing but a useful distraction on the side. After all trying to get his Owatonna Eagles teammate into bed is less work and more play. When tragedy rocks his family, his charmed life crumbles, and the only person he can turn to is the same one who claims to hate him.

Jacob Benson has only known hard work and stifling conservative values his whole life. Born and raised in the small rural community of Eden Crossing, Minnesota, he's the only son of a hard-working but struggling dairy farming family. Jacob is using his skills in hockey to finance his way to an agricultural science degree. These four years at Owatonna U. will probably be the only time he has to enjoy life, gain acceptance about his sexuality, and live openly before his inevitable return to the farm. Running into a pretty rich boy like Ryker Madsen is putting a damper on his enjoyment of life away from home. Ryker's flip, conceited, carefree attitude grates on Jacob's every nerve. So why, if Ryker is everything he dislikes, does he want nothing more than to explore the sinful dreams that his annoying teammate stars in every night?

Ryker

Owatonna U Hockey (Hockey Romance)

Coast to Coast (Arizona Raptors 1)

Coast To Coast

When opposites attract, this bottom-of-the-league team will never be the same again.

A stipulation in his father's will forces Mark back into the arms of a family that disowned him and leaves him one-third owner of a hockey team facing financial ruin. He doesn't even watch hockey, let alone like it, and wants nothing more than to head back to New York. Then there's the new coach, a stubborn, opinionated, irritating man with superiority issues and questionable music taste. Butting heads with Rowen becomes the new normal, but it comes with passionate debate and an all-consuming lust.

Challenged to rebuild one of the worst teams in the league into a future cup contender, Rowen can't pass up the opportunity. Never in his twenty years of hockey has he ever seen a team managed so badly or coached players overflowing with resentment and bigotry. Yet there's something about this team and this city that compels him to roll up his sleeves and start dismantling. If only Mark, one of three siblings who now own the Raptors, wasn't so damned rock-headed yet so damned appealing his job might be easier. It doesn't look like either is willing to give in, but one night in a dark, desert hotel changes everything.

Coast To Coast

Arizona Raptors (Hockey Romance)

1. Coast To Coast
2. Across the Pond
3. Shadow and Light
4. Sugar and Ice
5. School and Rock

Boston Rebels

Top Shelf (Boston Rebels 1)

Acting on the attraction to his best friend's brother has always been off the table for Xander until a passionate hookup with Mason at a beach resort begins a love affair that burns long after summer ends.

Mason specializes in assisting same-sex couples on their journey to becoming parents and fighting every rule that blocks his way in the stuck-in-the-past agency that hired him. Living in his brother's pool house is rent-free, and every cent he earns he saves for his dream—that one day he'd have his own company helping others. The downside is that he has to see his annoying brother every day, the upside is that his brother's teammates from the

Boston Rebels make regular visits. The eye candy that passes Mason's window is almost enough to make him consider dating a hockey player, but not just any player though. Ever since Xander —his brother's childhood friend—came out as gay at a press conference, Mason's puppy love has turned into a burning attraction he can no longer ignore.

Hockey has been one of Xander's main focuses since he was old enough to balance on skates. Well, hockey and Mason Kingsley, but Mason was always unattainable. Now that he's about to see thirty candles on his birthday cake and is no longer hiding the fact he's gay, he's ready to find a soul mate to make his life complete. A summer vacation is just what he needs to have time to think, but when the Boston Rebels arriving in paradise with Mason in tow, thinking is the last thing he needs. One torrid night under a balmy moon and rules about not messing with his best friend's brother vanish on a warm, tropical breeze.

Summer romances don't generally last past Labor Day, but with the new season about to begin Xander and Mason are going to have to face the world and decide if their love is real enough to withstand everything.

Boston Rebels

Lost In Boston (Free Prequel Novella)

1. Top Shelf
2. Back Check
3. Snowed
4. Royal Lines
5. Blade
6. Rental

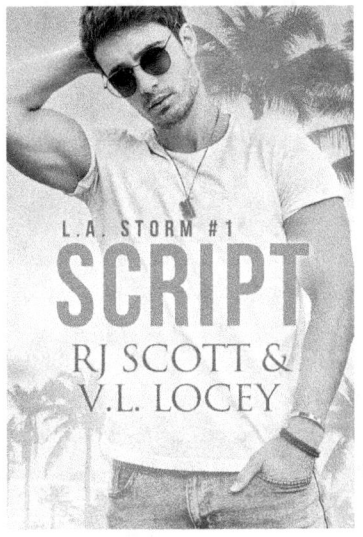

Script (LA Storm, 1)

Script

Hollywood A-lister Finn might be Canadian, but he needs Cameron to show him how to hockey.

Actor Finn Kerrigan is at a crossroads. After growing up a soap star, then starring in a hugely successful trilogy of action movies, he's finally given the chance to read a heartfelt and passionate script that could change his life forever. The role would be enough for people to see him as a serious actor, and maybe even win him an award or two (and no, a golden raspberry award for his action movies doesn't count). Once established as a serious actor he's sure he can come out of the closet and finally live his truth. When he lies to get the part of a hockey player on a struggling team, he suddenly has nowhere to hide. He might be Canadian, but the last time he skated he was ten, and no, he doesn't have hockey in his blood. With only a month until filming starts, he about to be exposed, but partnered with a player who's supposed to be giving him tips, he doesn't realize how many of his secrets will come to light. Falling in lust, one heated kiss at a time, is inevitable, but giving Cameron up at the end of the shoot could break his heart.

Cameron Chavkin is the face of the LA Storm. And the body, and the hair, and the smile. He's at the prime of his career, men and women want to be with him, and he's skating better than he ever has before. His house sits next to a famous rock star's mansion, his garage is filled with expensive cars, and he's even been asked to mentor a once-famous actor in a new hockey movie. Life is pretty sweet. Until the bad boy of hockey meets Finn, a man on the edge with more secrets than Cameron has endorsements. Knowing better than to get involved, Cameron is swept up despite himself, and when it's time to say goodbye to the Storm's most eligible bachelor is finding it hard to follow the script.

Script

LA Storm

Off The Ice (Chesterford Coyotes, 1)

Off The Ice

A coming-of-age love story with high school, hockey rivalry, friendship, family, and coming out.

Soren's life changes in an instant when he and his younger brother are adopted by hockey royalty. Making sense of his new life is hard enough, but when he's enrolled in a private school it means facing a whole new set of problems. Navigating friendship, family, and hockey is one thing, but being attracted to the boy who vexes him is a whole new thing.

Felix has a reputation to protect. He's the kid who seems to have everything but looks can be deceiving. Spinning lies about his perfect life, he's created a fantasy world that even he has started to believe. Only, it's not long before everything crumbles, all of his pretty lies are revealed, and only his closest rival sees through his pain and stands by him.

Fighting is easy, friendship is hard, but love is everything.

Off The Ice

Chesterford Coyotes

1. Off The Ice
2. On Thin Ice
3. *Dance on Ice*

Also By RJ Scott

For a full list of ebooks and links please scan the code above or
visit rjscott.co.uk/rjbooks

Meet RJ Scott

RJ discovered romance in books at a very young age and realized that if there wasn't romance on the page, she could create it in her head. With over one hundred and fifty books published, she is a full time author of gay romance.

She lives and works out of her home in the beautiful English countryside, spends her spare time reading, watching films, and enjoying time with her family.

The last time she had a week's break from writing she didn't like it one little bit and has yet to meet a box of chocolates she couldn't defeat.

www.rjscott.co.uk | rj@rjscott.co.uk

NEWSLETTER - rjscott.co.uk/rjnews

facebook.com/author.rjscott

x.com/Rjscott_author

instagram.com/rjscott_author

amazon.com/author/rj-scott

bookbub.com/authors/rj-scott

goodreads.com/rjscott

pinterest.com/rjscottauthor

Also By VL Locey

For a full list of ebooks and links please scan the code above or
visit vllocey.com/stories-from-vl-locey

Meet V.L. Locey

V.L. Locey loves worn jeans, yoga, belly laughs, walking, reading and writing lusty tales, Greek mythology, the New York Rangers, comic books, and coffee.

(Not necessarily in that order.)

She shares her life with her husband, her daughter, one dog, two cats, a flock of assorted domestic fowl, and two Jersey steers.

When not writing spicy romances, she enjoys spending her day with her menagerie in the rolling hills of Pennsylvania with a cup of fresh java in hand.

vllocey.com
vicki@vllocey.com

Newsletter - vllocey.com/newsletter

facebook.com/V.L.Locey

x.com/vllocey

instagram.com/vl_locey

bookbub.com/authors/v-l-locey

goodreads.com/vllocey

pinterest.com/vllocey

www.ingramcontent.com/pod-product-compliance
Lightning Source LLC
Chambersburg PA
CBHW070845260626
47170CB00007B/2504